CHOICES

JP ROSSELLE

The EC Publishing LLC books may be ordered
through booksellers or by contacting:

EC Publishing LLC
116 South Magnolia Ave.
Suite 3, Unit F
Ocala, FL 34471, USA
Direct Line: +1 (352) 644-6538
Fax: +1 (800) 483-1813
http://www.ecpublishingllc.com/

Ordering Information:
Quantity sales. Special discounts are available on quantity purchases by corporations, associations, and others. For details, contact the publisher at the address above.

Printed in the United States of America

TABLE OF CONTENTS

CHAPTER I

REAGAN'S QUIET WAR

It was a beautiful late September morning; the Miami Marina dock was where we would cast off on our latest adventure. Captain Mike, one Bahamian crew member, Jack, his girlfriend Cindy, Evette and George, two divers, plus Christina and myself. We were off to the waters of Panama looking for more of Sir Francis Drake's lost treasures.

Our first stopover would be Key West. Evette and George would leave the boat here as George was on probation and could not leave Florida. I could tell it was hard for Evette to leave the group, but she seemed committed to doing her part to make things work out between her and ex-husband George.

Key West had changed quite a bit since my sailing here 15 years ago in the "Princess", most of my relatives had moved north. One location I took Christina to see was the Heritage House. This house which my uncle, Captain George Carey, built in 1834, is the oldest standing structure in Key West. The house's location goes back almost 200 years, when Pirates first found a freshwater hole at the same place where my uncle built the house. It was here standing in front of this house that I first mentioned that I would one day write a book about my family's history.

My Dad always said that the second sailboat he built was named after our great Uncle George. It was said that my Uncle, Captain George Carey had built this house for his new bride. Uncle George had said it was by chance he was in the right place at the right time to find her. It was the year 1832 when my uncle was night sailing just miles off the eastern coast of the Florida Keys when he spotted a ship that had rammed one of the many reefs. Uncle George was able to rescue the crew, its few passengers, and, of course, the cargo. The ship that had run up onto the reef then, after a short time, broke apart and sank. There were said to have been five German sisters aboard the wrecked ship. My uncle married the 15-year-old and the other four were married off to four of my uncle's crew. Oh yes my Dad named his second sailboat, "PIRATE".

We spent one night in Key West and the next morning, the 8 of us shoved off for Cancun. It wasn't long before we were in seeing distance of Cuba's northwestern coast. Of course this too brought back memories to when I had sailed into Baracoa, Cuba in 1974. On that trip, we tricked the Cubans into believing that our sailboat had run into bad weather, during which time our main sail had ripped. My cargo was a beautiful young CIA woman whom we secretly exchanged for a Cuban General's daughter. That successful mission freed the way for the General to defect to the west.

Seeing Cuba again reminded me of why I had chosen the name "Defiance" for the new boat. It was Drakes last vessel's name but also marked my personal resistance to the moves that Castro and the Soviets were making. Neither Christina nor the crew knew of my first contribution to the CIA. I hadn't done it for the CIA, but as a favor for my friend Bob. Oh the memories.

Cancun was the biggest tourist beach I had ever seen. Much bigger than the Rivera. Again the beach was nice but nowhere as beautiful as the pink sands beaches of Harbor Island's east coast.

Cindy and Christina loved Cancun and would have been happy to spend more time there. I knew our next stop would top Cancun. Belize was the second most beautiful beach in the world. Once reaching Belize, Jack & Cindy, Christina, and I rented a bungalow right on the beach. We stayed for two beautiful days.

We were now ready for our next stop which was to be, seas wise the roughest part of the trip. It was on this trip that even I got seasick, me vomiting all over the bridge, and had Captain Mike doing the same. The smell again reminded me of my 1974 Cuba sailing trip. On that trip I had Janet shut up in the cabin for almost 16 hours durning rough weather. I don't have to tell you what that cabin looked and smelled like the next day.

Today the seas were rough with some waves 10 plus feet. The rough weather lasted the three-day trip. Christina must have lost 15 pounds after being sick and sicker for those three days. The trip was the worst sea voyage I had ever experienced. There was nothing that I enjoyed about the trip. I heard Christina say several times if she lived through this trip, she never wanted to set foot on a boat again.

The rough seas lasted until we pulled into Costa Rica's Limon harbor. The harbor only had a lite chop. Once we docked, both girls headed for a taxi. No kiss good bye, just a wave without looking back. Jack thought all this funny and said they'd be back tomorrow. I should have been hungry but I wasn't, a cold beer while sitting at a stable table sounded good.

The six of us walked into the American bar. Richard was there with Montibelli and Ian. The first thing that Richard said was that the woman from the Park Hotel had been there three times looking for me. I left the men at the bar and walked the one block north. At the Park hotel I got a warm welcome from the receptionist and a pile of notes from calls that she had started receiving from the night before. I asked to borrow the small hotel office to return the calls. The first was Lourdes, Lourdes said that the Colonel had called saying it was urgent that I call him back. Lourdes said the Colonel wanted to know where to send the helicopter. Lourdes said that the Colonel also had talked with Jerry. I called Jerry and Jerry said that the Colonel said that Castro had sent a Battalion of his best into Nicaragua, seemed the battalion were Castro's most seasoned and decorated group from Angola. Jerry said that they could reach our Nicaragua sector by Thursday, which gave us only two days. The Colonel had said that Ortega and Castro wanted to seal off the southeastern flow of arms, and Castro had stated they would make the many mercenaries think twice about taking the CIA's blood money.

Jerry said the Cubans numbered four to five hundred. Jerry said he had contacted Fernando and told him to head all his people to either our landing strip or Costa Rica. Jerry asked me what I thought Fernando said? I said he probably said they'd be staying. Jerry said that Fernando said that he needed to meet with you face to face. Jerry said he didn't know what to do, so just in case, our C-130 from Andros was sitting on the Limon runway. Jerry said he also took the liberty of sending every available man and supplies on that same C-130. I told Jerry that I would be on the way to the Limon airport. Call the Colonel and have him somewhere I can send him a coded message. I jogged back to the bar and Jack knew by my face that we would be on our way. I told Richard not to move the Cessna while I was gone, and to please stop by the house and tell the girls that Jack and I had gone fishing. Jack and I stopped by the boat, picked up a change of clothes and some gear and headed to the airport.

The C-130 seemed packed, even the Colonel's Rangers that we're in the process of training our men to parachute were aboard. I approached the three of them and said this wasn't a practice mission and they could and maybe should stay on the ground. The three of them just smiled.

We got up in the air and I started sending my messages thru the cockpit's computer system. It wasn't 30 minutes when we were landing on our Nicaraguan strip.

This was only the second time I had been on Nicaraguan soil. Fernando was there with several of his men. Fernando said that he and the men wanted to stay and fight. Fernando said that Castro's men would be slowed to a snail's pace while receiving heavy losses on their way. Hell Fernando said, he had laid out over 500 land mines. No he said, we will not run. As I looked, the C-130 was already being unloaded.

I told Fernando that this was different than hit and run. There will be casualties here I said, you are outnumbered 4 or 5 to 1. Fernando said that since he and his men, our men, arrived the contra numbers were growing by the day. Fernando said their numbers were now 400 plus. Mostly young men and women without much experience but full of heart, fight and armed to the teeth. Fernando smiled and said that they were the best fed army he had ever seen. We had recently delivered over two hundred live pigs and other farm animals. Fernando reminded me of Jerry's complaining that his returning C-130's smell reminded him of the smell of a circus. No Fernando said we will stay and fight.

Years ago, the CIA had attempted to mine the Managua harbor; it was a terrible failure. The small mines had only sunken seven fishing boats. The plan had been to keep cargo vessels and troop carriers out. Fernando asked that this time we do it right! Not secretly, but in broad daylight. Now so that the Cubans now here, will be thinking how they will get home.

We had been on the ground in Nicaragua for only two hours and it was time to go. Jack offered to stay but he was reminded that one of the things we were to do at our planned stop in Limon was to set up the radio in the small house that we had purchased for Evette. The house was on

Limon's highest hilltop overlooking the main cargo port of the Limon and the banana port of Moin. Jack understood how important this new radio set up was. The radio equipment was located in Limon's customs, ready to be picked up. The equipment would help us, especially during the next days. Not only could this equipment enable us to send and receive messages to and from our people in Nicaragua, it was able to communicate with passing ships and aircraft. The equipment was also equipped to intercept and would record all radio transmissions.

We took off from Nicaragua leaving the 26 men and a load of supplies. Our heading was back to Limon. Once in the air we were diverted to Honduras. The Colonel would meet us there.

The Colonel didn't look worried, he looked excited! While still parked on the runway the three of us talked sitting in an older open air jeep. The Colonel said he had brought with him a contribution of ranger snippers. The snippers were, of course, all volunteers. The rangers were accompanied by four other men who I thought were CIA. The Colonel said that the Director had sent them. Jack was there with us and I told Jack that those four men would have to get own their ride. Jack and the Colonel got my message.

I told the Colonel of Fernando's request to mine the harbors, the Colonel said he'd have the supplies delivered in Mandeville within 24 hours.

The C-130 was again refueled and would again fly south having the rangers parachute in over Fernando's position. Our C-130 would do a stop and go in Limon to drop off Jack.

One of several of my coded messages were to Evette. The message read, "sorry the honeymoon is over, you are urgently needed in Limon". I felt confident that Evette wouldn't let us down. George would be staying at his parents' house; I was concerned that George could get into trouble while he waited for Evette.

By now, our C-130 was headed north to Manderville; I hoped Christina had gotten my message. Women were something that wasn't high on my thoughts at the moment. I was thinking what was the fastest I could get my hands on the newest G.D. technologies'. G.D. had already installed a special power source, and receptacles in all four of our aircraft. The aircraft were ready but as things go G.D. was behind on its testing. G.D. said they were in the glitch mode. I planned to mine two of the three Nicaragua ports. Blue fields would not be mined, as long as it was not used by the military or receiving military supplies.

The Colonel had promised delivery of the first 30 such mines within 24 hours.

I came to a quick agreement with G.D. Their technical group were on the way to Mandeville.

Only twenty mines showed up the first day, we would load ten on each of the two birds that we had on the ground at Mandeville. Since our aircraft didn't have any other identifying marks other than camouflage and our Cat on the tail, I was sure that places like Nicaragua and Panama thought we only had one such plane. We would be sending two C-130s. We were now only waiting the G.D. technicians to install a system that we now called TESS. TESS was now much more sensitive than the original. It was now a one-component system that was housed in a case that was capable of self-destruction without causing damage to the crew or aircraft. Before TESS was activated an altitude guide line was required. Once the altitude guideline was breached the self-destruct device would destroy TESS. This along with other protection devises were built into TESS's security system. The altitude guideline was in case of a crash of the aircraft.

We hadn't heard from Fernando; Evette was now in Limon and had seen Silvia, who said that Peter had left on a small Cuban cargo ship that had made a Limon stopover five days ago. This information had me thinking two things, one that it would be Peter leading the way for the Cubans and that my buddies Richard and Ian were asleep at the wheel. Most likely drunk at the wheel.

Jack communicated that it could be 24 hours before he had the radio set up. I wasn't going to wait. The G.D. technicians gave the green light and we'd be off. Both of our targets were on the west coast. The Colonel was to give all commercial and friendly military the heads up on an upcoming electrical interference due to a break in the ozone.

Our two C-130s flew through Honduras then out over 50 miles to the west then circling back hugging just 100 feet above the water. Once within about 100 miles from our targets the TESS devices were enacted and each plane would move to its target. The dropping of the mines did not go un-noticed. Both planes took on antiaircraft fire, neither suffered any major damages.

Two Soviet helicopters were dispatched but we were long gone by the time they finally got up in the air and of course, with the activation of TESS, their helicopter's nor their ground radars were functioning.

We had dropped 10 mines in each of the two ports. Our mission was a complete success. We were refueled in the air as not to add any possibility of any attempt on the TESS technology. Prior to descending to land, both TESS's were reset and placed on alarm mode. Once the alarm mode was set, it would take a new code to disengage the alarm. As yet, Even I didn't have that code.

I arrived back in Mandeville to find Salinas there at the airport. It was good to see her even though some one had to have disobeyed my orders. Salinas was not alone, she had come with her personal body guard. Heads would have rolled if she had made the trip alone.

The Mandeville house was empty of anyone except one lonely guard. There was no word from Fernando and the men. Surely by now they had been face to face with those Cubans. Although the C-130 was equipped with Tim's computer and its communication, my first thing I would do once entering the house was to visit my office and contact Lourdes. With the door open behind me, Salinas had walked in and asked if she was correct that those were bullet holes in the C-130's tail? I turned and she came into my arms. She said she tried her best not to worry about me but that everyone always talked about the chances I took. You have a wife and five children waiting for you in Nassau she said. Please don't forget us.

Our embrace was interrupted by Lourdes voice on the phone, "Captain Jim, are you there" she asked? Yes, Lourdes I said. Please she said, read the scripted message coming in.

There had been no loss of life on our side. The Cubans were now camped just two miles on the other side of the main land mine lines. The Cubans had suffered at least 40 casualties. The Cuban's losses were from the mines and our six ranger snippers. Fernando had planned well, he had let me know that they had also placed well over two hundred remote controlled mines. With this news I carried Salinas off to bed.

The next morning just after 11:00 a.m. I received another call from Lourdes. Check the computer again she said. My Adams apple sunk to my stomach until I read the new message. Last night Fernando had sent a two-man envoy carrying a white flag into the Cuban camp. The men, one a Haitian Doctor, offered to assist with their wounded and gave our agreement that we would allow nonmilitary helicopters to come in to care for and evacuate the wounded.

The Cuban's commanding officer did not accept any assistance. Instead he sent his own message back that gave what he thought was our small group, 24 hours to surrender.

Fernando wouldn't give the Cubans the time to de-mind their camps. The next morning the Cubans were gone, they hadn't broken camp, they were just gone. Fernando said the Cubans must have lost another 60 men when he activated the remote controlled mines.

The Managua news didn't mention the Cubans, only the mining of the harbors, the news claimed a full force attack by the U.S. even showing that same old photo of our burned-out C-130 claiming they had brought it down during the fight.

I wouldn't see the photo until the next day in the New Orleans newspaper. The photo was the tail section of the our C-130 that the Colonel had lost six months before. I imagined that the Russian, Peter had taken that photo during one of his many trips into the Nicaraguan side of the border. We hadn't heard any news of Peter. I hoped he made it back. I would have hated to start all over getting to know a new man.

All the news was good, we did have some canvas tail covers made to put over and cover all three C-130's tails while on the ground.

Of course, the U.S. denied having anything to do with the attack or mining of the harbors.

Jack had now got the radio set up in Limon, and communication with Fernando and his group was good. Jack and Evette had also intercepted several conversations from the closest Sandinista camp that still had over 30 wounded Cubans. Seemed that even the Cubans were hesitant to send their own helicopters to recover their dead and wounded. The whereabouts of the remaining Cubans did have me worried.

If I was Castro, this wouldn't be the end of it. The air waves went silent; Castro had sent four MiGs in to clear the mines. Not one of our stinger missiles had even been fired, the MiGs flew just over the tree tops dropping some form of scatter bomb that activated many of the mines.

There had been lots of our 50 Calabria shooting but no trails of black smoke. The MiGs did a good job and it seemed that Fernando's men would be facing that now 300 or so Cubans plus 100 or so from the regular Sandinista force.

I had decided to send one of our birds to sit at the Honduran base as to assist with any wounded that we would have.

Again traveling through dense forest, the Cubans met heavy fire from our grenade launchers, mortars and of course the snippers. Fernando's group would hit and run. The Cuban patrols sent after them would not return. Fernando had surrounded the Cubans; the Cubans had underestimated our forces.

CHAPTER II

ACCIDENT IN MAIMI

I was at the Mandeville house getting pieces of information bit by bit about the battle. The phone rang as it had all night, Lourdes said that there had been a car accident in Miami. It was Lori and Malcolm. Both had been taken to Mercy Hospital, Lourdes didn't know how bad it was. Lourdes said that Tommy would be her next call. I hung up the phone, it was 1:30 a.m. Friday morning. I woke Salinas and told her the news. By the time it took me to get Bubba out of bed and to the car. Salinas and her body guard were sitting in the back seat.

During our flight to Miami we receive more news, it wasn't good. Fernando had been wounded; it was Fernando that called asking for the C-130 to come in to pick up our wounded. Lourdes said that Fernando sounded ok and had said that we were still in control of the area but that we should anticipate the bird taking on ground fire on the way in. I told Lourdes to get the bird in the air and call the Colonel to at least have a Navy Med Copter in Limon to transport the most seriously wounded to Panama.

An hour into our Miami-bound flight, we got an update on Lori and Malcolm. Neither were critical, both had bad bone fractures. We would be landing at the Miami airport instead of Opa-Locka because of the better distance to the hospital. Tim would meet us at the airport and take us to Mercy.

Still in the air, Lourdes said that the Bird had landed and taken off from our Nicaragua base with 16 wounded but that Fernando was not aboard. We had no word on his wounds or injury.

Arriving at the Miami hospital, we visited Lori first; Chubby was by her side. Lori had suffered a broken left thy bone and cuts and bruises. Lori was, of course, upset and was crying, along with asking about Malcolm. Salinas stayed with Lori while I went to see how Malcolm was doing. Malcolm was now in his second surgery; the nurse said Malcolm's left side was badly broken up. The first surgery was his hip, now she said they were working on his left leg. Both his left arm and leg had compound fractures. The Nurse said that Malcolm had also suffered a head injury and that they were watching closely for internal bleeding and or swelling. The Nurse said Malcolm was conscious and talking when they brought him in.

I called Lourdes for any news and that she needed to let Malcolm's family know that I was here with him. Lourdes said Malcolm's Father would be arriving in Miami at about 2:00 p.m.

Lourdes said that Jack and his two divers were helping the wounded that had arrived in Limon and said that a wounded Haitian Captain had informed them that we had lost at least six of our group, at least one ranger snipper and over 20 of the contra's. The Haitian captain said that the Cubans had suffer a terrible punishment. The captain said that Fernando had walked into one of his jungle traps and had received a head wound when he was lifted by one foot and rammed into a tree. The captain said that Fernando had well over 70 prisoners.

It was now 9:30 a.m. Friday morning. I had just got to see a sleeping Malcolm and was able to speak with his Doctor. The Doctor said that the main worry was the head injury but that so far it was looking good. I didn't ask about football as I knew Malcolm was at least out for the season. Lori said they were on the way home from the Thursday night sock hop only 4 or 5 blocks from the house when a big car came flying through a red light at 25th road. It wasn't Malcolm's fault, she said.

I would have to go and take Salinas to the apartment, even with the keys it could be difficult for Salinas to get the elevator to stop at our floor and open the elevator door. Cubby would stay at least until I returned. I kissed Lori and told her that I loved her and we were off.

On my way out of the hospital Salinas and we ran into an old friend, it was Tim from the Miami Daily News. Tim remembered Salinas from his fishing trip. Cat had given Tim the story about the Rape and Murder that our Lucy had been involved with. Tim of course wanted to know whom we were visiting at the hospital. I only mentioned that we were there visiting a friend that had been in a car wreck. Tim asked if I knew that my name was in today's Paper? Of course I said no and Tim asked for a few minutes of my time. I said I would have Lourdes call him later in the day.

Salinas and I Left the hospital in a Taxi, it was only a five-minute drive. On our way in to the apartment I picked up a newspaper from the lobby. The headlines read, "Cuba losses MiG to Contras", apparently for whatever reason one of the four MiGs that Castro had sent to Nicaragua did not return to its base in Cuba. The article went on to say that since the US Congress had now started to once again fund the contras, that Castro had sent ground troops for the first time into Nicaragua. Not just advisors as they and the Soviets already had there, ground troops.

The Sandinista's claimed to have shot down one of the CIAs cargo planes delivering arms to the Contras. They claimed that they had rescued and taken prisoner an American CIA spy. That same photo of our burned C-130 tail section was the only photo in the article. In the photo, one could only see the Cat on the tail, the Cat and its traveling bag were distinct. The article had mentioned arms being sold to Iran, using those funds to assist the contras. The news article had a long list of people that a Congressional Committee was going to hear from. My name appeared on the list that included Generals, Senators, Congressmen, and, of course, a certain Colonel and the Director of the CIA were also on the list. The selling of arms to Iran was illegal, the transportation of such arms was a gray area.

Southern Cargo Services or SCS was an off shore company of which I had no paper contact. By paper I meant, I was not a stock holder nor officer of the company. The news article was worrisome. The Colonel's and Director's names were the most mentioned in the article. Congress was calling for a full investigation. Just as soon as I read the article I called Lourdes to find the Colonel.

Lourdes called back with a message that the Colonel could meet in Washington, D.C. The words that jumped out of my mouth were, "not on my life." I said he could find me in Nassau.

Lourdes said she had heard from Fernando and noted that he was ok and the fighting had stopped. In all we had lost 8 of our group, plus 22 of the contras. Fernando said he had 81 prisoners and calculated that the

Cubans had lost over 50% of their men. Fernando wanted to know what to do with the prisoners.

By the looks of things, I thought it best to leave for Nassau just as soon as possible. I would first go back to the hospital and wait to see Malcolm.

When I arrived at the hospital, I first stopped to see Malcolm. Chubby was outside of Malcolm's room. Cubby raised his hands as to say it wasn't his doing. When I walked into Malcolm's room, there was Lori and, to a great surprise, young Mr. Crowlbe. Malcolm was awake, not looking so great but awake. I moved in toward the bed and took him by his right hand. Malcolm squeezed my hand and mumbled that he was sorry. Lori started to cry and young Brian put his arm around her. Looking at Brian I asked if that was his favorite arm? Brian quickly removed it.

Looking at Malcolm, I told him that we had been lucky. We all were going to be just fine. The Nurse came in and said that Malcolm needed his rest. Malcolm closed his eyes as we walked out into the hallway. Brian was pushing Lori's wheel chair and I asked him what had brought him to my back door. Lori answered saying that Brian was studying at the UM. Yes Sir, Brian said, I transferred here and ran into Lori and Malcolm at the sailing club. What a coincidence I said. Yes Sir, Brian said. I knew right off the bat that in this case it was no coincidence, he was here for Lori. I looked right at Lori and asked if she had been seeing Young Brian. Lori looked at me and said no Sir. Well I said if he asks and you want to go, just remember your curfew. Lori stopped the chair and stated to cry. She held her arms outward toward me. I bent down and took her into my arms and she asked if I still loved her, I whispered "until the day I die". I let her go and she smiled. Now young Brian I asked, you got time to stay with Lori a few hours so that Chubby can go get some sleep? It's been a long night for Chubby, I said. Brian said he be more than happy to watch over Lori.

Since I had gotten into the taxi from the apartment I had noticed I was being tailed. It didn't look like a professional but a tail just the same. I wanted to see if they were armed so I went around the corner and doubled back. Just by his face when I was pointing my Beretta at his head, I knew he must be a reporter. I checked him for a weapon of which he didn't have. I asked if he was working with Tim and he said yes. Where is he I asked? In the parking lot, the young man said. Let's go have a little talk with him I said. Yes sir, the man said.

As we walked up to Tim's car he got out. I said I thought we were friends. Tim said I was a hot ticket. Tim said he had let it drop the year before but now it was going to be him or someone else that got the story. I looked at him and said to print what he knew to be true, but to stay his distance from my friends and family. Your future will depend on it I said. I then looked at the young man that had been following me, you I said were lucky today. It won't be so the next time. The young man acknowledged by saying yes Sir, but Tim didn't say a word. I walked back to the hospital entrance and Chubby was waiting to give me a ride. Chubby asked where too? I said the apartment. I asked about the family and Chubby said all was fine. Lori was fine too, accept for the accident. Chubby said that Lori saw Malcolm as a friend; they saw each other once or twice a week. The other young man had stopped by the house but Lori did not invite him in. I looked at Chubby and said not to protect me, let her do the things a young girl does. If she finds a man, then it will be what it is. Chubby said she's still only a 16-year-old girl.

Chubby asked how the fight was going? Me looking straight ahead asked? The fish, the women or the Cubans? Chubby laughed. I told Chubby that I thought we had seen the last of Castro sending any Troops into Nicaragua. Not for a good while anyway.

When I got back up to the apartment I called in to Lourdes. I said to send word to Fernando that he should feed the Cubans and those who could march should be sent back only with their boots and pants. If Fernando had any of their wounded, he was to contact Managua and have them pick up their wounded in Honduras. Lourdes was to arrange the transport. Yes, one of our birds would fly in, pick up the wounded Cubans and fly them to Honduras. Lourdes said that our bird had already picked up three of the Cubans most seriously wounded and took them to Limon. Fernando had said they wouldn't have lived if they had not. Lourdes said that she now had also heard from Christina, it seemed she had recovered from the trip; Christina wanted to come back and be with Lori. I thought that an excellent idea.

Salinas and I wouldn't stay the night, I had wanted to see Malcolm's father, but it wasn't to be. I was sure Malcolm's father would stay until Malcolm could travel and then take him home to heel up. It would be up to Malcolm to get himself back to Miami. This time his mom wouldn't be so likely to let him come back. Time will tell I thought.

It would be dark before we arrived in Nassau. It had been a long few days. I got to see the children, they were happy to see their mother. Wendy Michelle was now a big girl that for the first time called me Papa.

In the shower I realized again what a beautiful girl Salinas was, four months pregnant, but beautiful. In bed after the shower Salinas asked if I would bring Lori here to Nassau to recover. I said that nothing had changed, Lori would stay the course with her family in Miami. Salinas said she just wanted me to know that Lori was welcome here. We slept the entire night without one phone call. When I opened my eyes Salinas was missing from the bed. Was that good coffee I smelled? Funny how a smell like coffee does things to your body, well at least to mine. Salinas was now sitting out on the porch, Wendy Michelle and Johnny were up and playing. Betty was also there, she got up to greet me. Salinas also got up hugged me and said how nice it was to have me home. Sitting there, I could hear the waves arriving on the beach, the chickens, the horses, and, of course, the children.

CHAPTER III

THE COLONEL'S MEETING

It was now 8:00 a.m., wouldn't you know it, the phone started ringing. First it was Lourdes, she was calling from home, then it was Tim from Omni Terminals, then Jody from the New Orleans terminal, then Jerry calling from the airfield in Manderville. All were calling about the reporters that were looking for information. The only bird that was parked at Mandeville was inside the hanger. Jerry said we looked like a ghost town there. Tim from Omni talked with the reporters and had told them that the only relation I had with Omni was that I had helped him get started when he had been fired years ago by Harrison. Jack told the reporters that he had been in the transport business long before he had ever met me. Jack told the reporters that he had been working for McLean Transport when they had closed and it was a natural fit that he'd take the terminal and start his own business. That part of the fire seemed to go out with a few small buckets of water. All three locations were asked if they knew my whereabouts? So far so good. I got the message that the Colonel would be in Nassau by nightfall.

The beach house had been empty since before Cat's death. It had been cleaned and repainted. The Colonel and I would meet there at 10:00 p.m. I had made arrangements to have that famous 28 foot Donzi anchored about a half mile off the beach house. Yes I had purchased that same Donzi from that infamous 1971 trip and named it "CHOICES". One of Mark's captains and one of Salinas's house guards would stand watch; the watching was more to ensure that someone wasn't out there taking photos of me meeting with the Colonel.

The Colonel showed, it was the first time I'd seen him without his uniform. The Colonel looked as if he was 10 pounds lighter, even in the dark. It should have been a meeting celebrating a great victory, instead, the Colonel said that a CIA captive had sold us out. The Colonel said my name was thrown around too. The transport from Panama would now be moved to Haiti. Why Haiti I asked? Reporters don't like to hang around a lot down there he said.

The Colonel said that he felt the President would deny any involvement leaving him and the Director out to dry. The Colonel said that the Director had already denied any knowledge of arms sales to Iran. The Colonel said for me not to worry as I didn't exist other than a few mentions of the Traveling Cat. That's how the President speaks of you Jim he said. The Colonel said that the President had said that myself and my group were still our best chance of winning down there in Nicaragua. The Colonel said that I had mined those ports even before he had gotten the chance to inform the President. The President learned of the operation from the newspaper. The Colonel said that the President didn't approve when he learned that TESS was involved. That's why I'm mainly here Jim he said. The President said I was not to use TESS again for any of my operations. I reminded the Colonel that TESS belonged to me. TESS was not a part of the vehicle agreement for which thus far I had only received just over half of the agreed payment. I then mentioned that I was now owed almost 5 million for transportation, not to mention the over $3,000,000.00 of my own monies spent fighting the communist. Before the Colonel could continue I mentioned that congress had just approved $100,000,000.00 to assist the contras. I asked where that money was going? I looked at him and said that the money I spent was my contribution to the cause, the monies that are owed must be paid. The Colonel noted that his part was the $5,000,000.00 for which he had brought payment in full. He pulled the check from his jacket pocket, I stood with my back facing the water and took the check and placed it on the table. I told him that I trusted this was a payment for services, not silence. The Colonel said the payment is because you earned it.

I thought it the right time to voice my concerns about the arms sales. I said that in my opinion, Congress could, would close its eyes and look the other way if all monies received were accounted for. However, that being said I would lay odds that for many, a government pay check and a good retirement plan just wouldn't be enough.

Tell the president that only mad dogs bite the hand that feeds them; I'm not mad. If you get his ear, tell him that G.D. hadn't received the government's investment money to go forward with his star-wars project, the TESS project has no government finance nor ownership. The vehicle has the technology and G.D. can produce the results he wants. If spent right, $50,000,000.00 would be plenty for the contras, the other $50,000,000.00 should go to G.D. Tell the Secretary of State that an agreement that is sealed by a hand shake doesn't mean, I'll do my best. It means you can count on the agreement being fulfilled.

Enough was said, the Colonel said that the first Haiti shipment would be ready the following Thursday. The house had been darkened for our meeting. We said our goodbyes at the door, and he was off into the darkness.

CHAPTER IV

MIAMI BOUND VIA DONZI

I went back to the porch and flickered the agreed code with the lights and of course took my check. The anchored Donzi signaled back and I heard the engine start. Just hearing the engine brought back memories of that 1971 trip I had made from Key West to Nassau and back. The trip being mostly in the dark, one would not forget the sounds, the spray of the saltwater or what raced through my mind on the way over nor how my plan had changed nor my thought's all the way back. It was all about the choices.

I was pissed that I felt that I couldn't be in Miami. The main airport and even Chalks could have reporters or even some government personnel watching for me. Hearing the Donzi's engine I knew what I was going do. The next morning I would have my machanic, Carlos give the Donzi the once over, and I'd head to Miami.

When I returned home to the hill top beach house I spent a few hours in my office on the computer. Jerry was to start loading the C-130 he had in his Mandeville hanger, we'd be making one more trip to Panama and then to Iran. Jack from the New Orleans Terminal was to load up three trailers of old tires and deliver the cargo to Jerry in the cover of night. The C-130 in Honduras was to come back and loaded to resupply Fernando.

The next morning, before Carlos had even started checking the boat for my trip, I called for Bob. Bob being smarter than me, he was not mentioned in the news article. Still Bob was out of town and I had to share my needs with Roger. Rodger said he would do as I wished. The plan was set and in motion.

I left out of Nassau Harbor at 9:00 a.m. in the Donzi, the weather was beautiful. Red sky at night sailor's delight, red sky at morn sailor's take warn.

I was rounding the northern tip of Andros in no time and then on into the Gulf Stream. I had used plenty of sun block as there wasn't a hat that was going to stay on my head. There would be no turning back to recover a hat that ended in the water. When we were younger we didn't have sun glasses, I couldn't even remember having a pair on Rusty's and my big sailing trip to Nassau. These days I had several good pairs and was wearing one. I had on a long sleeve cotton shirt and long paints. I would stay wet from the spray that hit me on every bounce from swell to swell. The Donzi cut through the Gulf's swells, her skipping over almost every other. Most of the trip I was on my feet, with a good grip on the wheel bending my knees as the Donzi came down cutting into the water. I only slowed down long enough to grab a cold coke then back to ¾ speed. From being wet all morning I didn't even notice the hot sun, it wasn't until 2:00 p.m. or so that I realized that my face was going to be burned. Burned from the sun and the wind. I had headed a bit too much to the north and quickly made the slight correction. I was coming up on the Key Biscayne light house, oh the memories. As I thought about it, I had visited that light house with every girlfriend that I ever had. I promised myself I would get back there soon. I rounded Key Biscayne and headed to the Coconut Grove Sailing Club. I hoped that Robert was there, he would set me up with a visitors mooring until I had a better place. Even though the Morgan was docked on the water way, I was still a member there at the club. Me not paying much attention to what day it was, I was surprised to see the dock and club quite full. Me being in a stink pot, a 28 foot shiny black, sleek looking Donzi got Roberts attention. He was just about to pull away from the dock in the launch with a group of people that he would be dropping off at their boats. He recognized me and at first yelled that he would get a spot on the dock shortly. I yelled back that, I'd like to moor her for the night. Robert motioned me to follow him. Robert pointed me out where to hook her too and he stopped on his way back to pick me up. It was funny, my body was now 36 years old but my eyes were still that 17-year-old boy. There was only one seat on the launch, it would have been sitting next to a beautiful young girl but her father took one look at me and changed seats with her.

Now I was sitting with her father on my port and the boats side rail on my starboard. Robert, when he saw what had happened just laughed. Shaking his head Robert said, I'd knowd him 28 years and aint nothing changed. Me smiling and him still laughing, we were the only ones aboard that knew what he was talking about. The launch came into the dock on the port side and I was the last to stand. When I did Robert also stood and we hugged. It's been too long, I said. I asked how he was doing and he said that the only things around here that don't change are you and my Jim Beam. I was surprised that Robert asked about Lori, he hadn't heard about the accident and said to tell her he'd be looking to see her here soon. Robert said that Lori had several admires that included young Carson, a Spaniard and Brian Crowlbe. Robert said that Mr. Crowlbe wasn't a member here and his sailing yacht, as Mr. Crowlbe called it was docked over at the Coral Reef Yacht Club. You knows, Roberto said, wheres them rich peoples go. I told Robert that I'd take care of him at the bar. Robert thanked me and said that my stink pot would be just fine where it was.

It was a pleasant trip up to the bar as Paul was still here. Look what the cat drug in Paul said. Paul came from around the bar and gave me a hug. You look like crap he said, you haven't changed a bit. The bar was almost full with one seat left at the bar. Paul put out a cold beer and said he should have known it was me in the Donzi. Looks like you've been out all day he said. Still wearing the same cloths and sun glasses, looking in the club mirror I could see I had quite a good burn. We better get some aloe on that burn a familiar voice said. Still looking in the mirror, I said and a hot shower too I trust. It was June, I had asked Lourdes to have someone that I could trust to pick me up at the sailing club. I stood and kissed her, then telling her that she had forgotten what a young boy had taught her 20 years back. June taking my seat said we'd see about that later. I of course was referring to the kiss I had received from June. June and I stayed for one more beer. Paul telling us that he and Penny too had a new son, Paul said they had named him Captain Jim. Yes, they would call him Captain. Son of son of a sailor Penney said. It's a good name I said. It took Paul a few moments and then he said, oh my God, your that same skinny girl that was chasing Jim when he was still in high school. Paul said; your father sure didn't like Jim. June said as far as her father was concerned, things hadn't changed much. With that, June got out of my seat and headed out the door. I looked at Paul and said Women.

June asked where I would stay? I asked, what about your place? June said she didn't think that would work as her sister had moved in and I was again on her dad's bad boy list. Besides June said she was working again. And dating I asked? June said yes, she was looking for someone full time. What she said, I've seen you maybe 3 times in as many months.

June was right, she needed to find someone. I hoped it would be someone that would work with me raising our daughter.

June would drop me off in my apartments garage. I asked her if she wanted to come up? She said she wanted too but would not. I then understood about that not so good kiss at the bar. I opened the door and she said, I know, call if I need anything. Yes I said, and she pulled off.

Getting up to my apartment was easy, I used the stairs to the first floor then catching the elevator. Once inside the apartment I set the air down low and headed to the shower. Here I was again by myself. I thought about it all while in the shower. I reminded myself of how many times I had promised myself that I could just go and leave this all behind. I could then hear the phone ringing. If I would have had company in the shower, I would have let it ring. It was Christina, she wanted to let me know she was at Chubby's with Lori. Lori had been discharged this morning. Christina wanted to come and see me. As much as I would have loved her company I said I'd stop by Monday morning and see them both. Christina put Lori on the phone, and Lori said she was doing fine, saying the Doctor said she would be in her leg cast for six weeks. Lori said that Malcolm's father was staying at the Holiday Inn. Lori thanked me for sending for Christina. Lori said she missed me terribly.

I hadn't eaten all day, I wasn't in the mood to go out so I put on the TV and would watch some Football.

5:00 a.m. came around, I put on coffee and turned on the computer. Jack in Costa Rica was asking about continuing on to Panama's Boca del Tora. Jack said there was a small airport there on the main island. Jack said he would prefer to wait there as Limon's American bar was getting old for Cindy. I sent back the ok.

Fernando was on his way to Limon. He should be there within 24 hours. Things in the southeast of Nicaragua were quite. Our dead were coming out with Fernando and I would have Tommy there waiting to take the dead back to Haiti. Fernando would accompany them.

Jack from New Orleans had made their night time delivery to Mandeville and the first C-130 was loaded just waiting for the second C-130 that had arrived from Honduras to be reloaded. Today they both should take off with separate destinations. Jerry said that there had been a group set up in the woods, just on the other side of the fence filming the entire Mandeville operation. Jerry said they could be spotted a mile away and that they were staying at the Motel 6 just down the street. Jerry's comment was "real professionals". I just hoped the filming was good.

I had left the Colonel's check with Salinas with instructions to deposit it in a Nassau account, once cleared Lourdes would transfer that money to the Caymans.

The Fishing and Tourist business was still raking in the money. With Peter now running 100% of the show, we now had three tourist boats and six fishing boats. Salinas had stepped right into the business assisting Peter and Janie. Janie managing the shops and the Michelle & Deanna Charity. There were plans to open a small hospital wing that would be donated by the late Catherine Johnson. Cat's name would also be added to the charity's.

Both tourist shops were also doing well and Lee, well Lee was still flying back and forth from Andros. The construction company had now purchased a Cessna of its own that would also keep Paix supplied.

Since the Vehicle was brought up, Lee moved his construction crew back to the other expansions of the Andros Navy base. My three engineers were still working with the Vehicle almost 16 hours a day.

My friend the base commander had decided that since there were no more monsters down there, the Navy would take over bringing the other item that was down there up. I hadn't heard any news about the Soviets sub that was hanging around so maybe they had gone.

Lucy and her family had now moved back to Andros and were managing their almost like new hotel. Business there wasn't booming but then again they only had the four rooms.

It was still early enough for me to call Malcolm's father to catch a ride with him to the hospital. I woke him up saying I could be there in 20 minutes and would buy him breakfast at Denny's. I walked to the Holiday Inn, and Malcolm's father and I were off to breakfast. From there, we went to visit Malcolm. Malcolm was glad to see me and again apologized for getting Lori involved in the accident. I assured Malcolm that it wasn't his fault that the other car's driver was taken to Jackson Memorial and was still in a coma. The other driver, the young man's blood alcohol was three times the legal limit. Malcolm was doing better and had gone through three operations. He was scheduled to be discharged the next day. As I had imagined, Malcolm's mom wanted him home.

I would catch a taxi from the hospital, going down town to Burdines where as I had in the past, long ago, I was dropped off in front of Burdines on one street, walked through the store and caught a taxi on the other street. From there I taxied to Chubby's house.

The girls were happy to see me, the children had left for school. It seemed I hadn't seen Christina in weeks. Both girls looked better than the last time I had seen them. The girls asked how long I would be in town I said that I was on stand by and it could be a few days. Christina walked me out as I left and asked if she'd be going with me? Somehow Christina had gotten the idea that I was mad at her for getting sick on the boat, but I was not. I told Christina that I wanted her to spend time with Lori. I told her that I had missed her and that I would not head to Panama without her. Christina latched on until I pulled her off.

My next stop was to see Roy, man was he pissed. Roy said that I was looking for it and I had found it. You thought having four kids within 12 months was trouble, he said. Roy said I had stepped on my own Dick. Roy said I would be going to Washington to represent myself. After Roy calmed down we sat and we mapped out a plan. I told Roy about the C-130 moves, and he said I must have thought this out by luck; it sounded good to him.

Delote, Hassen and Sells had been and still where my accounting firm. Roy said this would be a true test for the accounting firm.

Roy's plan was not to hide or run but for me to contact the subcommittee and offer to go and visit them behind closed doors. If what their looking into is arm sales to Iran and where the money went then Roy said we'd have nothing to fear.

I had Jerry contact someone that could arrange my visit to Washington. The subcommittee was anxious to speak and meet with me. The perimeters of the questions would be limited to their business at hand, the Iran Contra Affair, as they were calling it. I would appear without council.

Today was Monday and I wanted to insure that our C-130's had been loaded, taken off and had reached their destinations. The Panama C-130 would be unloaded to be reloaded with the new cargo, then bound for Iran. I would not visit the subcommittee before the C-130 bound for Iran had arrived at it's destination. Jerry said the flights would be completed Thursday at the latest. I would visit Washington DC Thursday night, meeting with the subcommittee Friday at 10:00 a.m. All was to be secret but I knew that it would not be. I would need to be low key until then. On my way back to the apartment I purchased a pint bottle of Jim Beam. This of course was for Robert at the sailing club.

Dinner would be pizza while watching Monday Night Football. The next morning, I got started as the sun came up. I retrieved the Donzi, took her by the Dinner Key Marina and while the attendant filled her up with high-test, I checked oil and everything else I could. Once the Donzi was ready and I had purchased a hoagie, a six pack of coke and a bag of ice, I was off. The weather looked good, and the bay was as smooth as silk. Heading out and now on the east side of the light house, I flew past several fishing boats that were on their way out for the day. My face had just about gotten finished peeling from the sun burn and it looked like I would get the new skin burned too. The trip went without a hitch. I was entering the Nassau Harbor by 4:30 p.m. I wouldn't go to the dry dock but to the city docks. Pete, still working there after all these years, answered my radio call for a slip. Pete didn't recognize the boats name nor my voice. Pete gave me a slip number and I asked if he didn't have something closer to the bar? Captain Jim, Pete asked? Well its not barnacle Bill I replied. Pete laughed and said just to take any slip that was vacant.

Pete was there to catch my bow line. I stepped off the boat and Pete jumped on to finish tying her off. Me I was on my way to the bar.

It was funny but when I walked in I had to slap the bar to wake Willy. Can't someone get a beer around here I grumbled. Willy in his seventies came alive and then came around the bar and hugged me, lifting my feet off the wooden floor. Hell Willy said, you looked better 20 years ago. I countered that I couldn't say the same for him. We both laughed. Willy went back behind the bar and got us both a Pauli girl. I's told you, you should have just moved over here and left all thems white folk. I's told you didn't I Willy said. Yes Willy, you certainly did. Then Willy laughed and said that being around thems white folk I had lost my brown skin and said it was the first time he ever seen my skin a fallen off. You's look like one of them tourist Willy said still laughing. Willy said that Michelle, Deanna and Cat were up there in the clouds just a laughing too. Yes sir Willy said our Bahamian King Fish had gone and turned white on us. I was at the bar drinking with Willy until all the fishing boats had started returning. Otis had called Salinas to send someone for me. Otis had stopped by and said hello and reminded me that I had a home. I was having way too much fun talking with Willy! That was until the law showed up. The law being Salinas with Michelle in hand. Michelle came and grabbed my leg and said, come home papa. That was it, it was time to go. It was after 9:00 p.m. when we got home and I went right to bed and to sleep.

The next morning, ah that coffee smell, Salinas was up and sitting on the porch. When she saw me, she came an hugged me thanking me for coming home. After my coffee, it was off to the shower. I told Salinas of the decision to go to Washington and talk to the subcommittee. Salinas offered to go with me and hold my hand. I smiled at the offer. Somehow I thought the committee seeing how young Salinas was could cast more doubt than they were already going to have.

I would have all day today and part of tomorrow to spend with Salinas and the children.

Soon the phone started ringing, Lourdes said that Bob had called, the Colonel, the Director's secretary, and the Secretary of State too. The best part was a message from the Bank of The Caymans of a wire transfer of $9,000,000.00. This was the balanced owed from the Vehicle's delivery monies, paid in full. Just maybe someone figured I was about to blow the whistle and they thought that maybe by paying me what they owed, I might think about it and change my mind. $9,000,000.00 was a lot of money but my mind was all set.

Bob wanted to know what I was up to? The Colonel too. I wouldn't call back the Director, the Secretary just wanted some kind of comfort. I assured them all that they need not to worry.

Bob knew what I had asked of Rodger and knew I had a plan, he seemed calm, besides, he knew he had nothing to worry about me ever hurting him. Bob said the others, all of them were worried what I would say.

The Colonel said that he wanted to meet me that night in Washington to hear first-hand what I was going to tell the committee. I said I would call him from the Hotel but I would not.

Tommy would pick me up in Nassau and I would fly Delta, Miami to Washington DC. Tommy would be waiting in Washington to fly me back just as soon as I finished my little talk.

Thursday night I kept to myself, and Friday morning, besides having my coffee, I didn't eat anything before going to my meeting.

CHAPTER V

TESTIFYING IN FRONT OF THE SUBCOMMITTEE

I had seen what I thought was a congressional inquiry and expected a bigger room and more people. I had been armed with only my Beretta until it was taken from me as I entered the building. The Guards weren't too happy about it, nor was I.

There were 4 men and 1 woman sitting with their name boards in front of them. There was also a man sitting on the side who looked like a court reported. We were all introduces and then it started.

I stated my full name and gave my address as Paradise Island, Bahamas. I was asked why I lived outside of the U.S. My answer was that it was agreed that the question line was to stay on the Iran Contra Affair. The man that asked the question looked at the others and said he withdrew the question. The next question asked was what my profession was, I again said that I would answer the question, however, this too had nothing to do with the proposed questioning. I'm an adventurist I said, I fish, search for treasure, and do some consulting. The next question asked if I had ever sold arms. I answered, that I had not. I was given the photo of the burned-out C-130's partial tail with the cat on it. What can you tell us about this photo they asked? The photo, I said is the tail of a older C-130 that had caught fire while on the ground in the southeast of Nicaragua. When was the photo taken another man asked? About six months ago I stated. How do you know another man asked? I was there on the ground less than 24 hours later I said. What were you doing there they asked? That's an easy question I said. I was there to rescue the Colonel and the plane's crew. Who sent you they asked? Well I answered, no one sent me, it was the CIA

Director that had called asking for my assistance. If you permit me to talk I think I can clear up my role in all this. They said go ahead. The Colonel contracted a company named Southern Cargo Services, I do consulting for that company. The Colonel wanted the company to land the plane to remove a few bigger items that couldn't be delivered to the Contras via parachute as had been done several times before. SCS said they would not land in Nicaragua and the Colonel rented the plane and provided it's crew. I was called and told that the Colonel had lost the plane on the ground and was taking on ground fire. It was hastily done but what happen was that SCS sent another C-130 in to rescue the Colonel and crew. That's how and when I saw the burned tail section. Were the crew saved the woman asked? Oh yes mam, the second C-130 just went in, landed, made a U-turn, picked up the Colonel and took off again. Why were you aboard the woman asked? Well mam, I knew the pilots of the second plane, I believe their thinking was that if I was going, it must not going to be very dangerous. The woman smiled and said that the Director had called the right man for the job. I answered yes mam. Then other photos were passed to me and another man asked? Do you know any of those people? Of the ten or so photos I knew 4 men. One was the President, the Colonel, the CIA Director and the Secretary of State. The others I did not know. Did any of these men ever mention the selling of arms to Iran. The selling of arms has never been brought up by any of these men I said.

We understand you travel in a privet jet, is this so the woman asked? Mam I came to Washington on a Delta Line Commercial Flight, business class. I do not own a plane or Jet. Sometimes my clients want me in a certain place quickly and they send transportation. The women then asked about my peeling facial skin. I looked at her and said I like to fish. I added that the fishing in the Bahamas was the best in the world. Do you like to fish mam I asked? Then I got one of the surprises of my life. The woman said that her father had taken her fishing out of Nassau on a Yacht by the name of the "Nassau Queen". The woman said it was one of her fondest memories of her father. Do you know the boat she asked? Yes mam I said, I knew that I had recognized the woman's name from somewhere. The last name was Kaplan, the woman's mother was the lady that had given me the house on Eleuthera. The house where Charles and Madilyn were now living in. Yes Mam I said I know the boat and your parents. The woman smiled and closed the notebook in front of her. One of the others then cleared his throat and asked If I had ever heard the name the Traveling Cat. Yes sir I said, That's a name I sometime use when doing business. Why do these planes carry your emblem on their tails he asked? I then told the story of Rusty and I crossing the Gulf Stream some 21 years ago. I mention the emblem on the sail of the boat that my Dad had built. Yes it's the same emblem, many of the business that one would think are mine are friends that I have assisted in getting started. Your money where does it come from the man asked? Well as we said at the beginning, these questions were not to be about my privet life. It's a known fact that I have been involved in locating treasure. I have been a part of two such finds and still have the passion for searching the ocean's bottom. Treasure and an inheritance has paid my way. In 1983 I sold out of most of my business at that time, only to have the IRS seize over $800,000.00 of my belongings and retirement fund. My disagreement with the IRS helped me make the decision to live in the Bahamas. I'm a U.S. citizen born and raised in Miami while my Dad's mother's family have Bahamian roots. I served in the U.S. armed forces during the Vietnam War and I'm a patriot. I have not nor would I sell arms to Iran. I then asked if there were any other questions and there was only one. I was asked if I thought the Colonel and the Director were also patriots. My answer was that I liked the Colonel and yes thought he was a patriot. I said I would not comment on the Director. I was thanked by the committee for my visit and asked if they could count on me in the future? I said that it would help if they kept my name out of the news. The woman said they would see what they could do.

I left the room believing that I just might have a friend on the committee and that they for the most part had believed my story.

I picked up my gun on the way out of the building and was on the way to the airport. Tommy was there waiting and as I walked up his stairs, he asked where too. Miami I said, Miami.

During our flight Lourdes called and said that the Colonel asked that we return to Washington. Lourdes said the Colonel mentioned the name Kaplan. Lourdes said the Colonel had said that name would turn me around. Lourdes then said there would be a limo waiting at the airport. I hesitated then said that we would return with an ETA of 40 minutes.

As the leer landed and was still on the tarmac heading into the gate, Tommy said there was a limo signaling for us to stop. I told Tommy to do so. The leer stopped and Tommy let down the steps. The limo pulled alongside and with the window going down I could see the Colonel and the Congress woman inside. The driver of the limo got out and came around to open the door. I was hesitant to get in but what the heck I'd done stupider things. Once inside the Colonel spoke first saying that Liz had said I had done a good job in front of the committee. Hell Liz said even I almost believed every word you said. Liz asked the Colonel to give her a moment with me and the Colonel stepped out of the limo. Well, Liz said I finally get to meet the famous King Fish. She said both her mom and father had told her stories that they had brought back from the Bahamas. How is your mother I asked? For being 80 and without my father damn good Liz said.

To the point she said, I want to hear about TESS. I know all about the Vehicle and the President's Star War Project, but I understand you have successfully used TESS on two occasions. Does it work she asked and when can we see a demonstration? TESS is not a government project nor property I said. TESS is an ongoing work that is in the start-up mode. Pardon me for asking mam but who is we? I also am a member of a patriot group she said. The CIA I asked? No she said we don't have agents, we gather and act on information that is used to protect our nation. An example I asked? We ask what if she said. What if, in 10 years the President's dream of a laser satellite could knock down a ballistic missile? The Soviets have thousands of missiles she said. If the President's system could knock out 90% it wouldn't be good enough she said. Your Nassau might not be hit by a nuke but the title wave would wash right over it. Hell she said with a smile, if the Cubans and Soviets knew you lived there, Nassau could even be on their hit list. If all incoming missile's guidance systems could be put out of order or changed once in flight, then that is a game changer. Can TESS do this Liz asked? I looked her and said that I didn't have the capability to check their group. I knew your Mother and Father as they were good fun loving people that knew how to have a good time. Do you fish mam I asked?

Is fishing the criteria you use to judge a person's motives she asked? I'm not asking or offering to buy TESS she said. We want to know its capabilities so we can plan ahead.

It was the Director that attempted to steal TESS from you she said. They were the Director's hand-picked men. Did the President know I asked? Only afterwards she said. And why is he still there? I asked. The President needs the Director a bit longer, she said. The Director has testified under oath that he had not known about the arm sales. Ever been diving I asked? Always the King Fish she said. I want to meet the Traveling Cat she said, and yes she said, I know how to fish and can scuba dive too. Good I said, how do I contact you. She gave me her card, on the back was her privet number. If you can't reach me on my private number, then have Lourdes call my secretary. You know who Lourdes is I asked? Oh, yes she said we've been watching you now for some time. Liz then stuck out her hand and said, well then, I'll be waiting for your call. I felt the woman already knew what I was thinking. I opened the door and the Colonel standing on the other side gave me that army salute and got back in the limo. Before I turned to climb the steps, the limo had gone. As the steps came up and the door closed behind me, Tommy asked what that was all about. That I said, was a woman that knows what she wants. Tommy made the comment that she was most likely 20 years too late. Maybe so I said, maybe so.

Tommy wanted confirmation that we were still heading to Miami? I confirmed. I called Lourdes and asked her to find me Bob. Tommy said we'd be at Opa-Locka at 4:00 p.m. and I told Lourdes to have Christina ready to leave for Panama by about 5:00 p.m. I had just promised myself that I wouldn't be sleeping alone anymore.

Lourdes said that Jerry had called and said both birds had gotten off and that the supply drop-off was on its way back. The Panama delivery should have been filmed as it was unloaded and reloaded for Iran. I was anxious to get the feed-back of what the Miami Newspaper had to say about Tim spending all that money to track used tires being shipped from Mandeville to Panama and then farm equipment from Panama to Iran. I would like to be a fly on that wall. I smiled as I thought about it.

When I arrived at Cubby's, Lori had on a pair of short shorts. Lori even with her cast on from her upper thy to her calf looked good. Lori had gone to class, only missing two days. Her cast must have had three hundred signatures on it including a drawing of a Traveling Cat. I promised Lori that she would spend her two weeks Christmas break with me. She asked if we could go to Harbor Island, just the two of us, I agreed.

Lori and Christina had been and cut their hair; both cuts were the same. They almost looked like twins. A little short for my liking but I said and they did, look great.

The kids were there and they asked about Thanksgiving and Christmas. I promised to be there for Thanksgiving and ask what they wanted for Christmas. Sam as his friends from school were calling him, said that Chubby said they must write Santa a letter with a wish list. I told the children that I had written many such letters when I was their age. I had arrived in a taxi and it was still there waiting. I kissed the children, then gave hugs to Chubby and Lilly. Lori walked me outside whispering that she was jealous and that during the summer break she wasn't leaving my side. Lori kissed me then gave me a swat on the butt.

Once in the taxi I gave the direction of the apartment. Christina asked If I was picking up clothes and I said we were not leaving for Panama just yet. Christina said she had missed me. Christina had two bags and I had just me.

Once in the apartment I checked the messages, the recorder was full. Lee, the Admiral's secretary, Lourdes, my Dad, Robert from the Sailing club and June.

I called my Dad first telling him I had just come from testifying before the subcommittee and that I was fine. He invited me to the family cabin for Thanksgiving. He was worried about me.

I called June, she answered the phone saying she was sorry how she had treated me the other day and wanted me to come by the house. June said her father said that if I needed a good attorney he would take the case. I told June that I appreciated hearing from her as it had bothered me how we had departed.

Lee called and said that the Navy said a sub, they figured, Soviet, had destroyed the Vehicle's sonar ball that was left down in the channel. I had suggested to the commander that the Navy retrieve the sonar ball before they lost it. Looked like they waited just a little too long. Lee said the Commander had asked for me. I asked Lee how our engineers were doing and Lee said they were still working almost 20 hours a day. I noted that I hope someone from the Navy was there close by. Lee said this was another reason that he had called.

CHAPTER VI

CIA TAKE OVER OF THE VEHICLE

The Navy had backed off and a new group was there working with our people. Lee commented that it looked like our Ex-NASA people knew the new group. I asked about the security and Lee said that the security had also been changed to a privet group.

I then called Lourdes and told her to call Fernando and send me 6 of his most trusted men, this ASAP. I need them on Andros.

I then called the Admiral's privet number, his secretary answered. She said he was gone for the day, I said I needed to speak with him tonight. She then put me on hold. I didn't like the sound of new personal working at the Vehicle and why replace the Navy's security. My stomach just didn't feel good about it. The Admiral's secretary came back on and said that the Admiral said to call him tomorrow. I asked if he would be in town all day tomorrow? She said yes. Will you be visiting us she asked? I said yes.

I then Called the Colonel's office and got a recording. I called back Lourdes and told her to find the Colonel and have him call me.

It was too late to catch Robert at the sailing club but I called anyway. Paul at the bar answered and said that Robert had left the message that two men that looked like dicks, as Robert said, were there asking questions about you and any boats you owned or used. Paul said those two men had visited before he had gotten there. I told Paul to put a few beers on my tab for Robert, you know I said, the same tab you set up when I was 16 years old. PauL laughed and said some of his best memories were from those days. Still laughing Paul mentioned the time that Mr. Andres asked what was the biggest crawfish I had ever caught in the Bahamas? You said 4 foot and the entire bar laughed. Everyone, except for your Uncle Bob, Carson and myself. With everyone laughing, you got up and left. Paul continued and said Mr. Andres, as I walked out had called out to me, not to go away mad. You came back two minutes later with that photo of you and two friends holding that crawfish. When Paul stopped laughing he asked about Rusty? I said I hadn't seen or spoken to him in years. I told Paul to give my regards to Penny and thank Robert for the heads up. When I hung up the phone my head had drifted way back in time, way back. I could clearly see Johnny, Rusty and I holding that Crawfish.

Christina and I got that hot shower that I was looking for but things were more business-like than before. I asked myself if this started after she had gotten seasick or after she heard me promise to spend the Christmas Holiday's with Lori? The though only stayed there a second and I looked at my watch and got out of bed. It was still early and we hadn't eaten dinner. I jumped up and said we were going to DadeLand's Burdines, it was 8:00 p.m. If we hurried, we could just make it. Christina was up and we were out in three minutes. Christina knew what Burdines was for; clothes. Christina and I were heading to D.C., Christina wasn't built like Karen, but there weren't five girls more beautiful than she was. The store stayed open until we were finished buying. There were two dresses that if I had to choose between the two I couldn't have.

We left Burdines and stopped at the Studio for Dinner. To our great surprise the restaurant had closed down, No way I thought, how could this be? Bob must have been upset. 1800 club here we come.

When arriving back to the apartment from shopping and dinner, it was late and whatever it had been, Christina had settled down.

The Colonel of course had called and Lourdes had left that message that she couldn't reach Bob. Lourdes's message said she had even spoken with Bob's wife. It was hard to believe but Bob still had the same wife for the 20 years I knew him. Wow, she must be a saint, I thought.

I called the Colonel and said that I was on the way to D.C. tomorrow and wanted to visit with whoever was in charge of the Vehicle. I said it was urgent. The Colonel said the Admiral would be a good start.

The newspapers hadn't let up on the Director nor the Colonel, seemed they were both taking a lot of heat. My thought was that the Colonel could take whatever was thrown at him but I wasn't so sure about the Director.

It was in my mind that the Director must have been pushing 75 years old or maybe more.

The next morning Christina made coffee and then went to work on getting ready for the trip. I had no planned time for return as what I had in mind could take a while. Christina was dressed to kill. Both of us would be taking Kevlar. I would be wearing a concealable vest while Christina would bring her dress jacket.

By 12 noon we were sitting in the Admiral's waiting room. As usual I had left my gun at the street side door, I did not feel comfortable without it.

Someone must have called the Admiral about the beautiful girl in the waiting room, because he stuck his head out to check the view. When he did, he also saw me. The Admiral stepped out and came and shook my hand and said to give him 30 minutes to finish up a meeting he was in. The Admiral was talking to me but his eyes didn't leave Christina. Christina had stood when the Admiral had stepped out of his meeting. Christina was wearing a short black dress that stuck to all her curves.

Normally the Admirals guest would have exited out the back door of his office, not this time, the Admiral wanted his company to get a look at Christina on their way out. Christina was quick to say she was my wife.

The Admiral asked his secretary to keep Christina company while he and I talked. I followed him into his office and he turned and again shook my hand. As he was seated, he said, I hear it was a job well done the other day. I looked at him and said I had only told the truth.

The Admiral said that they had lost the Vehicle's sonar device and wanted me to build another just like it. He asked if this was possible? I said I thought it was, using the Vehicle's built in sonar. And radar the Admiral asked? We would have to get the vehicle airborn first I said. The Admiral asked when we could do that? I then said that I was ready to call my engineers back. If he wanted to hire anyone of them he was welcome to. I told him I didn't like the changes that recently had been made as far as the new engineers and security. I was blunt, I said that I felt the project was in danger. The Admiral said he had approved the changes that were requested by the base commander. The Admiral said that both groups had been checked out by Navy intelligence and the CIA. I asked if the President had been informed. The Admiral said he had met with the Director. I said I would hate to be the one that authorized any changes that led to any inconveniences with the technology. No matter I said, my people would be there until weeks' end. And the sonar device the Admiral asked? I'm sure your people are capable I said. The Admiral almost looking angry asked for a completion date for the construction project. I said that Lee had sent a newly revised list of completion dates for each section of the base. I told him if he didn't have a copy, I would insure we delivered him a copy within 24 hours. The Admiral had now forgotten about any skirts as he didn't offer his hand nor get out of his chair when I was leaving.

When Christina saw my face, she knew I wasn't a happy puppy. We exited the building me not knowing exactly where to go next.

I called Lourdes and she said the Colonel had called and said that he couldn't get to the President and he was sure I didn't want to see the Director. Lourdes said the Colonel said to try Liz.

I hadn't planned on calling Liz, not until well into the new year. It looked like she could be my only way in. I called her privet line, she answered and said she hadn't expected my call so quick. I told her that I was in D.C. and needed to see the President. Liz gave me the name of a restaurant and said she'd meet me there at 12:30 p.m. I agreed.

I called back Lourdes and now asked for the rest of my messages. Evette had called saying that Peter had returned to Limon. Looks like Peter had been wounded in Nicaragua during our skirmish and had been treated in Cuba. Evette said that Silvia had been sent looking for me because Peter wanted a meeting. Silvia said that Peter said that I was behind all his troubles.

Jack had contacted Lourdes saying that they were anchored just off Boca de Toro Island, noting that the airport was usable but no docks and only one rustic hotel with a you catch them we cook them restaurant. Lourdes said the reception from the boat wasn't that good.

Jerry had called and said that his second bird was on the ground and was on hold for my approval to pick up the six men that Fernando had waiting in Limon. I told Lourdes to authorize the flight but that the bird must stop in Nassau an pick-up as much crawfish as possible to deliver to Richard. I figured that since I had stopped Richard from visiting Blue Fields, he would appreciate the crawfish. Richard and Ian keeping in good favor with all the Ship's Captains was imperative. I then said to add several cases of Bahamian rum and a few boxes of Cuban cigars.

The call that I wasn't expecting was from Mr. Crowlbe, no not young Mr. Crowlbe, the grandfather. I had forgotten his relation with the President and thought it might have been wiser to have gone that route. I called the number that was left with Lourdes. Mr. Crowlbe answered, first asking how Lori was then myself and the rest of the family. He asked if I had received their last wire transfer and then said of course we had. Mr. Crowlbe said we had some unfinished business and asked when I could come out his way. I asked if he enjoyed fishing? He answered yes of course. I said we'd have to plan a fishing trip on one of my boats. Mr. Crowlbe noted that he too had a fishing boat docked in Fort Lauderdale. Then Mr. Crowlbe finally got around to asking what he had called to ask, young Brian isn't getting into any trouble down there is he Mr. Crowlbe asked? I said that I hadn't heard of any trouble and asked if he wanted me to keep an eye on him. Oh no Mr. Crowlbe answered, I just didn't want him to cause you any trouble. No sir I said, and if your implying something with Lori, she's free to come and go just long as she doesn't miss any of her planned activates, no drugs or drinking and is home by her curfew. Yes, well of course Mr. Crowlbe said. I told Mr. Crowlbe that I'd be tied up until about the middle of April and we get together then. He said he'd be looking forward to that meeting. It wasn't strange that he called asking what he asked. What he really wanted to know was if young Crowlbe was bothering me enough for Brian to somehow get hurt.

Christina and I walked into the Restaurant where we were to meet Liz. The maître asked my name and led us to a small table for two. I mentioned there would be three of us as we were meeting Congress Woman Liz. The maître was caught off guard and led us to another section where the space between tables was much larger. The table which was marked reserved was set for four. Liz was almost 30 minutes late. I stood and introduced Christina as my wife. Liz apologized for being late as I pulled out her chair. Liz looked at Christina and said CIA wasn't it. Christina looked directly at Liz and said yes mam, ex CIA. Well Captain, Liz said, what can we do for you. I need to see the President I said. Just as the words had gotten out of my mouth, I added, well I'll be damned. Walking at us from across the room was my old friend, Bob. My next words were, if it isn't the great white hunter himself. Bob looking like a tourist with that, well maybe the same Cuban cigar in his hand, walked up and kissed Liz on the head and said good afternoon dear. Then looking at Christina said, Christina isn't it? Christina said yes sir. Then looking at me with a big smile said, well Captain Jim I stopped in because I saw that 20 foot wooden sailboat of yours parked outside. I said 21 foot, Bob laughed.

Liz said to Bob, that I was just saying that I needed to speak with the President. Oh Bob said, it must be important. All of a sudden, I felt that I had been trapped. I had walked right into it. I looked at Bob and asked, you don't have any plans to barrow something that doesn't belong to you, do you? Bob kissed Liz and asked if she'd mind showing Christina to the little girl's room. Liz stood and said come Christina. Christina looked for my approval and with the nod of my head she got up and went with Liz. Bob asked, you trust that woman? I countered with, you stealing the vehicle's secrets or the vehicle its self? We're protecting it, Bob said. Bob then said, the part you have, did you steal it or are you borrowing it? I looked at Bob and said, what I have didn't come from the Vehicle and no, I did not steal it. Did you pay the Nassau government their 25% Bob asked? Not exactly I said. I looked at Bob and said he was crazy and playing with fire. Where have we heard that before Bob asked? The laser weapon Bob said where is it? I handed it to the Secretary of State I said. In the White House Bob asked? Yes, I handed him the instrument case and the weapon in the Oval Office of the President. Bob sat back and said, this is why we are doing what we're doing. The weapon, Bob said has gone missing. Does the President know I asked? With a sarcastic tone Bob asked? The President. Bob got up, I did the same as the women returned to the table. By now the waiter had brought a bottle of Don on ice and asked if we were ready to order. Bob looked at Christina and said fish or beef then quickly said he had forgotten she was from Manila. Bob then ordered for us all. Some habits are hard to break I said. Yes Bob said, like playing with fire. Christina, Bob asked, does the Captain still sleep with that gun under his pillow? Christina said she didn't know that the Captain slept.

We had a good lunch, there was no more talk of business. When we finished lunch, Bob asked if we needed to continue our little talk. I looked at Liz and asked if the Soviets had blown up the small sonar sphere? Liz said no, they had just taken it. The new engineers, there yours? no she said the security is ours. The engineers work for the CIA she said. Liz asked if I still wanted to see the President? I said no. What about that fishing trip

Liz asked? It will have to wait I said, I'll be going south for a month or so searching for more of Drake's treasure. Ah the life of a pirate Bob said. I thanked Liz for the lunch, I didn't pay. Bob said he'd see me again soon and we departed. My first call from the plane was to our Miami's Tim, then Jack then Lourdes. My call to Tim was to check our computers that they were still secure. Tim said he would at once run a test program that would check the system and indicate if there had been any attempt to hack into the system. Tim said the program run would take about an hour.

I knew what we did in the next hours, maybe even days, we would be somehow monitored. No matter what kind of friend Bob was, Liz couldn't depend on that I had changed my mind about the Presidential visit. I wasn't going to the President but I was going to attempt to stop them, both sides from getting any more from the Vehicle than what they already had. I felt sure that by now the Vehicle's computer box had been breached if not completely changed out for some form of decoy. This I felt the reasoning why the control box hadn't been turned over to G.D.

Once in the air I had told Tommy to be diligent having our flight plan show Miami but that to change direction at the last minute for Fairbanks. I was headed for G.D. to consult with the technical group that was working on TESS. Once on the ground and still aboard the Leer, Tim Called and said our system was good to go and there had been no bugs. I then sent my pre-prepared message out to the gang.

I hadn't called out to let G.D. know that I was coming. Christina was coming with me, as we walked through the airport she was wearing that long heavy weight jacket.

We reached G.D. just after 4:00 p.m., I knew the chance that we were too late for that little talk but if it could, it needed to be now. I was announced at the gate and was let in though the walk in. I had asked the taxi to wait and handed him a $100.00 bill. $100.00 dollars wouldn't last long but he said he'd wait. Once inside the facility we were directed in a different direction. Here the security was better, I was removed of both guns. In the waiting room, we were met by the head engineer. The engineer had met with me several times but had not met Christina. Christina was asked to wait and the engineer and I proceeded into another room that was one side glass, looking into their lab.

The first thing was my questions about TESS. What progress had been made. The engineer asked me to be seated while his people prepared a small show. The engineer reminded me that the TESS I had in all three C-130s could not be invaded in any way. The security was such that any attempt to remove or alter would result in itself destruction of 100%. This part I knew and understood. The engineer said that they had moved forward integrating a multi laser beam into TESS, the laser he said is designed to eliminate the heat seeking threat to TESS. It wouldn't stop the small arms or 50 Calabria rounds from hitting their target, but anything with a tail fire or thrust should be knocked down. The technology he said would require a modification to the C-130 itself that would reduce its cargo space and cargo weight. You might want to look at scrapping your present aircraft and start with a newer production he said. Something to think about he said. I asked about the up-dated cost, he noted it had already cost me over $12,000,000.00 this with them having been delivered the basic technology. How much I asked? Another $5,000,000.00 to get installed and working he said. All three aircraft I asked? He said yes. I told him to stop the show, I didn't need to see it right now. I then asked the next question, knowing what you know now, what would it cost to complete the star-wars project. The engineer said they hadn't even started nor looked into the cost. The engineer said that G.D. was spending millions in using the new technology. Already we are using it in almost everything we design he said. Chips have become smaller and smarter, cell phones, computers, cars even NASA is using some of this technology. I trust you have received some kind of dividends for all of this he said with a smile. Then he said, you haven't even looked have you. The engineer then said $200,000,000.00 to design and test the system and most likely billions and years to get it to work. I asked how long it would take to install the first upgrade for TESS?

We can start just as soon as you land the first aircraft in our back yard he said. I thanked him for his time and said the first C-130 would be here within the week. I also asked him to rethink their security. The engineer walked me back to Christina. I again thanked him and he said to stop by at any time.

The taxi being still there, we left the plant and headed back to the airport.

My thinking had somewhat changed since my G.D. visit but still I wanted to somehow stop both groups from going any further. It wouldn't take an army to fly the vehicle right out of the facility, what it would take was a NASA pilot that could fly by using a radar that so far we couldn't match up with. We only had a small time window to work with as I had told the Admiral that we would be soon be pulling out our people.

I decided to inform the Admiral that if he still wanted that sonar device and possibly some form of the vehicle's radar I would take on that project.

We arrived back in Miami, it had been a long day. With nothing much in the apartment's kitchen, I had called and invited Lori to have dinner with Christina and I. I was planning to leave for Panama tomorrow p.m. Lori had already left for the Thursday night football game, Chubby said that Brian had picked Lori up having dinner first then going to the game. Christina liked what she heard but it didn't sit well with me. Christina and I had a quite dinner at Joe's.

The next morning Christina shopped for the trip to Panama while I contacted the Admiral offering him my services. The Admiral said that he appreciated my change of mind.

Christina and I would arrive on Boca del Toro just before dark Friday evening. Jack wasn't with the crew as he was off on the project that I had given him. Tommy would drop us and fly on where he would play a role in my plan.

CHAPTER VII

THE HUNT FOR DRAKE'S TREASURE

The "Defiance" was at the Chiquita dock, where their barge would pick up and deliver the Islands daily workers. Chiquita's small barge type boat had the carrying ability to haul a car or small truck plus about 40 or so workers and their goods returning home. The area was full of many small islands. From this spot the Chiquita workers would canoe to and from their homes. Captain Mike was happy to see that we had brought along fresh supplies. Jacks wife Cindy, was more than pleased to see Christina with me.

Not knowing the waters Captain Mike said we'd start off at day break. We pulled away from the dock and anchored just between the dock and the next island.

It was great to be back aboard. Still I worried about my plan and for the first time I wasn't sure how I felt about Lori. It shouldn't have, but it did bother me, the thought of her being out with Brian.

The next morning, we headed out to where I directed Captain Mike. We traveled no more than 40 miles when we were at the location where the point had been marked on the paper that was found in Drake's sword handle. We were only 30 yards off shore of a small island. The depth was marking at no more than 20 feet. A depth that even 300 years ago a fair diver could dive down and at least tie a line on a treasure box. The men on the boat had inflated a rubber boat and placed a 20 HP Johnson outboard on it. The rubber boat would pull us along the shore line starting at 30 yards from shore going the length of the island.

It was the second day that we found one and then another ship. Both had been burned to the water line, both appeared to have been intact when they sunk. Needless to say, we were elated with joy. I was sure these were Drake's ships. Here again the treasure if down there would be buried under all the debris that had taken these 300 plus years to fall apart on top of our treasure. Yes, our treasure. Unfortunately, I knew the Panamanian leader and just as soon as he knew, if and when, he knew of our discovery we would lose it all. Not having Jack's advice and expertise I quickly decided to anchor over what I thought would be the Captain's cabin of the largest ship. It took us almost that and the next day to put together the hoist that my brother Bob had built. The lift was electric driven that had the capacity of lifting about 2,000 pounds. The fourth day the three of us were in the water connecting and moving mostly large planks of wood. My hope elevated as we found pieces of the ships wheel and on the first day working in the water, found the Captain's small deck cannon. To me this meant that if the original group of men hadn't gotten back to the ship after the death of Drake then, no one had been there as yet.

That night we heard the news that Attorney General Meese had publicly announced that the selling of arms to Iran did actually happen and only a small percentage of profits were used to fund the Contras. The Attorney stated he would be looking to prosecute those responsible. The Director had already testified four times that he had no knowledge of arm sales to Iran, nor how the Contras had been being resupplied prior to Congress approving their newest funding. Lourdes said that an ex-Air Force General testified that he had informed the Director six months earlier about the arms sales and that much of the money was being spent on arming the Contras. Lourdes said it wasn't looking good for The Director nor the Colonel.

There had been some good news though, Roy had gotten a judge to let George leave for Costa Rica. Roy convinced the judge that George's wife had a good paying job that required her to be in Limon for months at a time. George would need to check in at the American embassy in San Jose every 30 days. This of course would make Evette more comfortable.

The two divers were in charge of catching us dinner. I was hoping for crawfish and they didn't let me down.

We moved debris around down there for four more days before we thought we should be about where the captain's cabin should have been. The last item we had found that looked promising had been that small cannon. We had been anchored there eight days. Jack's wife was getting worried as we hadn't heard from him, I too was kind of anxious as to what was going on with my plan. All I knew was that Lourdes said the one bird was parked up north. I took that as the Andros C-130 had been moved to Fairbanks while the other big gun bearing C-130 in Mandeville had been moved to Andros. Those had been my orders.

We were now into our 11th day and running low on supplies. If we didn't find anything today we would be pulling up anchor and heading into Boca del Toro for supplies.

It was just after a hot lunch of fish chelow that Richard and Dan moved a large plank and there laid a pile of goodies. We had planned for days how we would bring up any box that we found but it was not to be. We had the crew drop over one of our 300 pound test bags and we started filling the bag. The three of us went up with the first bag following it as the electric hoist brought it up and aboard. It was just what we thought it was, a King's treasure. The hoist measured the weight as 324 pounds. No gold bars, just jewelry. It was now almost 3:00 P.M. We put on our double tanks and would do one more dive. We were down there another hour before we couldn't find any more. No, we weren't sure but we were done for the day. This time the goods that we brought up weighed 243 pounds. Here again, no gold bars, only jewelry. It was funny, there wasn't a drop of alcohol on the boat to celebrate. If we weren't eating fish our food for the last two days had been from a can. We decided to make a run for Limon. We didn't need to mark the site and there was no reason to return to Boca del Toro. I wouldn't be happy until we were out of Panamanian waters. This time we really were pirates. I could tell that Christina was worried about the seas, yes, we hugged the cost line but it was still rough. Not like a month ago but still rough. For Christina it was déjà vu, yes she was again seasick. This time it would only be hours not days.

It was almost midnight when we pulled into Limon's harbor. Believe me, I too was glad to get away from those rolls and waves. Again, once docked Christina and Jack's wife Cindy were off to catch a taxi. I had called Lourdes to send one of the C-130s to Limon. I wanted it to be a touch and go landing so the bird was to refuel at the Honduras Air Base that we had used several times. If our C-130 had departed within an hour of my call, our ride out should be here within two or three hours from now. The timing, all had to be just right as if not our arrival and movements might look like we were moving something else. I would walk to Richard's house as Christina had taken the only taxi sitting at the dock. There was no cargo ship in port so the activity was low. With no sailors, even the bars were closed. With no sailors, even the three policemen that Limon had would be sleeping. I woke Richard and had him drive me home to pick-up my land-rover. I shook Christina and asked if she wanted to go with me? She shook her head and moaned no. Richard didn't yet know what he was doing, when we got back to the boat I then told him we would be moving 7 bags to the airport. Right away I could see what Richard was thinking. I said the cargo was not drugs. Contraband yes but not drugs. Richard said he was just doing a favor for a friend. We waited until the C-130 roar could be heard and we left the docks in both cars. Four bags in my land rover and 3 bags in Richard's car. Richard and I both had one each well-armed ex-navy seal plus the one crew member. The five of us were on the way to the airport. When driving onto the tarmac the plane's cargo ramp started down. We moved the 7 bags up the ramp. The two divers and myself were heading out with the cargo. The crew member was to drive my land rover back to the house. I waved Richard my thanks as the cargo ramp went up. The plane's motors never being shut down, we started moving on the run way when I was buzzed in the cargo hold and the captain said there was a taxi chasing the plane. I told him to circle around. As the plane slowed and turned to the port I could only see the taxi's lights. The taxi stopped and out came running at a trot were Cindy and Christina. Christina wasn't carrying a bag and they ran right up the cargo ramp as it came down for them. As the girls came aboard the cargo ramp again raised to close and we again were taking off. I unfolded the seat next to me for Christina but she sat in my lap and put her right arm around my neck and her head on my left shoulder. Cindy got a seat and strapped herself in.

Once in the air our next stop would be George Town, Cayman Islands. When we reached our planned altitude, I tapped Christina to let me up, buckled her in, and I went up to the cockpit. I then called Lourdes to let her know that we were air born and that we should make the Caymans before 9:00 a.m. It was planned that the banks armored truck should meet us on the tarmac. Lourdes said all the arrangements had been made to my instructions.

As I returned to Christina, I noticed that she still looked a little green. The cargo hold wouldn't give us any chance to talk as the noise level was too high. I sat next to Christina and again she put her head on my shoulder.

It wasn't long before we landed and sure enough the banks truck was there. We loaded the truck and then rode with the truck to the bank. The bank back doors opened and the truck backed in. This bank unlike Nassau had walk in mini vaults. Similar to a safety deposit box, but here there were two combination locks and two key locks. Here the bank inspector weighed the bags and I opened the bag of his choice. The banks weight was about 8 pounds less than ours. I figured that extra weight had been sea water. The girls had gone to find a hotel, I guess we were staying for the day. Cindy was anxious to hear from Jack. She hadn't asked and I hadn't said where he was.

With my last visit to DC and meeting with Liz and Bob, I then was in the opinion that I didn't want either group, the CIA nor the Congress woman's secret group to have the Vehicle's special tools. It was going to be Tim's and Jack's job to get the Vehicle to catch a cold as Tim had put it. The key was that Tim though it was possible to pass the cold or virus by a wireless connection. This not leaving any trace of where the virus had come from. Me telling the Admiral that my engineers would be exiting the project gave us only a small window to do what we could. Tim had given instructions to the remaining engineers what information we required to build a new sonar device for the Vehicle. Jack and the extra security group were there to insure that Tim, if suspected of anything, wasn't detained.

All had gone as planned, but we wouldn't know if we had succeeded until the CIA engineers went into the controller to get the information that Tim had requested. At present Jack was in Nassau and Tim back in Miami.

I called Lourdes from the bank and told her to get Tommy to pick-up Jack and bring him here to George Town. The C-130 crew and the two security men would head back to Andros. Richard and Dan chose to spend the night and catch the next day's commercial flight to Miami. I paid both men an advance of $50,000.00 toward their share of the treasure. The divers including Jack would receive a tax free 10% of the total value to be split three ways. Captain Mike his crew were to split 5%. I would give Christina her first cash ever and planned on giving Cindy cash too but would talk to Jack about it first. I knew that Tommy bringing Jack here would be greatly appreciated by both Cindy and Jack.

When I got to my hotel room, me turning on the shower got Christina's attention getting, her too into the shower. Christina said she had almost missed the flight. She said she pulled herself to leave the house as she knew how I didn't like to sleep alone. She didn't have to but reminded me that one of my three best girls was 5 months pregnant and the other had on a leg cast. It was her that was going to ensure that when I rolled over at night someone would be there. I wandered if somehow she felt the same. In my case, she hit the nail on the head.

The next day Christina and I were headed back to Limon. Jack and Cindy would second honey moon for a few days right where they were.

Once in Limon I would meet with Fernando getting to see that embarrassing scare on his head and him telling me of the most glorious battle of his life. Fernando said that he would go and fight anywhere with his men. Fernando said his men and even the young Contras were fearless warriors.

Christina mostly stayed at home by the pool still getting back her land legs. I didn't visit Evette and George, I wasn't sure whether Silvia's cover had been blown. I would wait to run into Peter. Captain Mike had departed for Belize; I didn't want the boat sitting in Limon. Captain Mike said he saw a break in the weather and took it. I imagined that the Captain would be visiting some of the local bars. I sent the message to only stay two days and head on back to Miami.

It was my second day back in Limon, a Standard Fruit employee showed at our gate. The Message was that a Mr. Shoemaker was in San Jose and invited me to come up and visit. The employee said that Mr. Shoemaker would send his privet jet. I wasn't too interested but said that my wife and myself would love to come visit. It was arranged that we'd be at the airport at 10:30 a.m. Christina was now feeling much better asking what she should ware. I reminded her that San Jose was a high-altitude town and got chilly at night. Christina asked if we would spend the night? I said yes. Christina asked if they had a McDonalds? I laughed.

Christina looked like a million, from Limon we boarded a leer that was similar to Tommy's. We were in the air climbing for only 30 minutes, then we were landing. We were met by a Company driver and taken to their headquarters. The building looked brand new, the driver speaking English confirmed that Standard was in the process of moving their world headquarters from San Francisco to here in San Jose. We were met at the front door and escorted to Mr. Shoemaker's office. Mr. Shoemaker, an older man welcomed us and said to call him Eric. Eric's secretary opened a siding door and it looked like we were having lunch in his office. It was a great view, it looked like we were having Lobster. Yes, another word for crawfish. Christina and I just smiled as less than a week ago that had been our main food aboard the "Defiance".

Eric was nice and asked if we had enjoyed the trip in his Jet. Christina said it wasn't every day that one got such treatment. I was glad to see Eric smile and not get Christina's true meaning. I kicked her under the table, she kicked back.

Eric said that his two supper cargo ships would soon be ready and said that he understood that Mr. Bozzni had informed me that one of the two ships would be calling Moin. I acknowledged that Mr. Bozzni had talked about the ships calling port here. Eric said that Sea Containers had offered a reasonable buy out for the refrigerated containers that Standard was planning to off hire. Eric said that they had estimated the cost of the off-hire repair would be higher than the cost to purchase. Eric said they'd like me to set a shop in Limon and start rebuilding the older units. The older units were to stay in service at least three more years. Eric asked if I would do this? I said to open a shop for a project that may last only 24 months or so may not be feasible. Eric said he would move all their major container damages here if the repair price was right. Eric also said that he had spoken to his counter parts with Chiquita and DelMonte and both said they would also support a repair facility in Limon.

I didn't make any commitment but told Eric that I would meet with Chiquita and DelMonte and let him know within two weeks. Eric said they were counting on a positive reply.

During the conversation about where we had all come from, Christina had said she was from the Philippines. Eric said that Mr. Bozzni and Mr. Crowlbe had both mentioned that I had fallen in love with a local girl while working in General Santos. Eric said that all in General Santos were doing well and mention that Mr. Bozzni said that I still owned the richest 1000 plus acres on the island. Eric was speaking of the Santos Plantation. I asked about the Tuna factory and business and he said that they were working on an expansion plan for the factory. Eric said he was aware that the factory was still owned by me and was hoping to negotiate a purchase. I let him know that in the present 5-year lease, there was mention of expansions and the relayed price increase based on a square foot of any additional space. I again said that the factory would be held by me at least until Mrs. Santos had passed away. Then and only then would there be any possibility of a buy sell agreement.

We thanked Eric for the fine lunch and business offer. Eric offered his leer to take us back to Limon but that due to the heavy fog over the mountains, the plane would need to leave San Jose by 4:00 p.m. This in order to get back before the fog set in. We thanked him for the offer but said we'd be staying the night in San Jose. Eric didn't extend the offer for tomorrow.

From Mr. Shoemaker's office, their driver dropped us off in the center of town. We got a room and then went walking. We located a McDonalds and a Pizza Hut. We decided we'd have an early dinner at McDonalds', catch a movie then visit Pizza Hut. While eating pizza, Christina asked what was to stop the owners of the Tuna business from building their own Factory. My answer was simple, the lease and the fact that I had purchased all the land from the factory north to the river. In five years, I could go back into the tuna and or shipping business. I said I didn't think they'd want that factory available to competition.

We had a great evening, reaching the hotel at 2:00 a.m. When entering the room, Christina opened the large unscreened window. The cool air came blowing in. Christina then walked in and turned on the shower. That hot shower and then crawling under those clean sheets with Christina was wonderful.

The next morning, we ate an early breakfast and then caught a bus to Limon. The down-hill ride took only two and a half hours.

Limon was hot and muggy, this compared to San Jose. Once at home we change and hit the pool.

At about 5:00 p.m. I headed down to the American bar, 5:00 p.m. was a universal happy hour. All the gang was there. Peter was now sitting with Ian's girlfriend. At least it had been Ian's girl. Looked like now it was Peter's. I sat down with Montibelli, Richard and Ian said that it looked like Peter was taking out his frustrations on Ian. Three of us laughed. Ian didn't think it funny.

Dookie, Peters driver was sitting at Peter's table. Looked like the Dook and Peter were arguing about money. I saw Peter take the keys from Dookie and Dookie got up and left. I stood and went and asked Peter if Dookie was a good driver? Peter said that he wanted to speak with me. Peter asked where I had found so many black men? Jamaicans right he asked? Actually, I said they were not normal men at all. They were Haitian Boogeymen that were on loan from the "PRINCESS OF DARKNESS" herself. Peter laughed. I said to laugh if he wished. I thought if he had seen Jena that night in Club Royal 17 years ago he wouldn't be laughing, especially if Jena had one of her voodoo dolls that resembled him in her hand. Peter asked if he could buy a round? Peter yelled two whiskeys. The drinks came and Peter took his glass and raised it. To enemies on the field and friends at the table, Peter said. To good friends and beautiful women, I said. We then both drank the glass in its entirety.

I glanced over at Richard and he looked to be in disbelief. Peter said he had just brought a house just outside of town. Peter said his new wife and he were going to have a baby. Congratulations I said. Peter said he'd like for me to bring my wife to meet his wife and see the house. What about a barbecue on Saturday afternoon Peter asked? Sounds good I said. I then asked if he needed any assistance in moving. Peter said he had hired a local group to move the furniture and radio equipment. This was one of the strangest things I ever heard of, Peter looked to need a friend so bad he was willing to accept his enemy to be that friend. Maybe it was Silvia that was pushing Peter for a friend. Well we would find out soon enough.

I reached home early and Christina was there waiting with dinner, she said she cooked. Seemed Christina had hired a neighborhood girl to teach her how to cook. Black beans, rice, chicken and sweet plantains. It was good and Christina was pleased. Me looking at what Christina was wearing made me want to quickly finish my food. I didn't know what it was called but what she had on was the thing that she had worn under her San Jose trip dress. It had two thin shoulder straps, it was black, hung loose and short. That was all she had on.

My next morning started early with a call from Lourdes telling me to check the computer and get back to her. I turned on the computer to warm it up and put on my coffee. Smelling the coffee reminded me of two things, the first was that last week we had gone even without coffee for days on the "Defiance". The second was the treasure. It hadn't hit me until now. Some people look for treasure all their lives, most of those never find what they were searching for. The cost for some that did find treasure was heavy, for some the cost was more than they would have traded the treasure for. This last treasure trip had cost me getting sea sick for the first time and drinking coffee that we used the same coffee grounds until it hadn't taste like coffee any more. Me eating Crawfish three times a day wasn't any sacrifice. Of course, I could have done without running out of limes.

CHAPTER VIII

BACK IN THE GAME

The coffee and the computer were ready, the message was encrypted, it took only seconds to translate the garble.

Tim had planned to infect the Vehicle using two separate triggers. One was time related and the other triggered when attempting to retrieve the sonar information he had asked for. Tim wasn't 100% sure it would work nor what the effect could or would be. By the look of the news I was reading we did get some reaction from the control box. The new CIA engineers had now replaced the power rods with the spares that were stored. The engineers were thinking that more power would increase the mobility and of course the laser's ability. For some unknown reason the control box had now started to smoke and everything had shut down. The Admiral was requesting our assistance. The Admiral wasn't the only one, Liz had called, and it looked like I would or at least could have my meeting with the President. The news I though couldn't have been better. I would have liked to sent back the reply that I was out fishing but I didn't. I told Lourdes, if possible to set the visit with the President's office first. The message was that I was out of the country and could be there any time after 11:00 a.m. Monday morning. According to the White House reply she could set up meetings with Liz and Bob. Lourdes was to make the Bob part clear. Then the Admiral, telling him that I was also seeing the President. I mentioned that if the White House appointment allowed me to see Liz and Bob first I would but, on the same time line, not before 11:00 a.m.

It was Saturday and Christina would get some early sun, then visit the town's open market. I had sent for Dookie, Dookie agreed to come to work full time for me. Dookie knew a lot about Peter. Dookie did just about anything for a buck. Dookie drove Christina to Saturday's open market then at about 2:00 p.m. we headed out to Peter's. To our pleasant surprise Evette and George were at Peter's house. Salvia was in the house and Evette took Christina in to meet Silvia. The way Peter introduced George, I could tell Peter wasn't impressed with George. Peter had a store-bought barbecue of which he had beef and chicken on the grill. Peter had a cooler of beer and the party had started. The house looked like it was just built. The problems were no electric nor running water. The kitchen was set up just like Angee's first house in Nassau. Here if it didn't rain Silvia would have to bucket the water from the nearby river. There was a 55-gallon drum that was half full of water, this for washing dishes, bathing and flushing the toilet. I wondered if Peter had done a good job planning to ensure that if the river ever overflowed that it wouldn't reach the house.

We had a fair time, when it was time to leave, we took Evette and George with us back to Limon. I had heard that Peter was rough on Silvia but I saw no signs of it. If Silvia was pregnant she didn't show it.

I had told Christina that I'd be traveling to Miami and then DC on Sunday. Christina had invited Evette and Silvia to the house to use the pool on Monday. I made it clear that Peter, under no circumstances was to be let in the house.

Christina said that Silvia had said that even when Peter wasn't out of town, Peter spent many a night without coming home. Christina said she felt bad for Silvia as Peter would most likely get AIDs from the prostitutes and pass it to Silvia. Christina asked if I would talk to Peter about it? I said I would not.

Evette and George seemed to be doing fine, George said that Peter had offered him drugs and because he said no Peter grew suspicious of his motives. Evette said that Silvia confirmed that she was pregnant. Silva had said that when Peter had come back from Cuba that he had changed. Not for the better or worse but changed. Silvia said that Peter's father had wanted him to return to Russia, Peter had asked to stay. Silvia said that either Peter hadn't gotten the radio to work or not, but that he hadn't used it since they had been at the new house. Here at their new home, they were not located on a hill and I saw no antenna. I hoped that there just wasn't much going on to talk about.

I hadn't got the chance to talk to Dookie about Peter. Sunday morning Dookie picked me up and drove me to the airport. Christina said she knew I was going to see Lori and even Salinas but to please not stay gone long.

The planned short trip that I did have with Dookie proved interesting and I sat with him for almost a hour while Tommy waited. I learned not only things about Peter but Limon. Dookie said that Limon had a section called Sinagita that was heavy into contraband and drugs. Dookie had been delivering Peter his drugs and that he was sure that Peter would look for him to return to work for him. I warned Dookie that he was not to have any drugs or women in my car and if he did it wouldn't be good for his wellbeing. Dookie said he had only assisted Peter with the drugs and would not return to Sinagita without my sending him there. I wasn't sure that Dookie would work out for me but his knowledge of what was going on in town had its value.

I boarded the leer and we were up and off to Miami. I was happy; I was going to see Lori. That would be my first stop.

From the Opa-Locks airport I taxied straight to Chubby's. Lilly was home and said that Chubby had taken the children to Mass. Lilly said that everyone, were doing just fine. In the same taxi, I left for the Church of the Little Flower. Once there I paid the driver, I walked in. It had been quite some time since I had been in a church. As I walked in I heard a spiss. It was Chubby, he was standing just inside the doorway. Chubby hugged me and pointed to the children. He then pointed out Brian. Brian wasn't sitting with the children he was a good 5 rows behind them. We weren't standing back there 5 minutes when Sam noticed me, he whispered to Lori and Lori turned to look. Once Lori saw me she stood and with her crutches started heading my way just as fast as she could. I met her half way down the aisle, Lori almost dropped her crutches on the floor when we latched on to each other. Needless to say, we made a seen. The priest that was talking at the podium cleared his throat. I turned to go back to the door but Lori grabbed my arm and pulled me back to sit with her. I looked at the priest and he said, considering my interruption, it was the least I could do. Most of the congregation approved. When seated Lori took my right hand and with her right holding mine she put both of our hands high in her lap. She then took her left arm and attached it around my right arm. Her head then dropped onto my right shoulder. Both Sam and Melody were looking at the two of us and smiling. Sam looked back at what I was sure to be Brian and waved. Sam must not like Brian so much I thought. I bent my head down to Sam and winked my approval of his action; Sam winked back.

As church came to an end the Priest was at the main door shaking hands. When we reached the Priest at the door, he said that he'd like very much to see the children at church more often. He said that Lori should be attending their weekly study group so to better know our Lord. He then said that I too should know God. I noted that Lori and the children could attend church as they wished. I then added that even as a young boy I knew God. I told the Priest that I also knew the Devil and that anyone bringing harm to my family would soon meet him personally. The Priest smiled and said to Lori that she should visit more often. We all walked down the steps with Sam asking if I really had met the Devil? I laughed and looked at Chubby and said that I once had him for a business partner. Chubby knew exactly whom I was talking about.

Of course, young Brian was waiting out on the side walk. Lori stood as close to me as her crutches allowed, I stopped and said hello. How's your grandfather I asked? He's fine Sir Brian said, he sends his regards. Brian asked if he could invite us all to lunch? Sam was quick to say that we already had plans. Brian then said maybe another time. Sam made a comment in Pilipino that I didn't catch.

From church the five of us went in Chubby's car out to lunch. We ate at the Coral Gables Country Club. I had joined this club so that the children especially Lori could take tennis lessons. Lori's swimming and tennis would be on hold for a few weeks more. Lori asked me to please not leave her again. I told her I was on my way to Washing DC. The Capital Sam asked? Yes Sam, the Capital. Wow he said it must be an important meeting. Not so important I said, just business with the Navy. Lunch was good and Lori wanted to show me around the club, she knew I hadn't ever been inside before. Lori showed me the grand ball room and said that one day she wanted to have our wedding reception in that very room.

Chubby dropped Lori and I off at the apartment. I don't know why but that cast looked awful sexy, I couldn't wait until she took off that dress.

We were a mess, there was no hot shower but I didn't even think about it. I didn't realize just how much I missed her.

I asked what the news was on Malcolm; Lori said he would call almost every night. Malcolm was healing well; he had undergone one more surgery, still in a body cast. Lori said she couldn't imagine how awful that must be. Lori didn't mention Brian but when I asked she said that he was nice to her but she no longer felt comfortable around him. She said he also called or comes by almost every night. Lori said Brian had asked if she could go to California with him during the holiday to meet his family. If not his family would come here. Sounds serious I replied. I told him that I love you she said, but he just seems not to hear me. He told me that you and I will never marry and that he could take care of me and the children. Sam, Lori said doesn't like him, not one bit. How about you, I asked? You like him? Well she said, I'm scared of him in way she said. At any moment, he is going to kiss me she said. If we could just stay friends that would make me happy but he wants much, much more. What should I do she asked? My friends at school asked me if this was Brian's ring? I told them that it belonged to you. Well I said, your in tenth grade and have two more years of high school and then on to collage. Brian might be in a rush as he's a senior in collage and most likely his family will want him back to work in the families Business. Kind of like me and you I said. I'm kind of building a business that you, once ready will be the heir. What I still have planned is for you to be the one that takes care of our money. Us being married she asked? Yes, I said. Then why do we have to wait so long to get married Lori asked? Please she said, marry me now. Why now I asked, so it would then be easy for you to say no to Brian or all the other boys that will be after you? Oh no I said, I'm going to make it hard on you. Your business pot just got at the least, another $10,000,000.00 richer. You found Drake's treasure Lori asked? Yes we found his "Defiance" I said. Was Christina there she asked? Yes I said. Did you bring me anything she asked? Yes I said and this time it's something you can wear. I got up and looked in my pouch. I pulled out a neckless that was wrapped in foil. I unwrapped it and held it hanging from my hand. Lori stood and hobbled to the mirror. Please she said put it on me. With only a night light on, I stood behind her and put it around her neck. I attached the hook and stepped back. The small diamonds, over 50 of them sparkled pulling every bit of light there was in the room. It's the most beautiful thing I've ever seen she said. She then turned and kissed me. Lori was correct and I agreed, standing in front of me, wearing only that cast, her ring and the neckless, she was the most beautiful thing I had ever seen. Kissing me chest to chest I reminded her of the first such time. It had been the Hilton in Manila. Lori of course remembered well. Back in bed, I asked how she was with her studies. Lori had made all A's. Lori, before the accident, had gone out for the swim team; her coach said her butterfly and freestyle time was the best sophomore times she had ever seen. I asked, what, she's a first year coach? Lori punched me for the joke. Lori said she knew that she would have to work extra hard once the cast was off. I asked if she wanted to go with me to Washington. Of course, she said. I said we should get moving.

I checked the phone messages and the computer. My 11:00 a.m. was with the Admiral, lunch with Liz and Bob at 1:30 p.m. and the White House for Dinner at 8:00 p.m. I sent the message back for Lourdes to ask about bringing a young lady to dinner. I didn't think I would get a no. With all that I gathered, I had picked out a bracelet for the First Lady. Lori and I headed off to Chubby's. I needed a haircut but wouldn't get one today being Sunday. Lori said she had plenty to wear but we would pass by Burdines on the way to the airport. Tommy would be waiting to get us into DC tonight.

Once in DC we got a limo, in Washington there were lots of limos. It was almost 2:00 a.m. when our heads hit the pillows. The next morning, I was out and about getting a hair-cut. When I returned to our room Lori was getting ready. I thought, that cast sure looked sexy.

Lori would sit in the Admiral's waiting room, the Admiral was expecting Christina and as I walked into his office, he stood and walked to the door. The little sister the Admiral asked? Kind of I said, their good friends.

The Admiral was of course concern not only about the Vehicle, but his job. It wasn't long ago I was warning him of his bad choices. He asked if the damage was irreversible. I said that I would do my best to bring the Presidents worries to a manageable level. The Admiral said that we had risen together with him approving my every move. Yes I said, right up to the last time. Without apologizing the Admiral said he wouldn't make that mistake a second time. As he walked me out he said he wanted to meet the young lady. Lori I said, this is the head honcho where our military is concerned. One of if not the most powerful in the world, I noted. Please to meet you Lori said. Why what happen to your leg the Admiral asked? A car accident Lori said. Your Ferrari the Admiral asked looking at me? Oh no, Lori said it was Malcolm Carson's son who was driving. Our Carson the Admiral asked? Yes sir I said. How is young Carson the Admiral asked? He is in a body cast Lori said. The Admiral just catching sight of the neckless, he commented on its beauty. Then looking at Lori asked what collage she was attending. I had already set it up that if he asked, Lori was to say that she was thinking maybe the Navy Academy. Well the Admiral said, what a recommendation the Secretary of the Navy would make. We'll have to talk more about this he said. The Admiral closed asking Lori to give young Carson his best.

Lori and I were then off for lunch, this time Liz and Bob were waiting. Bob stood and greeted Lori, Bob knew exactly who Lori was and about her accident. He immediately asked how young Malcolm was doing. Lori said that Malcolm was in a body cast and having a rough time. Bob said to give Malcolm his regards. Liz was quiet until she saw the neckless. Liz said she hadn't ever seen anything quite like it. Lori looked at me and said it was from the Captain's latest discovery. Bob then asked if I had found Drake's ship? I said we had. Bob with his cigar in hand leaned back in his chair and said, the adventure continues.

Bob said, Jimmy my boy we're in quite a jam. Liz had told their engineers not to process any information that your people asked for. Liz was afraid that pulling the requested information could somehow trigger a system failure. The information was not pulled, but we are still faced with such a failure. I looked at Liz and said that without investigating it looked to be an overload. I said it could be simple; the systems, as Bob called it, were designed to be cooled by their movement in the atmosphere or water while sitting or moving. Liz asked, you're saying it overheated? Yes mam I said, just as a car would if you were sitting in your warm garage with its door shut. If the car's engine was running at 3,000 to 4,000 RPMs, it too would overheat. Sounds too damn simple Liz said. It's a complicated piece of equipment and you're looking for a complicated answer, I said. Many times, I said, the most obvious is over looked. Liz then looked at me and asked if the damage was Irreversible? You tell me I said, my people haven't even seen the damage. When can you get back in the game Liz asked? Bob looked at me and said, he never was all the way out, were you Captain? You somehow knew you would be going back. Bob then said Liz was worried what I would tell the President. I will tell him the truth, the oversight was something that could have happened under anyone's control. If he wants me back, we'll go but the CIA engineers and the new security must go. Liz said she needed a compromise. The CIA goes but her people stay. If your people were in place to watch the CIA, why would you still need them when the CIA is gone. I'll use your words she said, it's simple, I don't trust you or anyone. I said the compromise will be that I have one man per security shift. Liz agreed.

Liz then immediately moved back to Lori. I understand you're a sophomore in high school she said. Lori said she was attending the same high school as I had. Lori said that when I had gone there, I only dreamed of adventure and didn't even carry a book. And you Liz asked? What do you dream of?

I dream of changing the world Lori said. Looking at me, she then said at least part of it. Where I come from many people don't have enough to eat. I want to go back and help pull my people into a better way of life. My small town will one day be a model city, she said. Have you ever visited the Philippines mam Lori asked? No I have not Liz said, I'm still working to insure we can pull this country up and out of our own people from going hungry. Because we have to spend so much defending our way of life it's difficult to manage that everyone gets a fair part of a better world Liz said. Yes mam, I understand Lori said. Liz asked if Lori planned on going back. Oh yes mam, Jim, the captain, still has business and property in General Santos. We will go back and do good things there. Plan on living there Liz asked? Lori said she would live where ever her husband lived. Bob then broke in, giving me a little help.

Lori nor I drank any of the champagne. We both ate a light lunch.

Lori and I got back to the hotel with time to catch a nap, well sort of. To get ready for the White House, Lori put on a soft strapless braw then a short black slip then that Black short dress with that skinny gold belt. The dress was short sleeves with a low neckline. Diamond pierced earrings, that Diamond neckless, and that Diamond solitaire ring went great with her dress. The cast now had almost 5 weeks and wasn't the cleanest thing I ever saw, but what the heck, Lori was still the most beautiful girl I had ever seen.

The White House limo picked us up at 7:30 p.m. I left my gun and case in the limo warning the driver of the rat trap.

We were greeted by the first lady and led into a sitting room. The first lady introduced herself as did Lori. The President's wife first asked about the cast, then the neckless. I was offered a whiskey on the rocks and Lori a coke. I was not surprised to see the President's wife wearing the broach that Cat had given her. Touching the broach She said how sorry she was to hear the news of Cat's death. I stood and took out a small box and said I apologized for the box but what was inside just might have been made by the same jeweler as a match to her broach. I handed her the box and she opened it. The bracelet was, as was the broach made with ruby's each encircled with small diamonds. I told the story that we had now found Drake's last ship and that is where the bracelet had come from. Oh she said I don't think the President will let me accept this gift she said. What gift the President said as he walked in. Lori and myself stood as the President walked in. The President all smiles, came to me shaking my hand. Well now the President said, who do we have here. My name is Lori she said. The President didn't mention Cat as the first lady had. But did get a good look at Lori's cast. The President said, if there had been room he'd have signed it too. A man came to the door and mentioned that dinner was ready.

It looked like Lori and I were having a privet dinner with the President and the First Lady. The First Lady started off by saying that it was her that arranged the privacy. Captain, she asked, you pulled your people from this very special Andros project, why? The truth is mam I had no way of getting to the President. I visited the Admiral and voiced my concerns. The CIA was brought in plus the Navy guard was called off. I've had nothing but bad experience with the CIA. I don't trust them, I said. What do you think happened over there she asked? I said it could be as simple as a miscalculation or it could have been planned to cover up something that had been removed. Something taken from the control panel could be a small as a dime I said. When I say simple, I understand the fuel rods had just been changed. The Vehicle, when moving or sitting in the ocean had sea water running through it. Pushing the throttle so to speak sitting in its hanger would be like running your car engine at high speed while sitting in your garage with the doors closed. Your car would over heat and first would start smoking and then if not shut down fast enough, the engine most likely would suffer some sort of damage and then shut itself down. Can it be fixed she asked? I suggest that the controller be sent to G.D. There we will find out what caused the problem. Either way mam, someone in the administration doesn't want that controller to get to G.D. The President broke in and asked what I was doing at lunch with the congress woman? I replied that I didn't catch a tail so maybe it was Liz that was being watched? About a month ago I reached out to a friend on how to contact you sir. As you know I testified to the sub-committee on the Iran-Contra affair. Liz was on the committee and I discovered that I had known her father and still know her mother. You see, Liz's mom and dad used to come down and go fishing with Cat. Anyway, my friend asked me to lunch and Liz was also there. What did they want the President asked? She wanted TESS I said. Liz knew that the CIA had taken control of the Vehicle and was concerned that the technology would be stolen. Liz knew of the laser gun that I had delivered to you at the same time I delivered the Vehicle's control box. Liz said that the Laser was missing. The First Lady broke in and asked the President if he knew where the weapon was? The President smirked and twitched his face to the left. The First Lady looked at him and said, go on, go find out. The President then stood and walked to the phone on a table in the corner. I couldn't hear the President as the First Lady continued to talk. How powerful is this weapon she asked? Well mam, I said we don't have anything to compare it with except maybe the system that the Vehicle has aboard. The Vehicle's laser couldn't be tested for its complete power as even the hand-held modal would pierce the facilities walls. This TESS she asked? Why would Liz want it. Well mam, TESS is what I had G.D. develop. TESS has been used twice by me in my C-130's. Although still a baby and still being developed, I successfully used TESS in the field. TESS blocks out the magnetic field and raises havoc with most electric devices. TESS so far has a range of 100 miles. The President returned and said that the gun had been moved to CIA headquarters for testing and development. The First Lady asked the President if he knew about TESS? Yes of course he replied. The Captain has used TESS in the field successfully two times, we had asked the Captain not to use TESS as this will would make it a target that our enemies would attempt to steal. The CIA attempted to steal TESS twice, I said. Once at the Fairbanks airport and once after its first official test. The first time I shot one of the Director's men two times, he lived and the second time, 4 men were killed, three of them also under CIA employment. The First Lady asked about the potential of TESS? I have spent almost $20,000,000.00 on development and testing. The Vehicle and TESS have the capability of making the President's Star-Wars vision come true. I had mentioned to the Colonel that of the $100,000,000.00 approved for the Contras, half of that should have been used to join with G.D. and start the development which to get a working modal could cost $200,000,000.00 and billions more to get deployed. The First Lady looked at the President and asked, well what do you think? I think the Captain doesn't show all his cards, we appreciate how he handled himself thus far. We will move the controller and the laser to G.D., I will arrange emergency funding. Will you oversee the project the President asked? I of course said that I would, but that the CIA personal on Andros had to go. What will you do with TESS the First Lady asked? I will continue to develop it. What if the Vehicle's controller can't be brought back she asked? I told her that I had found a log with a set of what looked like DVD disks. I've had one of my people working with IBM to convert their floppy disk to something we could transfer from theirs to one of ours. Of course, the language that they used was Latin.

What were these beings like she asked? Much like us I said, the smaller ones were super intelligent and compassionate. I don't know if you heard the story but we dug up a Seminole Indian Chief on Andros who was buried with a prosthetic forearm and hand. The missing hand had been taken by a 30-foot crocodile. A skeleton of one of these beings was found in the Vehicle itself. If there are or were larger ones, then they were bigger and stronger. In the early 1970s there were rumors of a being that was encountered in Nicaragua. This beastly being hunted and ate men while they still lived, it hunted them for sport. It too was said to carry two similar devices much like the smaller being. A powerful laser weapon and some kind of medical laser device. It seemed that our smaller beings were hiding from something. The TOTO channel was as good a hiding spot that one could have picked until in 1941 when a German sub running from a British Destroyer fired two torpedoes at the Vehicle in the channel.

The Captain of the Destroyer only witnessed the sonar of the encounter in which the Vehicle after reflecting the torpedoes fired back destroying the sub. The British Captain's report said that the Germans' Sub's torpedoes looked to be on the mark, but didn't explode until hitting the channels ledge. The strangest part was the speed in which the Vehicle darted away after the kill. The Captain noted a speed of over 60 nots. The rest was the history that has brought us to where we are. And the rest of the story the First Lady asked? Sorry mam I didn't mean to bore you. Oh no, I want to hear more she said. I looked at the President and she looked at him and said she was sure they had the time. Yes Captain, the President said go on with the story, the short version. Anyway I said, the British Captain just couldn't let it go and he was sent to the US meeting with our Navy. The Navy sent a small sub maned with 14 sailors down into the channel, it was never heard from again. In 1942 after the US joined the war, the US and Great Britain decided to build a Naval base on Andros's east coast. Besides appearing to be the home of this mysterious vessel, the TOTO channel was one of the largest and deepest in the world. It could have been used for German sub refuge and access to the US east coast. I told her that the Vehicle didn't permit the secret base to be completed and that the project was postponed. After the war was over President Truman sent in 5 Navy torpedo aircraft to destroy what he called the enemy vessel. All 5 aircraft were lost, a rescue aircraft was sent and it too did not return. The President then authorized an experimental nuclear bomb to be dropped at the sight. The bomb was dropped and it apparently did the trick. The Navy base went ahead and after all that time the radiation is now low enough to have permitted us to retrieve that same vessel. As I understand it, the autopsy on the being showed the cause of death as Radiation poisoning. Your story is fascinating Captain, you tell it with such a passion she said. Yes mam it has and continues to be quite an adventure. The President wanted to put an end to the story telling and added that with the Colonel out of commission he would like me to head up the Contra fight. The President said they had heard what a hurting we had put on the Cubans and was sympathetic for the families that had loss of life. We could have talked for hours more but I could tell that the President was ready to retire. At the end, we thanked the President and his wife for their kind hospitality. I had called the Presidents wife, Mrs. President and Mrs. First lady. At the end she asked me to call her by her first name.

Our limo was brought to the front door and a Marine guard opened the back door with Lori getting in on the starboard side and me going around to the port. Once I was inside Lori climbed into my lap with both legs now on the seat. Lori then asked me to kiss her and not to stop. The ride to the hotel was short, it was now almost 11:00 p.m. The cast didn't bother me that much but I could see that Lori was anxious to get it off. I asked Lori if by the next weekend the Doctor had taken off the cast if she wanted to make a short visit to see Malcolm. Lori said she wanted to see him but that only if I also went along. Lori knew from our conversations at the White House that I would be moving around quite a bit. Lori said that I didn't want her to miss any of her high school proms, she asked how many 16 year old's got to eat dinner at the White House with the President? No one will believe my story she said. I asked what would she tell them we talked about? Lori thought about it and then said she even had less chance of anyone believing that either. Lori said even if the President would have signed her cast, anyone seeing it would say that it was anyone's signature but the Presidents. Watching Lori undress and climb into bed, I wondered how I would drop her off at Chubby's tomorrow.

CHAPTER IX

DISMISSING THE CIA'S ENGINEERS

It was only weeks before Thanksgiving; I needed to see Salinas and the kids and either get back to see Christina or have Christina come to me. I knew I would be spending at least two or three days on Andros. Salinas was now at least 6 months pregnant. Her now saying the Doctors said we are having a boy. This baby would be number three for Salinas with her barely reaching 18 years old. With one with June and one from Cat, I would have 5 plus two that Deanna left me plus Lori's little brother and sister. That's nine children, I wanted to have at least two with Lori, of course by then I would be say 44 or 45 years old. Lori would then be 24 or 25. Hopefully a smart well educated 25-year-old.

The next morning Lori and I flew back to Miami, she already missed the morning class so I took her to the apartment with me. At the apartment, I check the calls and the computer and would sit there at the computer sending messages. Jack was now back in Andros with the six-security crew I requested. I sent for the return of our three engineers and Tim. Evette had sent word that Fernando and his people had returned to Nicaragua. Thinking that Costa Rica could be on hold for a few weeks I also sent for Christina. Christina should go straight to Nassau, I would pick her up there, where we would travel to Andros.

I would be meeting with Bob, he was concern as to how my meeting with the President went. The restaurant would be Joe's, the studio and Prince Hamlet now being closed. Lori would get to show off one of her new dresses from Burdines. When I saw her with it on, my first thought was that Burdines would love a photo of her in that dress with that cast. I had seen a sign on the main floor of our building for a photo shop here in the building. I thought I'd surprise Lori by calling and asking if they had time to take a few photos of Lori. Maybe it was just me but for some reason, I felt that almost anyone would see what I see. I called down to the lobby and they transferred my call. The shop was closing but said they would wait. Lori still having no idea that we would stop by the photo shop took her small bag and we were off. When we got downstairs is when I told her of my plan. Lori said she didn't want to stop. She asked please not to go. We walked in me dragging her by the hand. At first the camera man didn't look impressed, he must have thought, just some man wanting a photo of his daughter. Lori had taken a light jacket from Evette's and Karen's room and had it over her shoulders. I took the jacket from her and kissed her, telling her that I was in love with her. From the kiss came out that beautiful young lady that I knew was in there. The camera man then showing her where and how to stand made no comment about Lori or the Jewelry. He took some photos with Lori giving different possess and then said he was finished. I wasn't impressed, paid cash and said to call the phone number that I had given him when the photos were ready.

Lori and I then headed off to meet Bob for dinner. I had never seen Bob look worried, until tonight. I told him not to worry that his name never even came up. What about Liz he asked. I told him that the President asked what we were talking about at lunch. Bob said, you mentioned that we went to lunch? The President knew, I said because Liz was being tailed. Bob asked by whom? I said I didn't know or ask. I told the President that I had met Liz when I was testifying and that Liz mentioned that her parents had talked about their fishing trips with Cat. Liz's mom and dad had moved to the Islands. Liz's father died and her mom gave me their Island home. I told Bob that we talked about the Vehicle and TESS. Starting today I would take charge of the Vehicle and the Contras. I told Bob that I thought that the Director was on his way out. The Colonel was already out. I said their security could stay and that tomorrow I would dismiss the CIA's engineers. I told Bob that I would move the control board to G.D. for them to see what was salvageable. Bob said to tell him we hadn't lost the possibilities. I thought you didn't pick sides I said. Jimmy boy just because I show up to a lunch with her doesn't mean that I'm sleeping in the same bed with her. Bob added that we were both playing with fire, he said that in Liz's group that they called her the Dragon Lady. Dragon as in as fire breathing Dragon he said. Bob said that once when she had gotten upset, that his cigar that he was holding, lit up by itself. I hadn't heard his laugh in some time, it was good to see his since of special humor. Bob said a lot but I could tell he was careful about what he said in front of Lori. Bob's last words on the Liz subject were that she had said she was waiting on the fishing tip.

Bob then switch to another subject, air cargo. Bob said that Montibelli would need to contract our SCS services. Since that Panama run has dried up Bob said he was sure I wouldn't mind the extra business. I asked Bob if Montibelli was going to start shipping ice blocks from Limon? Bob laughed.

The food was as good as always, I would take Lori back to the apartment and then return her to Chubby's early tomorrow morning just before I took off for Nassau. Lori didn't ask a lot of questions about my business, I asked why and she said that she figured if I wanted her to know something I would tell her. I then told her for the second time that day that I loved her.

When I dropped Lori at Chubby's I had some special instructions for him that included better eyes on all the children.

I was on my way to visit Salinas and see the children. When arriving, I was surprised that Salinas had gone and taken the "Cat" for a sail. Betty said Salinas had been taking out the boat several times a week. Betty said that Salinas had even taken Willy out on his first sail. Betty said at first it was a way to win your approval but then it became something else, she enjoys it. Today Betty said she had gone out with Christina whom had arrived last night. Betty said it would be a good time for me to spend the day with the children. Wendy Michelle and Johnny were both the age that I could walk them down the beach all that way to the Holiday Inn get them a burger and walk back. Go on she said and get out of those clothes and put on the Island gear. Island gear for Betty was an Hawaiian shirt, shorts and tennis. So I changed my clothes and Wendy Michelle, Johnny and myself were off down the beach. You might think I would be without my Gun but I now had a water proof tourist looking pouch that was holding that stainless Walter 9mm of mine.

The children and I actually had a blast, both Wendy Michelle, and Johnny were good swimmers, we would jump in after one of those rolling waves then jump out and run up the beach until we found another wave just about to hit the beach. It was nice to be with the kids hearing them laugh calling me papa. Both had strong Bahamian accents. Salinas had told them it was a British accent but it was Bahamian. Every once in a while the children would talk to each other in French and laugh, they were talking about me and knew that I couldn't understand them. We reached the Holiday Inn, ate lunch and started back. Wendy Michelle said they had been laughing about my color, I had what I considered a good tan but still my skin was much lighter than theirs. Both had those big green eyes while mine were light blue. Johnny asked how I got such beautiful eyes. I told him I had gotten them from my mother just as he had gotten his from his mother. Johnny said that his real mama was in heaven. Yes I said, yes she is but Salinas is your mama now right? Yes sir Papa, both the children said. Johnny was referring to Cat as he was too young to have remember Deanna. Ah Deanna, just the thought of her and I out on this same beach had tears of joy rolling down my cheeks. I was smiling thinking that she was happy to see me with the children. The three of them were most likely sitting together up there watching us, them talking about old times.

Almost home I looked up the beach, and here came trouble, no, not that kind, it was Salinas and Christina. The children spotted them almost at the same time as I did and they both took off running toward them. When they reached Salinas they all hugged and kissed, the children pointing to me. Christina stayed with the children and Salinas came at a trot, A slow 6 month's pregnant trot. As Salinas arrived in my arms she said she had missed me and loved me more than ever. I already had the news but Salinas told me again. We're having a boy. I want to name him Jacques she said. That's James in French she said. Jacques, I repeated. She said yes. Jacques it is I said as I kissed her again. Salinas took my hand and we walked toward Christina and the children. Salinas said to the children that Christina was their Aunt Christina. Still holding Salinas by the hand I reached out to Christina and pulled her to me kissing her saying that I was happy to see her. Salinas then took both children by the hand and started walking back to the house. As Salinas dropped my hand Christina put both arm around me and kissed me again saying that after

Jacques was born, Salinas was going to take a break from having children while she had the next one. If that's going to happen you'll have a lot of hard work to finish first. So that's a yes she said with a smile? That's a, I'll think about it I said. Christina then hugged me and said that she wanted to stay the night in my old apartment for two nights to give Salinas some time with me. I said that unfortunately I would be heading to Andros in the morning and was planning to take her with me. I said that we had important work to start there. Christina said she thought things would change once the President had called. Christina said that at least Salinas would have one night. You making my plans now I asked? Christina said that between the three of them they were planning to keep me busy. One for all, all for one she said. Christina said that Salinas had told her the story of the three Musketeers.

We now had several cars and chauffeurs as we still had Cat's truck, car and driver, Salinas of course had her own driver. As I walked Christina up to the house, she said that she had a great time with Salinas on the Hunter. Christina kissed me telling me that she loved being a part of the family and wanted to make it official by bringing a child into the world. She'd be waiting for me at the airport at 7:00 a.m.

Inside the house Salinas was waiting for me to take our shower. First I was to see our three youngest.

Salinas and I passed a good night with her promising not to cry as I left but she did anyway. I promised to be back within a week and would do my best to stay a week and then spend Thanksgiving weekend here.

The next morning Christina and I traveled to Andros, the whole gang was here. I first briefed our people then visited the base Commander whom had already been informed that we were back and once again taking over the Vehicle Project. The Commander would be present at the change of the guard. The CIA engineers were stripped searched and escorted off the base.

Our first priority, was to remove the controller, our C-130 had arrived from having its TESS upgrade and would be used to transport the controller to G.D. Jerry would head up the delivery team. Jerry, being in charge of the operational side including the personal delivery. The EX-Navy Seal Jack, along with his two men and Fernando's top pick 6 would run security for the trip. The C-130 while at G.D. had also installed an extra gift from G.D. that included electronics that indicated when the aircraft was being tracked via ground, air and or satellite. Jerry and Jack, plus their men would leave for Fairbanks just as soon as possible.

Tim was in charge of the controller's removal and with our three Ex-Nasa engineers', would assess the damage before moving it to G.D. Once the controller was on its way to G.D. Tim could return to Miami while our three engineers would remove the newly placed fuel rods, replacing them with the originals. Lee having our engineers help was designing a system that would hold the Vehicle from being moved on its own power plus a sophisticated system that would allow the Vehicle to use sea water to charge the Vehicle's batteries and we hoped refuel the fuel rods. All this would require that G.D. supply some kind of replacement for the damaged controller that would allow at least the basics. No one, but the G.D. President and myself knew that G.D. and I had a spare controller and Laser from which G.D. was using to develop TESS. I believe the spare controller that G.D. would develop could be used without certain parts and capabilities.

The day had gone by quickly; Christina and I would be staying at the Andros house with Lee.

Once at the house, Christina contacted Lourdes for messages; of course, there were the usuals, plus the photo shop owner had asked if I would return his call. I called thinking his photographer had most likely damaged the photos, and the owner was calling to apologize. The owner said there was something about Lori that caught his eye and he was wondering if we could come back by so he could take a few more photos. The owner mentioned that if possible, Lori could bring with her several outfits, including a bathing suit. I mentioned that Lori would be having her cast removed on the following Monday and that since Thursday started a four day holiday, maybe we could work it in on the Wednesday before Thanksgiving. The owner, Mr. Horwitz said he'd like to take the photos with the cast. I said then maybe this Friday after school. Mr. Horwitz asked about Saturday morning. I asked if 9:00 a.m. was good? He said that would be fine. We'll see you then I said. Christina was listening and asked about the photos. I thought about it a moment and asked if she had brought with her that short black dress. The one you like she asked? I wouldn't go anywhere without it, she said.

Lourdes had also said that Evette and George were on their way to Miami as George needed to report to his parole officer.

I wasn't worried about the controller's trip to G.D. I knew it was in good hands. We received a call at about 8:00 p.m. from Jerry letting me know that their mission had been successful. They should be taking off from G.D. by about 10:00 p.m., they would make the stop over and pick up the package that I ordered and arrive sometime early tomorrow morning. I had hired a personal trainer that I would use to get Christina into a physical and mental shape that I thought would come in handy shortly. Christina's plan of her getting pregnant wasn't going to be as she and Salinas had thought.

Lee shared with us that he had met with the local Andros Governor requesting the purchase of an addition 10 acres stretching to the south. Lee was at the point of the Navy's construction contract that would infringe on our property. He said that on the additional sight he would need to buy and relocate three small homes. All had been negotiated except for the land owned by the Bahamian government. Lee's thinking, on which I agreed, was to move our northern fence and keep building the Navy's project on our property without transferring ownership. Our property and the Construction Company were not one and the same owners. Therefore, any future negotiations on the sale of that property, the Navy couldn't claim that the property owners had given permission because they had done the construction.

The next morning at the Vehicle sight we met with our engineers and discussed the plans for the future of the Vehicle, this assuming that the controller could be repaired. During this meeting Mira asked about TESS and where that technology had come from. I warned Mira and the others that as far as they knew TESS didn't exist. Mira said she had been told by one of the CIA engineers that TESS was an active system that we had developed. I let them all know that information that came from me would be on a need to know basis. If there were something that they needed to know, I would tell them.

CHAPTER X

THE ARRIVAL OF BULLDOG

Our C-130 arrived and once all were transported to the house, Christina and I returned to meet our newest person to join our group. Maria, a 35-year-old TI instructor with the Marines, would now begin training Christina. Yes, Christina would now be going through something like a boot camp. Maria was an 18 year veteran with the rank of Master Sargent. Maria had planned to be a lifer with the Core, until she was brought to my attention and I offered her employment. Maria, unsure she would adapt to or like the job took a year's leave of absents from the Marines. Maria was a good-looking woman that looked to me something like I imagined Joe-Ann may have looked like at 35, if she would have lived. Maria's nickname was Bulldog. Maria was born and raised in Puerto Rico and, of course, spoke fluent Spanish.

When introducing Christina to Maria, Maria asked if Christina was ready for her first run? Maria looked at me and said I could come along if I thought I could keep up. I liked this woman. Maria had Christina borrow one of the other recruits' backpacks and when Christina and I came down from changing, Maria was there waiting with 8 other new recruits. The 8 consisted of 5 Haitians and three Bahamians, yes three high school grads from our own Andros Island. One of the Andros recruits was a girl, she was the older sister of Carla that had been raped and murdered by the Navy personnel. Three of the 4 men that were responsible for Carla's death were sitting in a Bahamian jail.

Maria must have put 20 pounds worth of gear in Christina's backpack; then Maria started running. All 10 of us started after her. One by one the recruits started to lag-behind. Maria didn't stop, nor did Christina and I. While running, I was reminded of the stomach cramps that came at 3 miles. Maria was now almost 50 yards ahead of us when she stopped. I was exhausted and now relieved until Maria then started running back our way. Christina looked at me and asked, she must be kidding, right? As Maria ran by us she said for us to turn around and follow. One by one we past each recruit and they then turned and rejoined our group. Once we caught up to the last recruit Maria started walking. Walking along side of her, Maria asked the ages of each one us. When I said 37 she said she thought I was older. Christina still out of breath, laughed. Christina asked why she carried the pack? Maria answered that she was contracted to make her, the best she could be, a true Marine. A Marine, Maria said can run all day without rest, carrying everything on her back that is required to complete the task she is given. A Marine will sacrifice anything for a fellow Marine. Christina looked at me and said that she could take anything that Maria could dish out. As we reached the compound, Maria said she would meet both of us on the beach at sun up. Maria looked down at Christina's tennis shoes and said that we needed to find her some boots. Maria then smiled and saluted, saying, Master Sargent Maria reporting for duty Sir. I saluted her back saying welcome aboard Sargent. Maria then held out her hand to Christina and said that she was going to be tough but they would become best of friends. Christina shook Maria's hand and asked where she would be staying? Maria said she would share a room with Christina. Christina said that she was the captain's wife and that their bed was full. Maria apologized saying that she didn't realize that we were married. Christina asked Maria if she was or had ever been married. Maria said that she had been married once but it was an abusive marriage and ended in two broken knees from a bat. Christina said by the way Marina ran that she had made a good recovery. Maria said that the broken knees were her husband's. Maria said she would bunk with the new recruits.

The dock house was again full, with the three engineers staying at Lucy's parent's small hotel, we were about out of room. Lee asked about another house. Lee said bigger family bigger house. We talked about it and decided that the next house that would be built on the south beach would not be hurricane proof but more like the houses on the beach in Belize. Jack's wife had been picked up and flown over here to Andros today by

Tommy. Jack and Cindy had added their input to the thinking of a beach house. Seemed that Christina and Cindy had made the decision for us. We would build two small one bedroom houses right on the beach.

That night in bed Christina asked if I wanted her to be a Marine? I smiled and laughed and told her that she was to be the protector of the family. If anything happened to me she was to insure the safety of our family.

We would soon know if the CIA engineers had taken what they needed from the controller or if indeed what we have is the controller. The President had said that the laser weapon would be delivered to G.D. by now. By tomorrow we will have several answers that could put us in a much higher risk than we already are. The Colonel is finished and for the CIA Director, I only saw a small window before he would break and point his finger toward the President. This, if something wasn't done to stop him. Something like what Christina asked? Maybe a heart attack I said, he is and older man. Anyway I said you being in top shape will only be a good thing. Once Lori gets out of that cast I want you and Maria to train with Lori to get her even stronger than she was before the accident. I told Christina that I had added some additional security for Lori and the children and was in the process to do the same in Nassau. Hopefully Lori nor Salinas would even notice the extra measures.

Friday morning, we would get up and run as a magnificent sunrise showed its colors. The plan was just the 3 of us but, all of the new recruits were there ready for the run. Today Maria ran even further than yesterday. All of us ran further. This time Maria shouted as she ran. It was some kind of Marine thing, she shouted and then we repeated it. It reminded me of basic training at Lackland ABF some 19 years back. Back then in 1970, basic training lasted 6 weeks. I still have my group graduation photo. I wondered where some of the old group might be. Metca, Plumbe, Rayan and Burman. Burman and I were squad leaders, once while all we're asleep I had put a five dollar bill in Burman's dress blues top pocket. I left just enough of the bill sticking out that it would be seen during the weekly barracks inspection. My squad got a one-day pass, and Burmas's squad got KP. Burman went to the Synagogue on Wednesday nights. The first Wednesday night Burman arrived back to the barracks well after lights out. As he came in I quietly called him over and whispered that I thought someone had been messing with his bedding. Against the rules, Burman turned on the lights and ripped his bedding apart. When he did this, all he found was a few laughs. The next Wednesday night I again called him over and said again, I thought someone had been messing with his bedding. This time Burman attempted to get into bed without checking and found his bed had been short-sheeted. With Burman's cursing came the laughs of the entire floor. Short-sheeting was something that I had picked up at Boy Scout camp. Oh, the memories.

After a good breakfast, Maria would travel to Miami with Christina and me; there would be no break for Christina. Maria had traveled many times in a C-130 but never a leer jet. We got in early enough for us to get Maria settled into the third room of the Miami apartment. We would drop off Christina's black dress to a two-hour cleaner, then make it for lunch at the 1800 club. Lourdes had called Lori and let her know we were coming plus making a salon appointment for the two girls. We were at Chubby's when Lori came driving up in her jeep. Lori's first hug and kiss went to Christina then me. I'm sure Maria would have thought my kiss strange if Christina hadn't done some talking on the leer. Lori looked at Maria then me and said what I had thought. Lori said, she reminds me of Joe-Anne. I said it's the uniform, then introduced Lori and Maria. Lori, saying it was nice to meet her. Christina commenting that maybe after she got that cast off, Lori would change her mind.

Our plan for the rest of the day was simple, the salon then shopping. Lori would be the main attraction tomorrow morning but I was having Christina wear that Black dress. I had the hunch when the photographer saw Christina that he would want at least a few shots of her too. I dropped all the women off at the salon warning the girls working at the shop, no died hair and nothing short. The girls at the salon told me not to forget the Cuban coffee. That was my signal to leave, the girls agreed I should return in about two hours. I returned to the apartment and would check if my friends at G.D. had any news.

CHAPTER XI

THE CONTROLLER

The communications to G.D. needed to be sent through the computer to Lourdes then she would send to G.D. then back through Lourdes.

As I had suspected the laser weapon was delivered to G.D., but with it guts missing, someone now had the laser capability. This in itself was bad news, but just as bad, at least one part of the controller had been changed out. The part that was changed out was what messed with the magnetic north. G.D. said that the interchanged part, was from the Israeli manufacture, IPAC. If there was any good news it was that the part missing wasn't enough to duplicate TESS. G.D. stated that, although too early to tell, it looked like my theory of overheating could have been the cause of the failure. The Israeli replacement part was the first to melt down causing a chain reaction. G.D. said they wouldn't know for at least a week what if anything could be reused.

G.D. said that the Laser could be duplicated but to remember the power source. Even G.D. could be years away to building such a battery. The strength of the laser was directly related to the power source. The first TESS model's power source weighed over 2,000 pounds. The second version of TESS had almost double that weight. Both systems were encased in a thin layer of lead as both had high radiation levels.

I wasn't in any rush to have Mira taken into custody, there wasn't much she could carry out with my security there. At present, I didn't know of anything of value that was small enough to be swallowed.

I touched basis with Evette, she wanted to meet in privet. I thought she could be wavering on the Costa Rica assignment. Since we would be the lead with the Contras, we needed her even more than before. She asked to visit early tomorrow as George was sleeping late. It was agreed that Evette would come to the apartment at 7:00 a.m.

My two hours were about up, I parked and walked to the Cuban restaurant on the corner and bought coffee for the girls. I was pleasantly surprised when I walked in. All 3 had gotten work done. Lori's and Christina's hair didn't look any shorter, more like styled. They both looked like a million. Maria now, she got a haircut. The girls working spoke to Maria in Spanish. I asked Maria what they were talking about? Maria said they asked which girl was my wife? What did you tell them I asked? I told them it was on a need to know basis and that I didn't know. Good answer I said.

From there we would all pick up Christina's dress and then go shopping. Maria said she had all the clothes she needed. Greens, tans and blacks. We went down town to Burdines, Lori knew we were going back to take another round of photos and said she had everything she needed. So, we window shopped until we came to the bathing suits. Lori had two bathing suits, the one she had worn on the Rivera that I could put into my closed hand without it being seen and a one piece hide it all. Lori was looking at a two piece and looked at me. I looked at her and said she could try it on. When she came out, I knew that would be too much for any young man. By the look on my face, Lori looked at the sales woman and said we'll take it. Lori also picked up two more one piece speedo swim suits with matching caps. Christina had two good swim suits but seeing Lori in that black one-piece speedo, I asked her to also try one on. It had been my intention to get some Christina photos too, but her coming out in that black speedo did it. Christina asked if I liked it. I swallowed hard, and said it would do just fine.

The girls didn't want to go out to dinner, I think it was that they didn't want to add anything to their stomachs before the photos were taken.

We pick up a few sandwiches at the apartments downstairs deli and called it an evening. Once in the apartment, Maria got another culture shock; both Lori and Christina slept in my room.

The next morning Lori and Christina took off early. Lori driving my BMW, they would go to Chubby's for Lori to get ready and bring a few changes back with her. By the time they were leaving Evette had shown up, The three girls all hugging and introducing Evette to Maria.

Evette and I walked out to the balcony, and Evette started with the tears. Even up to this point I still thought she was leaving us. With tears rolling down her cheeks, I said to spit it all out. She didn't want to be with George any more. George had blown her cover to Peter, not Silvia's only hers. Evette said if George would have known about Silvia he would have blown that too, but he didn't know. Evette wanted me to send her anywhere but without George. Evette said she didn't even want to go back to him today. I decided to send her to Nassau with Christina and Maria. They could stay at my Nassau apartment. I reassured Evette that we would be fine, Peter most likely suspected her anyway. My biggest concern at the moment was that the radio would be left unintended for longer than I planned. Before Fernando had gone back into Nicaragua he was told that we would fly in on this coming Wednesday at 14:00 hours to pick him up from the Nicaragua strip. I would call the Admiral and get them to extend their radio coverage, it had been agreed that the Navy would cover Evette coming out for three days. Now it would be more like a week. I didn't get conformation but hoped to hear something back soon.

The girls came back and we were ready for the show to start. All five of us went down in the elevator and to the photo shop.

The shop owner Mr. Horwitz was there with two helpers and another mid aged well dresses woman. Mr. Horwitz had never met any of us. His attention right away turned to Lori of whom he had seen photos and then Christina whom he at first assumed were sisters.

They got started on Lori, at first Mr. Horwitz was positioning Lori and himself taking the photos. Within minutes the well dress woman stepped in and took over doing the positioning. As she moved Lori she told Lori that she wanted her to look at me and forget everyone else in the room. The woman then turned and asked all but me to wait in the sitting room. The woman was smart as it was like a light was turned on. Lori became Lori. Her smile, posture and even her complexion had changed. Lori went through two of her dresses and then started on the bathing suits. The woman that was doing all the direction was now smiling and having fun with Lori. I could tell that Lori was comfortable with her. I had seen Lori in a bathing suit with her cast on but here too, looking at her made my stomach feel good inside. Every once in a while, the woman looked over at me to see my reaction. The last photos were with Lori wearing the black speedo. Lori asked the woman if she was going to take some shots with Christina? The woman said, not today sweet heart. Lori said that Christina had a identical black speedo and she'd like one photo of them both together. It looked like just to please Lori the woman agreed and Christina was called in. Christina changed into her bathing suit and came back into the room. The woman walked up to Christina and like examined her curves then make up. The woman then turned to me and asked if we had brought along the neckless that Lori had worn in the first photos. Lori jumped right in saying that she had the neckless in her bag. The woman had Lori and Christina do several possess with Mr. Horwitz still taking photos. The woman then asked if she could take a few shots of Christina with the neckless. Do you want me to change into my black dress Christina asked? Not today the woman said we'll keep you in that bathing suit. The woman looked at Lori and said we're done with you today dear. You go and change. Lori then walked into the other room. The woman then asked Christina if she was comfortable? Christina looked at me and asked how she looked? As Christina looked at me, the woman realized both girls had looked for my approval. Several shots were taken of Christina with the neckless and without. The woman then had a few boxes that she had and looked until she took out a dress and asked Christina to try it on. The woman gave Christina everything from underwear to shoes.

Christina came out changed and the woman worked on touching up Christina's make up. They then took several photos and then the woman asked if she could take a few photos of Christina wearing only her full slip. Christina said she didn't mind and looked for my approval. I looked at the woman and asked why? The woman said that she represented several clothing manufactures and that Christina's posture and shape may help sell those clothes. Christina looking at me again said she didn't mind and I gave the go-ahead. Seeing Christina barefooted in that slip also gave me that funny feeling in my stomach.

When finished, the woman gave me her card and said that with my permission she would show the photos and see what interest they could get.

The woman said that she would like to manage Lori and she was sure since the clothes she was wearing were from Burdines that Burdines would love to have her as one of their young models. The woman looked at me and said that I had two beautiful girls. I joking asked if she needed a pregnant model? The woman asked if she was as beautiful as Lori and Christina? Salinas is the present Queen of Nassau I said. The woman smiled.

It was almost lunch time, we dropped off the girl's things in the apartment then walked to the Brickell Town House where they were still serving brunch.

Evette said, she wasn't going to return to George's parent's house not even to pick up any of her things. Evette said she would pack a small bag of things that she still had in her old room. Christina, Maria and Evette would catch a cab out to Op-Locka airport where Tommy would pick them up and take them to Nassau.

Lori would be staying, me dropping her off at Chubby's early tomorrow morning. Lori's appointment to take off the cast was at 10:00 a.m. I would be having and early lunch with Big Ted and Steve. Ted was running the behind the scenes security for Lori and the children. Although there was no threat, the possibility was real. I had also asked Jerry to find out all he could on young Brian. One of Ted's men assisted Jerry. I wanted to know what I could about Brian. Seemed young Brian was the favorite grandson of my friend Mr. Crowlbe. Young Brian lived in small but nice two bed room, two car garage condo in the grove. Two cars, a covetable Camaro SS and a 4-door BMW. He is an avid sailor having a 30 foot Catalina docked at Coral Reef Yacht Club. Young Brian also had a pilot's license of which he had his own signal engine parked at the Tamiami airport. Young Brian racked up at least 8 hours of flying time a week. The report said he was an excellent student, always on the Dean's list, not too many friends and no girl-friend. This noted except for the outings with Young Ms. Lori. Drinks Becks beer on the boat or sitting at the pool and doesn't carry or own a gun. Ted looked at me and raised his shoulders, then said, you can't trust a man that doesn't own a gun.

The men watching Lori and the children would have a few days off but Ted would be sending three men to Nassau for the 4-day weekend. I planned on staying in Miami until Lori, her group and myself left Wednesday after school for Nassau. Captain Mike which was living on the

"Defiance" at the Miami Marina would head the boat on over to Nassau, leaving Tuesday morning.

By now Lori should have gotten her cast off and finished her school day. Knowing Lori, she most likely reported to the pool to start working her legs. I called Chubby and Chubby confirmed that Lori said she would head to the pool from school. So, to the pool I went. When arriving at the pool I notice the jeep and that BMW of Brian's. I wasn't happy about seeing that BMW there, not at all. I didn't look for Lori, I just saw Brian. I walked right up to him and asked if Lori had invited him to watch her practice? No sir he said, but I knew she would be out here. I said from this point he should only see Lori if she invited him. If your invited its fine, if not its not I said. Your telling me to stay away from her he said. If that is what you heard I said, then yes. And if I don't chose too Brian asked? Then I said, your Grandfather will call you and give you some advice. Your life seems to be heading on the right track, don't let it get derailed I said. I then turned and walked about 10 feet away and sat down to watch Lori in the pool. Brian also sat back down, he looked my way, then got up and walked out.

Lori worked out the entire practice, she acted happy to see me, hugging and kissing me in front of her friends. The coach walked over and said how hard Lori had worked. The coach introduced herself as Margret, my name is Jim I said, Margret said that Lori always mentioned you as the Captain. By now several of Lori friends had walked on over, Lori started naming the entire team introducing me as the Captain. This is the Captain Lori said. Do you really dive for treasure one asked? Does Lori have a sailboat that she can take us sailing in? Yes she does, I said and now that she out of that cast I'm sure you all will be going out sailing shortly. One girl said are you going to marry Lori? Yes I said, just as soon as I'm old enough. This made all the girls laugh. Lori said you can swim like a fish, is that true? One girl asked if it was true that I had a 14-foot hammerhead shark for a pet. Now, now girls, the truth is the shark and I are only friends, no one owns that shark I said. When can we go out on our yacht one girl asked? I don't know coach what's a good day after this long weekend? Lori said how about the Saturday after next, after practice? All the girls said yes. The coach asked if we had room for the entire team? I said yes. It's a date then the Coach said. All the girls screamed with joy. Lori went with all her teammates to change. The coach stayed and said that many of the girls thought that I didn't exist. Well I said, it wouldn't have been the first time I was called a ghost. Lori said you found her working on a dock in the Philippines, with her, and her younger brother and sister living in an abandon fish factory the coach said. Yes, and did she also tell you she once saved my life I asked? No, the coach said we didn't hear that one. She'll be one of your top swimmers I said. She has the guts and stamina. Lori then came running out took my hand and pulled me away. See you tomorrow Miss Margret Lori said.

I walked Lori to the car and said I'd follow her home. No she said I have everything I need in the jeep. I'll race you to the apartment she said. She dropped my hand and ran toward the jeep.

Once at the apartment Lori went straight into the bathroom and turned on the shower. You coming she yelled.

We ordered pizza and watched Monday Night Football. Lori said she had seen me talking with Brian. Yes I said I told him that he should only be there if he was invited. Did you tell him not to call me she asked? No I did not I said. I wish you had Lori said.

Lori's left leg was just a bit smaller than the right, however, she didn't limp or favor it at all. The next morning, I got up early checked the computer, and sent a few messages. Lori got up and got ready for school. She said how great it was being out of that terrible cast.

I had received a message from the Admiral's office confirming they'd have an ear out on the Limon radio until the following Monday. My thoughts were, that I would send Christina and Maria to Costa Rica with Evette on Saturday.

Lori had gone when the phone rang, it was Lourdes saying that a Mrs. Shiner had called, requesting I call her back. Lourdes said that Mrs. Shiner was the woman at the photo shoot. Tim from the News had also called saying that he had some information he thought I would consider useful. I first called Mrs. Shiner back and she said that she wanted to represent both girls as professional models. Burdines would feature Lori in their weekly ads, but Christina would be on an as-needed basis. She knew that Lori was in school and had a full schedule but didn't know if Christina was available. I let her know that Christina has work, but we could make her available one day a week with a few days' notice. We didn't talk money, just the time that the girls would be available. Mrs. Shiner said she would send Lourdes two of her normal contracts. I said that was fine, I 'd look it over and get back to her sometime next week. Mrs. Shiner said that the photos were ready for my viewing at Mr. Horwitz's office. I figured she said that as a reminder for me to go pay the bill. I then called News paper Tim back, the last time we had talked it didn't go so well. I hadn't talked with him since I had set him up with our little farm supply run to Iran. It was Tim's cell and I got him right away. Tim wanted to meet somewhere like the sailing club where we could talk.

CHAPTER XII

THE DIRECTOR TURNS

We agreed to meet at 11:00 a.m. I arrived at the sailing club early enough to chat with Robert and catch up on what was happening there. As he had before, Robert said things just weren't the same without us boys. Tim showed and we stood out on the end of the dock. Tim said that he had suffered quite a setback at work over the wild goose chase I had sent him on. He mentioned that it must have cost me a small fortune to pull off. Tim said he had documented 21 trips that the same C-130 had made during six month prior to the last trip. Tim said it must have been quite some farm equipment order. I said that I wasn't involved in SCS's business. Tim said he had information that he thought I would find interesting. He wanted to trade information. He wanted the story of what had happened in Nicaragua with the battle with the Cubans. Tim knew about the downed MiG and a source had told him that Cuba had also suffer the loss of over 190 dead, 60 wounded and another 70 or so captured. Must have been quite a battle Tim noted. What you got for me I asked?

Tim said that I was about to come under a renewed investigation. That's nothing new I said, the Feds have been looking at me for years. This time it's different Tim said, this time its connected to the 2 CIA employees and their driver that had died in a car accident caused by a small explosion from something that the CIA men were transporting. Seems your wife had some connection to the men that were killed. Your wife does work for the CIA does she not Tim asked? Tim then stated that the police investigation also indicated that both you and your wife had just left the G.D. plant minutes before an explosion killed a third CIA employee there. The FBI said that both bombs were manufactured using the same materials and methods. I laughed and said that I didn't know where he got information that my wife is working with the CIA but it was false. As for the explosions that killed those men I have no connection. I will not deny or confirm that I was at G.D. that day but I assured him I had nothing to do with any bombs or deaths. Tim then said that the FBI had interviewed the CIA and that the Director indicated that it was true that his men were acting on their own but not true that what they were in the process of stealing or attempting to steal any Government property. In the case of the both expositions the Director said, the deaths were not connected to government property nor was it considered to be Top Secret. IF true Tim said then the deaths of all 4 men could be considered as second degree homicides. Punishable by jail time. That also meant that the families of the dead men could sue the responsible party or parties. Tim continued to say that his source had indicated that the Director had yesterday testified behind closed doors to a subcommittee on the Iran – Contra affair and that my name had come up when asked about a missing $9,000,000.00. Casey also supposedly said that now that the Colonel was out, that I was the President's go to person where the Contras were concerned. Tim said that even more surprising than all that was the fact that for the first-time the Director didn't protect the President. Tim said his source said they thought that the Director will breakdown under oath.

Well Tim asked, do I get my story? I said that although quite a bit of his story had large holes, I thought it at least was worthy of a fishing trip. I told Tim that this Saturday night there would be another special guest on the boat that just might assist with his story. Please I said call and make reservations with Lourdes. There's only one spot left. Don't forget what was said when I warned you. There's no forgiveness for whom hurts my family or friends.

From the sailing club, I drove back to the apartment. Before going up I stopped to see and pay for the photos. I smiled when Mr. Horwitz said that Mrs. Shiner was there the day before and wanted to take with her a few of the photos. Mr. Horwitz said that Mrs. Shiner looked at them all and was quite impressed, but the photo she wanted the most was this one. The photo that Mr. Horwitz pointed to was one of the photos of Christina with the diamond neckless. In this particular photo, the lights had caught Christina and the neckless perfectly. I've never in my life seen such a photo Mr. Horwitz said. The girl and the diamonds are brilliant. Mr. Horwitz said his favorite was still Lori with her short black dress and small golden belt, the cast and one tennis shoe. I asked Mr. Horwitz how much I owed and I asked if that included the negatives. He hesitated and then said yes.

I took the photos upstairs and looked at them all again. It was hard to believe that these two girls in the photos were indeed Lori and Christina. So much had happen during the short time that we all have been together. The neckless made me think, it still being here in my safe I went and got it and took several photos of my own.

While in the safe I thought about the possibility of the 4 bombing deaths investigations heading my way. I wasn't worried about the non-CIA death as Roy had made a privet anonymous settlement with the family. G.D. could stand to lose the most and its top leadership could be on the line for the homicides. All of this was too close to home and could affect my future plans. The one thing that could stop the investigation was to have the Navy and or the President declare TESS as Top Secret. I was sure that sometime before the exposure of TESS that the powers to be would put a stop to the investigation before TESS was put in danger. The other thing was that the President would need to stay clear of the Iran-Contra affair. The Director turning on the President and having some irrevocable proof could throw a wrench in all of this. Still looking though the safe, my mind zoomed back through the past. The 4 Rolex watches hanging on the wall were always an eye catcher. It was time for them to go.

I finally looked at my watch and saw it time to go and see Lori practice.

In pulling into the pool parking lot there was Brian's BMW. Defiant little bugger I said to myself. I wanted to mess with his car but I didn't. As I walked into the pool area, this time Brian wasn't sitting alone, this time his grandfather was sitting with him. Now what I thought? I looked for Lori and then walked up to both Mr. Crowlbe's.

Brian spoke first saying that I said I wanted to speak with his grandfather. Yes, you are right, I said. Good afternoon gentlemen I said. Let's get right to the point. Lori asked me to speak with Brian. She asked for him to stop showing up uninvited, to the house and the pool. Brian stood and said this wasn't so. The grandfather looked at me and asked if we could hear it from Lori. If I had been Lori's father I would have said no, but I was not her father. I looked at the grandfather and said that I thought that Brian, if he truly loved Lori should wait when the timing more favored him. I said that even if she said she doesn't want Brian's attention and did, his move now could seal any future possibilities. I will tell you both now that if she now says she's willing to see Brian, she can do so with a chaperone until she's 18. If she says no, then I will step in to insure her wishes. Think about it gentlemen I said. I stuck out my hand and said Tom. He stood and gave me is hand and said its always a pleasure. Like-wise I said. I looked at Brian and said, Brian, then I walked away and sat at about 10 feet from them. It wasn't ten minutes when they both got up and walked out. I knew that the old man had convinced Brian that I was right. I was also sure that we hadn't see the last of Brian.

When Lori and I walked out to her jeep here was a note on the window, Lori took it and read it to herself. She then held it out to me to see. I said that the note was for her. Lori then came to me hugging me. If you want him, it's still not too late I said. No she said, I'm right where I want to be. She wasn't crying, not a tear. She smiled and said she was in love with only one man and he was standing right in front of her. Lori said she'd like to stop by the house and help the children pack and get her things together. Tomorrow when swimming practice was over we would all leave for Nassau.

When we reached the apartment, I reached out for Bob. Rodger said Bob was at the UM tonight until 8:00 p.m. Rodger sent a message for Bob to get back to me. There were two messages on my phone, one from Mrs. Shiner and the other from Christina. Mrs. Shiner wanted to know if I had picked up the photos so she could start to do some marketing and Christina just wanted me to know she loved me. Lori heard both messages. The photos Lori said, we have them back? Yes I said as I walked and opened the safe. As I turned with the album in my hands, Lori was right there to receive it. Now only in her underwear, she took the book and jumped on the bed with it. Lori went thru the photos until she came to that same photo of Christina. Christina, Lori said is beautiful. Yes I said, almost as beautiful as you are. Lori stood and came to me asking if I was ready for that shower. After that shower I told her of my conversation with Mrs. Shiner. Lori said she would love to see herself in magazines. She then asked if we needed the money? I laughed and said havens no. Then Lori surprised me saying she didn't want to do it unless I wanted her too. Lori said she missed sailing and playing tennis. Lori said that Chubby had purchased a piano for her and the children to start lessons. This too Lori said she didn't want to do. Please she said, I don't want to hurt Chubby's feelings. I'll talk to him, I said. I don't think its Chubby she said, its Lilly.

We again stayed at home with me massaging her left leg. Lori admitted that it was sore and after tomorrows practice her leg will deserve a good break. Lori asked why I had hired the Marine to train Christina? I said that each family member would have a roll. Christina's will be the protector, Salinas the mother and you, you will manage the business. Lori said that Christina had told her that she too wanted to have a child. We have enough children running around for now I said. You will see when we get to Nassau. Lori said the first thing she wanted to do was to take out the Hunter with Salinas and Christina, just the three of us. Lori said they were all going to have a heart to heart talk. Don't go agreeing to anything to stop us from spending Christmas break alone. I've been looking forward to that for quite some time, I said. Also this summer's trip will be just you and I, don't go changing my plans, I warned. Lori smiled from ear to ear.

The phone rang and it was Bob, He said he was on his way over with a friend. What kind of friend I asked? A girl friend Bob said, one of my students.

Bob was there in thirty minutes; Lori had ordered a few dishes from the Italian restaurant. Bob's friend was named Carol. Bob came in still holding that same cigar. Lori sat and chatted with Carol while Bob and I talked on the balcony. Bob had already heard the news about the Director's behind closed doors testimony and said he was concerned but he seemed more interested in how the controller's repair was coming along? I asked if I was talking with Bob or Liz. Bob said he had heard that I would be talking to Liz Saturday night. Yes I said, I had promised to take her fishing. I told Bob if he wanted, I had room for him and his new friend. Bob then asked directly, would the controller be repaired and when? I told Bob that we would have somewhat of a working model sometime during the first week in December. In order for this to happen, we will need the entire project including TESS to be declared Top Secret. Bob said that given the circumstances he believed that wouldn't be possible until next year.

We need to see some progress on the controller before that he said. Just who is we I asked? We, Bob said, are the future, a group that's for more stability with the end of the cold war as they call it, where our adversaries understand that them having the Bomb capability just isn't enough. The Top Secret appointment after, we see progress on the controller sounds a bit like blackmail I said. You know how I feel about blackmail I said. Black mail is how we lost Michelle. If I can't get what I want I said, I'll have what I don't want. Your group won't be at all happy with what I don't want I said. Bob then stuck his head inside and asked Carol if she was up for Nassau for the weekend. Carol asked Lori if she was going and with Lori's yes, Carol turned to Bob and gave a thumbs up. Bob said finally I'll get a ride on one of those Hatteras's. I laughed and said he was behind the times. What he said, no more Hatteras? We still have the two Hatteras's I said but we'll be using the 54 foot Ocean Sport. Nice Bob said, Liz will like that.

It Seemed Bob and I were about wrapped up but Lori and Carol were just getting started. When looking at the girls sitting on the couch talking, I asked Bob if his girl friend didn't work for or was friends with any of his group. Bob said that Carol was just a student that was interested in living life.

Next Lori asked if she could show Carol her modeling photos? I went into the bedroom and opened the safe taking out the photo album. Lori sat with Carol and they looked at the photos together. Carol told Bob that it looked like I had found two super models. Carol made the comment that she thought Christina already looked like a high-paid model. Bob didn't even look at the photos only saying that he and I once knew a Bahamian girl that was a super model. Bob, of course, was speaking of Michelle.

CHAPTER XIII

THANKSGIVING

The next day went just as planned; Mike had left the day before for Nassau in the "Defiance". Lori, the children, Chubby, Lilly and myself would fly to Nassau that afternoon. Fernando should have arrived today with Jerry, his wife plus Lourdes her mother and two kids. Lourdes and her family would be staying at the Hill Top Beach house with Salinas, this due to the computer being located there. Lourdes would still be working as we definitely had things going on. Liz had made her own arrangements while Bob and Carol would stay at the Beach house with Lori. Christina, Maria and Evette were at my apartment over the restaurant. Everyone else would be staying in one boarding house or the other.

Lori and family plus myself departed Opa-Locka just after 6:00 p.m. landing in Nassau at 7:00 p.m.

Lori hadn't ever see the beach house before, unlike the Hill Top Beach house, this house was located right on the beach. Having only three bedrooms, once Bob and Carol arrived the children would be sharing a room with Chubby and Lilly. Bob didn't get permission to miss Turkey Dinner at his house so Tommy would be picking Carol and him up tomorrow at 5:00 p.m. Liz wouldn't be here until Saturday afternoon.

Lori loved the house, she had heard many of the stories about Michelle, Bob and I. It was hard for Lori to believe that Michelle had amassed such wealth. Since it had been years that I hadn't opened the safe here, I did so while Lori stood behind me. What memories, there was still quite a lot of sand on the safe's floor, this left from when Michelle and I stored the first loads of treasure we had found. The safe was quite large but much smaller than I remembered. My first gun, my grandfather's 32-20 was there loaded ready to use. I even found a diary of Michelle's that I hadn't even known existed. Old photos of Bob and Michelle and many others. Oh yes money, lots of money and jewelry too. There was no one left that could even open this safe but myself and maybe, just maybe Bob. I turned to Lori and said that everything in the safe would be handed down to her one day, even the diary of which I would not read. I didn't say it but it would have hurt too much. The house had been readied by Salinas with the refrigerator well stocked. There was an ice chest out on the porch full of freshly ice crawfish. We would stay in for dinner and not leave the house the first night.

With still no wall or fence around the house, we had Ted's men, one in the front and the other out back. During the night, the Donzi would be out there either anchored or making rounds. The security did their best not to be seen.

The next morning we would be picked up and taken to breakfast at Angee's. I had called Christina the night before, and asked them to meet us at Angee's after their morning run.

What a mess Angee was when we showed up. I thought she would never let me go from her hug. Angee looking at Lori told the group that she was the only one that could tell the story of all these years. I knowed the Captain from his first day on the Island Angee said. Then looking at Lori, Angee said and I knowed his first girlfriend too! All those green eye girls have gone and us dark eyes is whats got him now Angee said. Angee said I'd have to see her grandbaby before I left the island. I promised to visit Otis's new house as since the old house had been torn down and the new one built in its place, I hadn't seen it.

Christina arrived and she and I kissed, Angee said, oh Lordy, Miss Lori, yous going to let him get away with that? Christina then said, Angee it's me Christina. Angee said that after all these years she just couldn't keep up. Everyone but me laughed. I gave Angee the news that Bob would be arriving tonight. I's hope he aint gona boss me around because I'll have to put a whopping on him Angee said. This got me laughing. Angee said that in the old days Bob treated her as if she was his slave. Angee!, those boys don't have a drink in their hands, he'd yell, while standing over the balcony in his underwear. Angee looked at me and said yous remember

Captain Jim, yous remember. Yes Angee I said, I remember. That was when you could still cook I said with a laugh. Angee came and swatted me with one of her wooden spoons. Angee said that she had been at Hill Top until 2:00 a.m. this morning, we's been cooking up a storm, Betty and me Angee said. How many people coming to eat over there Angee asked? I counted 75, I said. Lord almighty Angee said, then saying that the men's were doing the dishes. The girls approved. By now Captain Mike had walked in with one of his crew. Mike knew almost all of us except Maria, Chubby, Lilly and the children. Mike hadn't seen Christina since that awful boat trip. Mike asked Christina if she had recovered? We had long finished eating but were still there when Fernando, Jerry, Jack, and their wives also showed up. Things were getting filled up. Lori wanted to get in a short sail before lunch. Lunch was to be served at 2:00 p.m. I was told that Salinas was on her way, the girls had their morning sail all planned. When Salinas came in, she made a scene, everybody even Lori clapped as she kissed me. In a loud voice, Christina asked, who was ready for a sail? As she said that, Christina passed out captain's hats to Salinas and Lori. I would hold back from the trip and let the captain's run the show, besides I thought it good the three of them being together without me.

Since I had opened the safe at the beach house, I decided to open both the apartment's and the hurricane's house safes as they too hadn't been opened for some time. As Christina was leaving I asked to borrow her apartment key. Angee would have the Hurricane house key. First I walked up stairs opening the apartment, here too, oh the memories. The safe here wasn't so big or complicated. Inside a loaded colt 45 gold cup, jewelry, money and paperwork. I didn't count the money but there were rubber banded stacks of $10,000,00. The money made me remember the night that I purchased the Paix Château from Baby Doc and Pilar.

From there I walked across the street to the Hurricane house. Unlike the apartment, I could tell no one had visited here lately. Here opening the safe, what I found made me realize that in some way I had dropped the ball. Here in the safe were many of Michelle's tapes that may have never been looked at. My first thought was to burn them. I certainly didn't want to see what was going on during those days but I just felt that I had to see her again. It had been some 18 years since her death. I set up the machine and placed in one of the tapes. I hesitated and then stopped. I removed the tape and replaced it back in the safe. The Hurricane house was stuffy, I walked up the stairs and opened the roof hatch to get some fresh air, the salt water smell brought me back. I thought about the good times Michelle and I had while searching for and bringing up the first treasure. Yes and how even then in a way Deanna was sharing me with Michelle. Things now were much more complicated but almost the same. Then like now I always had more than one girl. Fickle my Dad use to say I was, and he didn't know the half of it. I looked at my watch, no it wasn't that old Timex I had back then, that old Timex watch that as a boy I had found at Crandon's park on Key Biscayne was long gone. The one that I was wearing did tell me I needed to get going.

Thinking of old times reminded me that June said that she too would come and visit after her family's turkey dinner. I had asked her to bring our daughter but she said that Kayla would be spending the weekend with grandmother. I wasn't even sure that June would show. We had invited several people that said they might show. Lourdes said she had sent an invite to Jena. I figured that Jena had gone back to smoking and maybe changed her mind about becoming a mother. Roy had also been invited but he wasn't on speaking terms with me, at the moment. Seems the possibility of G.D. and even myself being involved in a possible criminal investigation didn't make him happy. Him owning some of the TESS stock didn't make him feel any better. Rusty was also invited, he said he'd love to come, but his mom and sister were coming in from out of town. I knew that his present wife didn't want him revisiting as she had it in her mind that our group had led him into the drug world. Beer at 15 by all means, but we never did any drugs.

I got to the city dock bar and there he was, Willy, I walked in and of course got a big greeting! Almost the biggest of all, no kisses but a greeting I wouldn't forget. Willy was the oldest of our group. The bar was over half full and Willy let everyone know that the King Fish was in the bar. Of course, many of my stories from back then had been forgotten. Not Willy, he didn't forget a one.

He would have started telling a few if Charles and Madilyn weren't there waiting for me. The three of us hugged, they too would be having dinner at the house and taking that fishing trip tonight. Already sitting with Charles and Madilyn was Montibelli. Montibelli had come in with

Fernando. Fernando, Montibelli said was aboard the Hunter with the girls. Fernando had been on the dock and recognized Maria and went out with the girls. Good for him I said. I told Charles and Madilyn that tonight they would meet the daughter of the past owner of their house. Yes the congress woman.

I stayed at the bar until the Hunter came in sight. We all walked to the empty slip and waited its arrival. The Captains brought her in like professionals. Charles was the acting photographer. Charles had out his Niki shooting away. The photo of the three captains would be special. Salinas with that big belly in the center.

From here we would all head on over to the Hill Top Beach house. The house was ready, the adults were served cocktails and the children a coke. I was walking around with Wendy Michelle and Johnny in hand. Lourdes was here with her mom and two children, I think we had 15 or so kids and so far 60 or so adults. Salinas and Lourdes were in the kitchen with Betty, Ah Betty, Betty when she saw me said you done this here party just so I'd have to do all this work. She then stopped what she was doing and came and hugged me. It had been quite some time that I had seen Lourdes. Tim and Joan also hadn't seen Lourdes, Joan hadn't seen Lourdes since we moved Lourdes and the family to New Orleans. Yes this was the first get together where we had so many of our friends and family.

The toast was made by Salinas, she said she didn't know everyone but hoped she soon would, she boldly said she was the woman of the house but not the only woman. Salinas said that all of us shared me in some way. Salinas thanked God that we had all made it here safe and mentioned that Fernando was taking a well-deserved break from fighting communism. Please she said give Fernando a hand. We all clapped as Fernando raised his beer. Welcome everyone Salinas said. I then would say grace, the same one my Dad always said " Dear Lord, thank you for this food and all our many other blessings, amen" Food was served. I was seated and a special plate brought to my table. On the plate was a complete broiled crawfish with turkey feathers mounted on its tail. Everyone got a kick out it. Betty said I could eat Crawfish every day. Christina said that's exactly what we did during our last several days in Panama.

I had an empty seat on my left, it was being saved for Salinas, Lori was sitting on my right and I lost track of Christina. Seamed we ate for hours.

The food just kept coming and coming. Desert was my favorites, key lime and pecan pies. 5:00 p.m. rolled around and a taxi pulled up with Bob, Carol, Tommy and even June. Bob had never seen the Hill Top House before, it was his and Carol's first time here. Of course the girls went wild over June. June looked great, when she got to me she said she was looking for a boyfriend. I asked her if she knew how to kiss a boy? June said an expert had taught her. She then jumped in my arms and kissed me. When June stopped kissing me she looked around and asked if there were any single men in the house? Fernando stood and said he was single. June went and kissed him too. Everyone laughed. The late comers were asked about food and all but Tommy had eaten.

CHAPTER XIV

LIZ'S FISHING TRIP

The plan was that several of us would pull out of the city dock at 10:00 p.m. The "Defiance" would have some of the same visitors as the last year plus Bob, Carol, Liz, Jack, Cindy, Tim, Joan, Fernando, Maria, Tommy, Evette, June, and Lori. Ok, quite a lot more people. This years the host would be Christina as Salinas said she was just too exhausted. There would be 25 of us aboard. Only 4 or 5 could possibly fish at once and the cabin and bridge were full. It looked more like a party boat than someone out fishing.

Liz and newspaper Tim showed up at the city bar on time. All were introduced, anyone that was to be on deck were to wear a life jacket. Liz came in a dress, but Christina took care of that right away. The boat pulled out with the real Captain Mike at the wheel. As we traveled I saw the Donzi not far behind. Bob said we had a shadow, I said yes, three in the water and one in the air.

We arrived at our spot and the anchor was dropped. The two crew members got the first fishing rods baited and ready. Liz was set to catch the first fish of the night. Both Liz and Evette hooked one at about the same time. I don't know who screamed louder of the two. Liz's fish was a good size hog snapper. Evette's was a small shark that we had to give enough of a headache for it not to be hungry anymore. Liz looked like she was done but we baited her hook with more crawfish and she was at it again. Evette said she was going to catch the biggest eatable fish. Lori was set and got her line overboard, Carol was next. When I tried to give a rod to Bob he signaled that the cigar in his hand was enough. Newspaper Tim stepped right in.

Christina being the host was kept busy making and serving drinks. Looked like everybody was talking about something interesting. Me I wanted to see Lori catch a big one and truthfully I was ready for a soft chair to fall asleep in. One thing for sure we didn't have enough sleeping space for everyone. Liz, Bob and Carol would share the smallest state room while all the girls the master. Us men would have to catch some shut eye, sitting if we wanted. Fernando and Maria hit it off from the start, I wondered why. The conversation that Newspaper Tim would have with Fernando would be sometime tomorrow morning, starting at brunch at the Holiday Inn. Looked like Maria would be going to that meeting too. Lori stayed up with me and fell asleep in my arms on the bridge. We didn't stay out all night. Newspaper Tim, Evette, and Lori were the fishermen on the trip. It was 3:00 a.m. when the anchor was reeled up and we were headed back to Nassau. When we arrived those that were in a bed kept right on sleeping. The others either went back to the boarding house or like Christina, Lori and I headed for the Hunter. Yes it had been Thanksgiving but both Hatteras's were out with tourist.

Captain Peter, as everyone in Nassau called him, said that we should leave the "Defiance" here in Nassau. Captain Peter, was in charge of everything in the water for the group. Peter said that if I could leave the "Defiance" there in Nassau, we could make a fortune making day trips with the tourist.

I was up early and had left for the airport, several of us were traveling to Andros. Computer Tim, Lee, Liz, Jerry, Jack, two of Jack's men and Fernando would all fly over in the Leer. Tommy was scheduled to get off the ground but we waited for Liz. I had told Liz that she would have to bring a letter from the Admiral extending her a Top-Secret clearance; if not, her trip to Andros wouldn't bear much fruit except for meeting TESS.

CHAPTER XV

SHOW OF A LIFETIME

Liz showed up, and we took off. The short trip took less than 20 minutes. Once we landed at the airport Liz noticed a C-130 then landing behind us. That one of yours she asked? Your safe I replied. Tim left with Lee in the truck that Lee had left at the airport two days before. We had one of our double cab pickups waiting. Liz would wait in the truck with Jerry. Fernando walked to the back of the truck and unloaded two long boxes. The rest of us boarded the C-130. The C-130 then took off going out about 5 miles and then circling back. We were at about 10,000 feet in the air and on the reproach when Fernando fired a heat-seeking rocket directly at our C-130. Just as soon as he fired the first one, he threw the carcass down on the ground and picked up and fired the second. The rocket firing startled Liz as she was now standing in front of the truck while Fernando was behind the truck. As the first rocket approached the C-130, it was struck and destroyed by a laser beam that shot from our C-130. Only seconds passed and the next rocket was also struck and destroyed. We then circled back around and landed. Liz stood and waited my return. As I walked from the aircraft, Liz walked my way meeting me half way. She asked if that was TESS? I said it was. She asked how many could it shoot down? I told her that TESS had multipole laser heads at six locations. I told her that there was a magic number but we as yet didn't know what that number was. Liz was impressed, not only that TESS had taken down the missiles, but that I was so sure of TESS that I had risked my life on it working. I didn't and wouldn't tell Liz that Fernando had removed the stinger's war heads before their being fired at our C-130. Liz asked about messing with the magnetic north. So far, we have a 100-mile radius, I said. We are also at about a rate of 75% of messing with any electronics within that same 100 miles. Some electronics that work on 24 volts seem to be protected. I then asked if she was ready for the big show. We got in the truck, what of us could in the cab, and the rest in the back bed. We were headed to the Navy Base. We were all passed at the base's front gate and drove to the Facility that housed the Vehicle. Omni Tim and Lee had prepared a small show for Liz. Lee had released the Vehicle's lockdowns while Tim installed a reworked controller into the Vehicle. The security checked our IDs and kept Liz's clearance letter. By now Tim and Lee were ready. By remote control Tim opened the Vehicle's doors. I pointed up toward the door and said ladies first and to watch her head. Liz was hesitant but stepped up and into the Vehicle. Then Tim, then me. The door closed behind us. Liz noticed that Tim was controlling the Vehicle's door with his lap top. I motioned Liz to sit down at the controls. I asked her not to touch anything as the Vehicle's tether and water lines had been disconnected. Tim took a cord that was connected to the laptop and reached in and connected the other end into the reworked controller. The Vehicle's panels and screens lit up. No windows Liz asked? No I said it moves using some advanced type of radar and sonar. The screens I said, show what was out there without physically seeing it. Kind of like its guided by a satellite but without the satellite. It could take a pilot years to learn to navigate the vessel I said. How did you get it in here she asked? It was preprogramed to the cave site guided to the caves entrance by a small buoy like sonar device. I noted that the buoy went missing a few months ago. We believe that the cave was enlarged to permit the vehicle to hide from something looking for them. You mean humans Liz asked? I'm afraid not I said. The cave was started long before humans had the capability of hurting them. I believe these beings were being sought by another larger meat eating being. Liz said you're talking science fiction, right? No mam I said. My people in Nicaragua are not only fighting the Sandinistas, they are looking for proof of a second type of being. The rumors are that in the early 1970s there were such beings sighted in the Southwest section of Nicaragua. Why they were there we don't know, but if they were there, they were most likely looking for something or our beings. Tim went though showing some of what we had working, he told

Liz that the weapon system seemed to be working but we dared not test it. I explained how the water pumps produced electric that could run most of the Vehicle's systems, the fuel rods would permit full power. The electric pumps also recharged the fuel rods. The engines were air or water cooled. When the CIA engineers, changed the fuel rods, they then wanted to see how much power they could get. They hadn't figured on the cooling. Liz walked through the small cabin and then wanted out. Tim started shutting down the system and the doors reopened. Tim disconnected our laptop and we exited the vehicle. Liz was surprised that the outer door position had changed. Yes I said, we had been floating and rotating in air without her even noticing.

Now I said, you've had your fishing trip, can I get the Top Secret decree? The President promised to fund the research, however, even with the money G.D. is on hold until they are in the clear for the deaths that were caused by a government identity attempted theft of TESS. I then said that I believed that the operation that led to the four deaths was sanctioned by the Director. Liz being Liz said the laptop stays in this room. If thats what it takes to make this work I said. Tim hand the Congress woman your laptop. As she took it in her hands, I could see her satisfaction. Yes it was quite a powerful moment for her. She then looked around the room and for just a second might of thought something stupid. They, as I'll put it were outnumbered and out gunned. I knew she would want to take the laptop with her but reminded her that the laptop contained very little of value. So she asked, can I walk out of here with it? If that would seal the agreement, then yes I said. Of course, the President will be informed that our work here is finished and that you are controlling the security and have the controller. The laptop stays she said as she handed it back to Tim. Tim asked, shall I place it back into the Vehicle? Liz said yes. We have an agreement I asked again. This time Liz said we do. I then stuck out my hand for the hand shake and got it. Two weeks she said give me two weeks. Tim then opened the Vehicle's door, walked in with and then out without the laptop. Liz asked when the vehicle could be ready for a test run? We need only three things I said, a complete controller, a new sonar device and a pilot. Timing she asked sternly? Money, I said back to her. What about TESS she asked? With the money we will provide the TESS technology to the program I said. I could see that it was still her intention to get her hands on TESS, but it would not be today. We exited leaving Tim and Lee to lock down and reconnect the Vehicle. Liz, as she walked by, said to her men that nothing was to leave the sight. This was almost humorous as we would be leaving almost nothing. As we returned to the airport Liz noticed that the C-130 wasn't on the ground. She asked about where it was? I said that it was on a routine training mission. This I was sure had her thinking that she had made the right choice.

We wouldn't wait for Tim and Lee, we boarded the Leer and took off back to Nassau. Tommy would return for Tim and Lee within the hour. Liz would be going back to her Paradise Island hotel room and then fly out on the evening flight. I offered her to go sailing with us but she said she had work to do. I figured more scheming.

Well, today was only Friday, it was agreed with Lori that today I would spend with Salinas and the kids. How unusual it was that the children wanted to spend the day on the beach. Salinas commented, just like their Father. Salinas was still exhausted from the day before dinner, she was 6 months pregnant. Lourdes and her two children also joined us on the beach. Lourdes said that she, her mom and the children were enjoying the country living. I asked if she wanted to return to Miami and she said that even though her ex had gotten remarried they didn't feel that he could be trusted.

Christina, Maria, and Fernando showed up coming back from their afternoon beach run. Christina had purchased boots when in Miami last week and was as she said, breaking them in. Fernando said he had, as I asked spent the morning with Newspaper Tim and would have their second meeting starting at 4:00 p.m. Tim, Fernando said was itching to get some of the stories started for his Saturday paper's addition. Tim had said that a taste in Saturday morning's paper would make Sunday a sellout. Christina asked Fernando if Tim was going to hear how he had got his head scar? I guess that Maria had heard the story because she also laughed. Fernando laughed and told Maria to add another 10 pounds to Christina's backpack because she needed to be more out of breath. Maria said that Lori had asked to come run with them today but that she had looked at Lori's leg and told her that it was still in the heeling process. Maria said that Lori's swimming was at this point the best exercise, as the swimming mainly worked the muscles not putting any weight-bearing pressure on the bones. Maria said that Lori has the spirit to make a good Marine.

Salinas yelled out from the balcony for me to get back to my today 's work. As I looked up there I saw June standing next to Salinas. Christina waved and the three of them continued on with their run.

Wendy Michelle and Johnny were both good swimmers and played well together. Wendy Michelle was a little bossy, Salinas said this too came from her father. When Salinas said things like this, I knew she meant me and not their real fathers.

Before sundown Tim and Joan came by the house to thank Salinas for the dinner. Tim wanted to make sure that I had put the small board and chip away in a safe place. Since I had on the same shorts and they looked a little damp, Tim asked to make sure I didn't still have them in my pocket. When Liz was heading down from the Vehicle's doorway, Tim had slipped the board and chip into my pocket. Tim said that my thinking was right on as the guards had them all empty their pockets and searched them as they exited the Vehicle's room.

I went to my room and retrieved what Tim was asking about. In handing them to him, I joked that I had dried them off using Salinas's hairdryer. Tim then asked about when the engineers would be back working again. I said that would be Monday. Tim said that he thought it would be at least a week before Mira could reproduce the board and chip that he had placed in the laptop. We knew that Mira had stolen part of the controller before it had burned. G.D. confirmed that the overload did cause the meltdown of the comptroller but that the meltdown had started with the part that someone had taken and replaced with inferior material. Mira and her associates had close to 90% of what they needed to reproduce TESS. We had modified the rebuilt controller knowing that someone would do anything to get their hands on the technology. We weren't sure who Mira's masters were but when she does take the next pieces, G.D. figured that it might take them years of extensive work and investment before they found that what they had wouldn't work. G.D. and I had gone to a lot of extra expense to match the material that their original theft had gotten them.

While Tim was with me, Joan was having a nice visit with June and Salinas. The girls were mainly talking about us men putting so many hours in when we didn't have to. Joan said that they had purchased a beautiful house just outside of Miami and Tim had purchased a nice boat as well. Joan said she had told Tim that he'd better be looking for a nice house on Eleuthera soon.

It wasn't long before Salinas and I were finally alone, we spent a nice quite night in.

The next morning, I stopped by the apartment hoping to catch Christina before they left for their morning run but I was too late. Evette was there still sleeping. I had woke her up, the three of them would be off to Limon later this afternoon. I would miss saying goodbye to Christina. Lori was meeting me at the airport at 7:00 a.m. where we would head on over to the Harbor Island house until Sunday afternoon. Lori was happy as I hadn't seen her alone in quite a while. I promised myself that this trip I would finish up on the new house's safe. Once on Harbor Island, Lori and I spent the morning on the beach and then walked down to the Pink Sands bar for lunch. Lori was wearing a red strapless bikini top with a short black skirt that covered her bathing suit bottom. With her hair in a pony tail she looked like a million. Lori's short skirt wasn't enough to hide the fact that her left leg had lost quite a bit of mussel tone.

While there, we made reservations for dinner as the hotel was as full as I had ever seen it. Lori said that the children were having a blast in Nassau and wanted her to ask if they could spend the summer there. Chubby had already made arrangements for the kids to spend the end of the Christmas Holidays at Disney World to see the New Year's parade and fireworks. I said that I would talk to Chubby about the summer but that she should count on spending at least a month with me on the Hunter. Lori reminded me that I had promised her time during Christmas.

We did return to the hotel for dinner, Lori and I walked down the beach at sun set and then back in the dark seeing several turtles on the beach laying eggs. At the hotel we ate out on the terrace as we both had walked over without shoes. Lori and I wore matching clothes as she had on a short flowered dress while I had on shorts and a matching flowered shirt. Dinner was baked grouper. Desert was of course key lime pie.

There was just something about that hot fresh water shower and then getting into that bed where the only sound one could hear was the small waves breaking on the beach. This I though was paradise.

Our 30 hours together pass by so quickly. When returning to Nassau Lori and the children, Chubby and Lilly packed up and would return with Tommy to Miami. Me I would spend another two days with Salinas and family then head to Miami.

Tim's Herald story was a big hit, the story sold all over the US. In the story Fernando was an ex-Cuban that had defected to the US. Fernando was actually a retired US Marine from Puerto Rico. The story of the harbor mining was full of blazing courage that had took the Sandinistas by surprise. Although we had over 100 Haitians on the ground and 9 rangers, the story only mentions a small, all voluntary multinational group that fought alongside a large group of Contras.

The huge Contra victory had been lopsided as the bad guys had over 200 killed or wounded and 73 of their group were captured. The good guys lost 9 men with none being captured. Fernando had told the story about his offer to permit soviet helicopters to come in and pick up the Cuban's wounded, this after the Cuban's first failed attack. The Cuban commander refused the offer and countered with an ultimatum for the Contras to surrender or die. That same night Fernando's men went on their first offense forcing the Cubans to retreat. That's when as Fernando said Castro sent in the MiGs. Fernando didn't claim that they had downed any of the MiGs, he only mentioned that Castro lost one of the four MiGs he had sent. Fernando said, days later the Cuban commander with 100 or so Sandinista reinforcements came back. The Cuban commander must have thought that the MiGs had softened us up Fernando said. As the Cuban's advanced they had sent ahead patrol after patrol. All had disappeared into the jungle. When the Cubans got well into the Contra controlled zone, Fernando's forces had just about surrounded them. The Cubans started taking on heavy loses and their commander gave the order to retreat. The Contras then quickly closed the circle trapping all but the 200 or so that escaped. The Contras then slowly moved in for the kill until the last 73 surrendered. Fernando said that they had sent many of the Cuban's with the most serious wounds to Limon. The other wounded were taken to Honduras where the Cubans could pick them up. The over 70 Cuban prisoners were given their freedom. Fernando had taken their shirts and gave them food and water for their march north. Tim's article noted that Fernando had wished that they could have marched their prisoners through the free streets of Managua as Castro had done in the streets of Havana with his prisoners from the Bay of Pigs invasion. Tim had asked why the Sandinistas didn't come at them with the Soviet helicopters? Fernando said that the US had supplied them with Stinger missiles that had a range of 5 miles. No Fernando said, we owned the ground and the sky.

Newspaper Tim had done a good job, both of us keeping our word.

Everyone soon returned to their homes or assignments. I spent two days with Salinas. Salinas had turned out to be quite a woman.

I went back to Miami to find Jena had come back to Miami. She knocked on my door my first day back. Jena said she had gotten Lourdes's invite but knew there would be to many people there. Jena asked about my arms selling problems and I told her that I trusted I was in the clear. Jena had heard about and then read of the Contra victory. Jena said she had many times told the story of us meeting Baby Doc in Nassau and us going to his rescue from one of the many attempts to rid him of ruling the Haitian people. Jena said she had run into Baby Doc and his "B-----" wife Michelle on the Riviera. Jena said that his wife, Michelle, would soon leave Baby Doc penniless and by himself.

I had hoped that Jena had changed her mind about being a mother, she had not. She said she had gone to see and signed the paper work at Roy's office. Thank the Lord that I was running late for Lori's swimming practice. Jena said she was counting the days when she could get pregnant.

I left the apartment thinking that for sure I'd better have Lori there during my time here to protect me.

I had checked all my many messages and walked Jena to her door.

On my drive over to the swimming pool I thought about the boat ride that I had promised Lori's friends for this coming Saturday. Mike had left with the "Defiance" from Nassau yesterday morning and should by now be at the Miami marina. Christina had left a message that she and Evette were fine and that she and Maria would be spending nights at Evette's. Fernando was back in Nicaragua; Evette had sent a message that all had been calm during Fernando's absents. Cindy had stayed in Nassau while Jack returned to Andros with Lee. Jerry and his wife traveled back to New Orleans with Lourdes and family.

CHAPTER XVI

TOP SECRET

Montibelli had somehow gotten a tourist visa allowing him to visit the US for up to 90 days at a time. He had flown in from Nassau to Atlanta, where his sisters lived. Montibelli also visited the Shah's son Reza and Reza's mother Farah. At the Shah's death, the Shah was the richest man on the planet. Farah still holding the family fortune together, saw to it that each of their four children had received cash of well over $500,000,000.00 each.

Montibelli had sent Lourdes a message that he would be staying at his house on Miami Beach starting this coming Monday.

Me I'd be staying put for a while as I was anxiously awaiting word from Liz on our Top Secret clearance for TESS. I had informed the G.D. people of my moves and hopes for the clearance within the two weeks as Liz promised.

It had only been a few days since I had seen Lori but as I walked into the pool area and she saw me she ran heading my way. As she did we both heard the whistle of the coach. I got a short kiss and Lori was running back to practice.

When practice was over the girls came on over and asked if we were still on for this Saturday's boat ride. I confirmed we were and the coach came over and said she had lined up a few of the parents to join the ride as chaperones. The coach asked me privately if I could hold back on all the extra attention for Lori while on the trip. Seems the coach was worried about what the parents would think about an older man dating such a young girl. I promised to keep my hands to myself. I thought I better have a little talk with Captain Mike to insure he didn't say anything improper to the girls or their mothers. The coach would for sure be on his radar.

Saturday came around and we had 13 girls, 4 mothers, two fathers and two coaches show up. This of course does not include Lori, Captain Mike, one crewman, and myself. We would leave the Miami Marina at sun rise, travel out the channel that ran along the Causeway and head out to the ocean traveling south. Our destination was the Ocean Reef Yacht Club. The girls had a blast on the trip each taking a turn at the wheel. I thought the two fathers were the most impressed. Once docked at the Ocean Reef Club we had arranged hot dogs and hamburgers at pool side. You wouldn't think these girls would want to use the pool but they did. Some of the seniors surly didn't look like high school girls specially in those bikinis. Lori wore that American, red white and blue one piece speedo. The coach too wore a small bikini that looked, pretty darn good. Lori said she now knew why I had agreed to take them all on the boat. I came back saying that it had been her idea. Lori laughed as she said she was not jealous of any of these girls. The trip back was also a lot of fun, all, had a great trip. One mother asked when we could take a trip over to visit Lori's beach house? I asked with or without chaperone?

The "Defiance" pulled into the Miami Marina at about 9:30 p.m., all the girls were exhausted. Lori and I said our good byes at dockside. We would stay aboard tonight making up for our lost time together during the day.

The next morning, we ate brunch at the Marina's restaurant. Then went straight to the Morgan for a day sail. Life was good, very good.

Monday morning, I took Lori home and she was off to class. I went back to the apartment to get caught up on the news. I hadn't heard a word from anyone in DC. Evette noted everything calm in Limon and Nicaragua.

After the Cubans were handed their heavy lost our resupply of the Contras doubled up for a few weeks then dropped off. At present our warehouse in Mandeville and Jack's warehouse in New Orleans started to become full of war supplies. All of a sudden, we had money sitting in off shore banks that came from the US treasury earmarked for the Contras. Nicaraguans that lived in the cities became weary of limited exports not being able to be shipped out and the imports almost ground to a halt, this due to the mines in the Harbors. The largest cities such as the capital were having their electric targeted almost weekly by the Contras. The large multinational companies that brought the farmer's products such as melons and bananas all but abandoned the country. Countries such as Honduras and Costa Rica largely started to benefit at Nicaragua's expense. It was notable that the war had started to turn more to the Contra's favor.

With more war supplies coming in and Fernando having been completely resupplied after the big fight, our aircraft few less and less supply missions. Jack from the New Orleans terminal was once again complaining that the war goods were taking up too much room. The storage money was good but as Jack said the war would one day be over.

With our aircraft now looking to only make maybe one monthly supply trip to Nicaragua, Jerry was now looking for and found other work. One such costumer was a company owned by Iran's ex-leader's family. The family having the money was suppling goods and weapons to assist Iran in it's Iran-Iraq war. This war was now in its 6th year with no end in sight.

As I learned that we were being contracted to begin deliveries to Iran, I put a hold on what was to have been our first trip. Doing business moving arms to Iran still might not be illegal but it could have an effect that would hurt our chances with TESS's top secret clearance . No, we would wait until we heard from Liz. Jerry would have to stall the business, me saying he would need my approval to start the moves.

The very next day guess who was calling up from the lobby. Right, my friend Montibelli. We talked on the phone like we were being listen to by others. We would meet at the Marina and take out the "Defiance" where we couldn't be heard.

Montibelli said his Israeli friends said there was a change of the wind coming. The arms race and the cold war were about to cost more money than either side had. One would need to outspend the other. Montibelli said that he and I were in unique position to obtain great wealth. The Soviet- Afghan war was going poorly for the Soviets. US Stinger Missiles were now being delivered to the Mujahideen's in Afghanistan and they were downing the Soviets aircraft at will. Montibelli said he knew of TESS and what it could bring to the table. Montibelli said that once TESS was fully developed that the US would have its superiority sealed. Montibelli said that the Israeli's also were working on a very similar system. Now's the time to make our moves Montibelli said. Montibelli was already talking as if we were partners. I didn't like it. I would hear what he had to say but I wasn't going in his direction, at least on the same ride. Montibelli didn't know as yet that I had put a hold on the new middle east flights. He then asked if I had remembered that he had said that he could keep my aircraft busy. Montibelli said that he had arranged for the Shah's family to start using our planes for all of their transport needs. Montibelli said that our friend Crowlbe would also benefit. I then told Montibelli that I was waiting for Liz to arrange the status of Top Secret for TESS. I told him that any future development depended on it. Montibelli said that I should stay clear of Liz. I repeated that everyone had told me the same of him. Its different with us he said, we are friends. I then told him of my decision to put a hold on the flights. He said that a week could make a difference in loss of life as our this weeks cargo was equipment that was desperately needed by the Iranians to protect the military and civilians from the chemicals that Hussein was using against the them. I asked how many such trips of that equipment were ready? Montibelli said two flights. I asked where this gear was located? Montibelli smiled and said both loads were in our Mandeville warehouse. I used the Defiance's computer and phone to send Lourdes the message. The protective gear and only the protective gear was to be at once shipped to Iran. I wanted it filmed and documented as to what the cargo was. Montibelli said we would be refueled while in air by the US Air Force. I looked at Montibelli, he raised his shoulders and hands turning his palms upward, and said, everybody likes money. The "Defiance" was returned to the marina and Montibelli was on his way with his now two body guards. Before leaving he said to give his regards to Salinas. Seemed that Montibelli had chosen Salinas as his favorite.

Yes, this all was risky, but under the circumstances I felt the right thing to do. I knew I would get more messages within the hour so I went directly back to the apartment. I had missed Lori's practice and had called Lilly to let Lori know I was at the apartment. Lilly said that Lori hadn't come home as yet. Just then I got a call from the lobby, it was Lori. Lori wasn't upset, more disappointed than anything. Lori said that during practice, the coach too was looking at her watch. Lori said that by the afternoon the entire school had heard about their boat trip. I told Lori that I had met with Montibelli, Lori still had a bad taste in her mouth for Montibelli for the case of Christina and most likely the other girl too.

As I suspected the phone and computer was a buzz. Lori and I stayed home and I tried to watch Monday Night Football. After that hot shower with Lori the football lost out.

The week past by and Bob had called asking for an urgent meeting. Sounded like someone was in trouble and he wanted me to go assist. Bob and I met at the sailing club at about 7:00 p.m. Bob said that the Director was scheduled to testify Monday morning at a senate subcommittee but that when the Director arrived to testify, he looked impaired. The Director couldn't get the words out. The meeting was adjourned and the Director had returned to his office. That same day a CIA Doctor went into the Director's office. After checking the Director behind closed doors, the Doctor said that the Director had suffered some kind of seizure becoming unconscious. Bob said the Director was taken via ambulance to Georgetown University Hospital. Bob asked what I thought? I said, I was sure that the Director would not recover. Bob said he thought the same.

Two days later the CIA Doctor wanted to do brain surgery, the family refused and wanted to move the Director to another facility. The next day when the family returned the Director had already had surgery. The hospital said that the Director had regained consciousness and signed the consent. The Hospital produced the authorization with the Director's signature and two witnesses. The CIA Doctor informed the family that the Director had a small tumor which they had removed.

Two days later Liz called and said that TESS was now a TOP SECRET project. G.D. and myself were off the hook. G.D. as Liz said would get the first 10 million within the week.

I called Bob for another meeting. Again the meeting took place on the Sailing Club's dock. I asked Bob point blank, If the President approved what had happened to the Director? Bob said that the number two man, the Vice Director had taken the rains earlier in the month. Bob said that it was all over Washington that the Director couldn't be trusted. So, was it him I asked? I won't and you shouldn't go there Bob said. The Director will soon be fired and number two will be the Director. Bob said he was surprised that the new man hadn't already contacted me. The new man knows you weren't a fan of the Director. And Liz I asked, she must have known? Bob said that when Liz heard the Director was slurring his words, Liz had called Bob and asked if You were in DC? Bob chuckled, I didn't. I noticed that Bob didn't have that cigar in his hand and I commented. Bob said that a sore had developed on his inside lower lip and the Doctor said it was most likely some form of skin cancer. Bob laughed and said he wouldn't be going north to have it removed. Bob then said something very familiar, Bob said the times were changing. The Club was opening up and I invited Bob in for a beer. That too has changed he said, I'm dieting. Doc says my sugar is too high. Bob said that the Doc was taking almost all his fun away. If it wasn't for Carol, he said there just would be no pleasures left. Bob chuckled and we said good bye.

I looked at my watch and I too would pass on the bar. I stopped in and said hello to Paul, he made me promise to come back with Lori.

I drove to Lori's swim practice; I had missed the most part. We left the jeep there and went back to the sailing club. Before leaving the jeep, Lori got a suit case from the jeep. What's in the bag I asked? My clothes She answered. I'm moving in with you she said, you need someone to take care of you. Besides she said, next week starts Christmas break. Two weeks no school she said.

At the sailing club, we were well received by Paul; Lori was a regular at the sailing club while taking pram lessons. Lori had made several friends there. Lori had asked that we move Malcolm's sailboat to the waterway and move the Morgan here to the Sailing Club. It was decided that I would dry dock Malcolm's boat for a rework, and we would move Lori's, as she called it, to Malcolm's mooring.

We didn't stay long, and I needed to get back and check my calls. Lori said that I could drop her off tomorrow morning at school, and she could catch a ride with one of the girls to swimming practice.

Once at the apartment I understood why Lori had decided to bring her clothes. Christina was waiting in the lobby. Lori wanted to insure that she'd be spending nights while Christina was here. Smart girl I thought. Christina was happy to see us both, we were also excited to see her. I asked about Maria and Christina had said that Maria didn't move because I hadn't invited her. Maria was my first call, me telling Maria that she was to stick with Christina like glue. Maria would be on the next flight to Miami. I wasn't happy about it but tried not to show it.

Lourdes had a long list. Montibelli had called several times including, Christina had seen him waiting in the lobby. Christina said Montibelli said hello and left. I called Montibelli and he invited me to Joe's. He said he had washed and was free of bugs. I got off the phone and asked the girls if they wanted to go to Joe's? With the thought that we'd be sitting with Montibelli, Lori ask if ok, she'd rather take Christina for a sail, moving the Morgan to the Sailing Club's guest mooring. I ok'd the movement of the Morgan and said that tomorrow we would move Malcolm's boat to Merrill Steven's dry dock. The girls would have to take the jeep to the Gables Water Way, and I'd pick them up from the Club after my dinner with Montibelli so they could pick up the jeep.

At Joe's Montibelli was sitting at a special table that was separated, space wise from the others. It had only been a short time since I'd see him but he seemed extra happy to see me. Once I was seated he put his hand on mine and said that I could now start working on moving the cargo. I mentioned my storage problem and he said it was all taken care of. Any land cargo could be directed to Lake Charles Louisiana; any inbound air cargo could also be directed into Lake Charles. Go on I said. Montibelli said that the airport administration at Lake Charles was only waiting for Jerry to fly over and sign the paperwork. We'll have a large warehouse and of course a good size hanger he said. Montibelli said we would also rent a warehouse on Lake Charles's port. This port warehouse would receive any cargo that we would ship via Crowlbe and could be used for any overcrowding that might take place at the airport. What do you think Montibelli asked? Three things I said, one, have the airport and port send the leases or agreements to Roy. Two, I don't like the refueling arrangements and three we won't be partners on the flights. I'll split the profits 50/50, but no paper partners. Montibelli agreed with the 50% and said that he would guarantee the refueling, whatever aircraft had to ditch due to lack of fuel he would pay all cost. That's very reassuring I said.

Once we had our stone crabs and key lime pie, I was off to the sailing club.

I beat the girls there by at least an hour, I stopped in at the dock master's office and requested a mooring for the night. The assistant Dock master walked out on the lawn and pointed out the mooring that we could use. The sailing Club bar had a good crowd, almost every seat was taken.

Then a Man looking my way, waved at me calling me, Bob. When I got a look at him I recognized him and then his wife Ella. The Man's name was Paul, he was an old friend of my uncle Bob's, Carson's and my Dad's too. As I walked over, Paul immediately stood saying he knew my name wasn't Bob but couldn't remember mine. He said he knew I was Paul's son and young Bob's brother. I remembered their' s names and said them both. Then I said mine was Jim. Paul from the bar overheard and said loudly, it's Captain Jim. I asked them about their son and two daughters, they said all were married and they had several grandchildren. They asked about my Dad and brothers? I brought them up to date adding that Bob had always talked about the great adventure that he had when he accompanied my uncle and his family on their sailing trip to the Bahamas on the "Pipe Dream". The couple I was sitting with had also taken their entire family on their sailboat making the trip along side of my uncle's boat. Ella asked if I was the one that had dated their daughter Jani? I told her that had been my brother Bill. Oh yes she said, as she remembered. Ella then asked if I was married? I said, I was in-between wives at the moment. I was sure Ella took it as I was single, I meant it as I said it. Ella then asked, children? I said 4 of my own, one on the way and 4 adopted. They both laughed and said I was crazy. I agreed. Then Paul asked if I was still working with my Dad? I answered that I had been out on my own for quite a while, 12 or 13 years I said. Then I asked about them and what they were up to. Ella said they were retired with a house on Fisher Island and one on Cat kay. I told them that I too had a few homes in the Bahamas. When I said that. Ella asked if I could be the King Fish? Oh my word, Ella said now it all makes perfect since, your Cat's husband! You knew Cat I asked? Knew as in gone she asked? Yes Mam, I'm afraid so I said. Cat became ill and passed away earlier this year. How did you know Cat I asked? Paul said they had heard about the fishing, and Cat had taken them out on the "Nassau Queen."

As we talked I noticed the girls pulling into the dock, I excused myself and said I would return. I ran up on the dock and caught the bow line as Christina threw it. Even before tying them off I pointed out our mooring. I gave the bow a push, throwing back the line as they slowly moved toward the mooring. As they pulled off I said I'd be in the bar. When I got back to the bar Ella asked if they were two of my girls? She of course meant two of my children? I replied with the truth, that's my two Philippine girlfriends.

Paul behind the bar had those great ears and laughed as I talked. The girls came on in, I introduced them all and I told Paul and Ella it was great to see them. I said that we'd come visit them soon on Cat's Kay. I paid my tab as well as theirs as we said good bye to Paul at the bar. It was good to see some of my uncles old group.

I would take the girls to get the jeep from where the Morgan had been docked.

The girls said they would order pizza while I used the computer and made phone calls.

We had the contact of the Major that was in charge of refueling and I made it clear to Jack that in no way were we to get out of range for a refueling depot on our first few flights. We weren't going to ditch for lack of fuel.

The first C-130 was loaded and once the route and refueling was agreed to, they could take off at will. As I got finished with the communications I thought, another adventure. I turned from my desk and saw two of the most beautiful women one could lay theirs eyes on. Both girls had on some kind of pajamas, if you would call what they had on pajamas. They both came to me and pulled me off to the shower.

The next morning we moved Malcom's sailboat to be dry docked, Robert towed us over there as the sailboat's engine wouldn't start. It looked like Malcolm might lose the school year if he didn't return soon. I asked Lori if she wanted to go up and visit Malcom on the next weekend but she said she'd go if Christina went along. I understood what she meant even if she didn't say it. Lori didn't want to leave me alone with Christina.

Christina's shape had changed since Maria started to train her. If Mrs. Shiner could now see Christina in that black one piece; well it made me think about the neckless that I had ordered. It was Saturday, the jeweler might be open until noon but we wouldn't make it. I wondered if it would be ready and how good it would look?

Maria would be coming in late today catching a taxi to the apartment. From getting everything ready with the order for Malcolm's boat repairs, the girls and I would walk back to the sailing club for our car.

We thanked Robert by paying for a 6 pack of beer at the bar. Paul said that after I had left last night, he had told the other Paul that I had been at Carson's side at his death.

Paul said that both Ella and Paul said how much they had enjoyed getting to know Cat. It was funny, as I thought about it, Paul behind the bar had met all my girls, from my first girlfriend Kelly until now, Lori and Christina. Come to think about it, the sailing club was like the old light house on key Biscayne, I had at one time or another brought all my girls here. Well, Paul said to Lori, I guess we'll be seeing a lot more of you, now that the Morgan is here. Lori said most likely starting in January as we were all spending the Holidays in Nassau.

When we arrived at the apartment, Maria was in the lobby with her small bag. Christina and Lori were already planning our big run tomorrow morning on the beach. Run 5 miles then have brunch at Sundays on the Key.

I checked my messages and one of them was Lourdes relaying a message from General Santos. Nilo had called and said that Mrs. Santos was ill and asking for me. Nilo said if I was to see her again I'd better come now. Nilo said Mrs. Santos also requested that I bring Lori. Lori had missed so much swimming practice already, but I decided to tell her and let her decide. I called Lourdes back and said to get the leer so that Lori and I could make the 7:00 a.m. flight from Chicago. I also requested at least 2 security men, either on the leer with us or at least get them to meet up with us ASAP. Lori and I would have to leave Miami within the next two hours. I told Lourdes to make sure we were on that plane to Manila.

CHAPTER XVII

GENERAL SANTOS WEDDING

I asked Lourdes to get the latest on our Iran flight and that I wanted an hourly report until we were on the Chicago flight. I didn't want to get on the flight without knowing. Once in the air and over the pacific we would be cut off from communications for about 12 hours. It was going to be close.

I could tell that Christina also wanted to go with us but she was a good trooper and didn't ask. Christina and Maria would stay in Miami or head to Nassau with Chubby and the family. General Santos now had telephone but I didn't know how long we would be gone. Lori and I were ready within the hour, Christina got that special kiss and Lori and I were off in a taxi to Opa-Locka airport.

We didn't have Tommy as our pilot, this year Tommy had taken the entire month of December off. It felt strange not having Tommy at the controls. Although Lourdes did her best, Lori and I boarded the Chicago flight without me knowing about the outcome of the Iran flight. I wasn't comfortable, but I also wasn't too worried. I was use to flying but in no-way was used to being in one place for so long. When Lori and the kids first had come over to the states, I hadn't accompanied them on their trip. It seemed so long ago but it hadn't been quite two years.

During the planes stop in LA, I was handed a note from the stewardess, it was from Lourdes, the note read, "aircraft arrived without any problems, refueled and again in the air for the return". One of Lori's shadows had accompanied us on the trip so far. He exited the aircraft at LA, and two of my men were now aboard.

The flight was long, we arrived in Manila, traveled to the national airport then on to Cebu then Davao, nothing had changed, not even the four seat airplane from Davao to General Santos. Yes, we had that same pilot and yes he had to first chase off the cows from the grass runway before we could land.

This time we had Nilo waiting for us. Nilo was happy to see us. He now had a driver with his new Toyota 4X4. We got loaded up and went straight to the Santos house. It was only the third time I had gone through the Santos security gates. The house was larger than I had recalled. Once there we were hurried to Mrs. Santos's side.

Mrs. Santos was bed redden and was aware when we entered her room. Captain she whispered, take my hand she said. Lori standing almost behind me then stepped forward along my side taking my right arm. Is this the girl you found living my old Factory Mrs. Santos asked? Lori answered, Yes mam, my sister, brother and myself lived there for almost three years. How are they Mrs. Santos asked? They're both in school doing fine Lori replied. Are you happy child she asked? Yes mam, I'm the happiest girl in the world. Captain, Mrs. Santos asked, have you married her as yet? Lori then held out her engagement ring. Mrs. Santos then said she was 14 when the General married her. He was a Lieutenant at the time she recalled. So what's stopping you from getting married Mrs. Santos asked? Lori said that I wanted her to finish school first. Nonsense Mrs. Santos said, I hear that just being around the Captain is an education. Just ask Nilo she said. Ever since the Captain sold the shipping line, not one ship has gone out with a full load, she said with a smile. Lori then said that I didn't want her to miss growing up. Mrs. Santos looked at me and asked to be alone with Lori. Mrs. Santos took Lori's hand as I left the room.

They were in there for almost 30 minutes when Lori came in and asked me to come back in. Mrs. Santos looked at me and said she had one final thing she'd like to do before joining the General. I ask you marry Lori now she said. Oh, she might miss a prom or two but she has promised me she will finish her education. Do you love her Captain Mrs. Santos asked? Yes mam with all my heart I said. Then its settled she said. I looked at Lori and asked if this is what she wanted? Lori looked at me and said yes, with all my heart. It was settled, we were to get Married here at the house, it would be a Christmas eve wedding.

It was a privet wedding, Lori hadn't brought with her a single white dress and there was no time to bring one in. Lori purchased a simple white dress from town. Lori was a beautiful bride. The local Priest preformed the ceremony and yes before I knew it, Lori and I were married.

Mrs. Santos said that it was customary for the bride to bring a Dowry to the husband. Lori's Dowry would be provided by Mrs. Santos. After the wedding, Mrs. Santos's man Juan delivered a plainly rapped box to me. I was to open it in front of her but, Mrs. Santos passed away before that had happened.

The wedding had been privet but the Christmas day funeral was for all of General Santos. Early that morning Lori and I made our Christmas calls. The children were now at the beach house in Nassau; I couldn't reach Christina but did get ahold of Salinas and the children. I had gotten Salinas some kind of expensive horse for Christmas, she was excited but said she'd rather of had me there than the horse. Of course, there was no mention of my new marriage.

The church was standing room only and the dirt streets were also full of people that wanted to show their respects. At the funeral, a man came and introduced himself as Jose Calderon. I at once knew the voice, it was Ninong the masked commander. I didn't let on that I recognized him, introducing him to Lori. Jose said that he brought with him two gifts, one for the new bride and one for the groom. Jose was accompanied by two men, one holding the two gifts. I also recognized both men as being a part of Ninong's old staff. Jose said that they were proud that I had not abandoned the girl from the docks and was happy to hear that we had married. Jose said that he wished that we could stay in General Santos and raise a family. Jose asked how long we would be in town? He asked that I give he and Nilo one morning before we departed. I agreed. During the Funeral, there were several people that spoke, Mr. Partridge was just one of those people. Most of what was said at the podium was about the General that had pioneered the city. Mrs. Santos was the woman behind the man. The General had been a young Philippine officer during Spanish-- American war which The Philippines gained its freedom from Spain. The General did not participate in the Philippine—American war but returned to Combat the Japanese during World War ll becoming a feared enemy of the Japanese. The Japanese name given to the General was then "Ibara" which in Pilipino translated into "Matinik" which translated into English was "Thorn" or Thorny. I just imagined how he could have gotten that name. As the older locals spoke of the General I looked over at Jose, Jose was smiling with pride. Besides me I knew three of the six men that started the movement of the casket toward the burial sight. During the trip the men carrying the casket were changed out several times, some only walking a few steps before being tapped on the shoulder to get relived. Seemed like every man in town wanted the honor of carrying her casket. Mrs. Santos would be buried alongside her husband and her only two sons that were killed fighting the Japanese. Mrs. Santos was the last of her family.

Lori hadn't brought along a white dress but that black dress had everyone looking. It was her shoe choice that slowed her down. I kept up with the casket but Lori and our two men had fallen well back into the crowd. The crowd was so that Lori wasn't even close as Mrs. Santos's casket was lowered into the ground. As the first dirt was placed on the casket it started to rain. The crowd didn't move. It was almost an hour when Lori made it up to where I was still standing.

As the crowd started back, someone had started to sing their national anthem. These were a proud people. One of my men had taken off their jacket and put it over Lori's head. Her rain soaked black dress stuck to her. We were walking back and had almost reached the house when Nilo returned with the pick-up. Nilo dropped us at the house front steps and then said he would see me at the agreed time.

The Santos house which had been bustling with people was now all and empty. It was odd but Mrs. Santos didn't have hot running water, air-conditioning nor a TV in the house. There was what looked like an antique radio but even it didn't work. Lori and I went upstairs to our room and got out of our wet clothes. We then went and sat on the balcony and talked while watching the rain. Lori asked, I'm I truly your wife? Yes, I said you most certainly are. Lori came and jumped in my arms and said she couldn't wait to tell the children! I got up and retrieved the box that Mrs. Santos had prepared. Lori and I opened it together. I had already pre-purchased and owned the farm and the house. Mrs. Santos had given me the old Fish Factory and I had purchased the property that stretched north from the factory to the river. What could this be? Inside the box we found the Generals uniform along with all his metals, his memoirs, lots of photos, cooking recipes, two bank books and her will. I had paid Mrs. Santos in Dollars in a Manila bank, in looking at that bank book, every cent that I had paid her was still there. The peso bank book, looked to be the monies that she had lived from, was of a modest amount. The will was very simple; everything was left to me. Attached to the will was a small hand-written note, asking me to take care of her house woman and Juan her driver.

Lori and I had never talked money before, of course she knew there must of been enough to go around because of our life style. As Lori looked at the dollar amount in the bank book, I again mentioned how important her continued education was to us and our family. Yes, I said our family. I told her that things between Salinas and I would not change. Christina, on the other hand, would no longer stay at the Miami apartment. Where ever we make our home, it will be yours alone. Lori came to me again and hugged me. I told her she was not to get pregnant and should stay with school and all her activities. I smelled food and went down stairs and found that Juan and the house girl had returned and were cooking us all dinner. The rain hadn't stopped and Juan said it might not until morning.

As Juan, had mentioned, the rain stopped at about 4:00 a.m. At 5:30 a.m. after our breakfast I noticed the head lights of Nilo's truck approaching. It was ship day and I would walk the docks and speak with the ship's Captain. There I would get the feel of what if anything wasn't going right. I was dressed as I had always done, and just as soon as the workers noticed me they were yelling the word "patron" which meant boss. Once I made it up to the ship's small office, I met with the Captain and chief engineer. The Captain was a replacement I had not met before, but the Chief Mate was happy to see me again. The Chief noted that things weren't terrible but that there were many small things like refrigerant leaks which the crew of his ship could repair during the trip. But then there were things like cargo that hadn't been connected to shore power and even banana loads that were just about frozen and prawns that were thawing because their container temperatures were set for bananas. Most of this the Chief noted were from human error.

The Captain said that the loading was taking much too much time and that he was sailing with only 80 to 85% of capacity. The Captain noted that they had complaints from the receiving fruit companies that the quality of the fruit had also dropped. I asked if they had lost any prawn cargo and the Chief said that they had returned two prawn loads that were damaged. He noted that both loads had problems with temperature settings. He said that the partlow chart indicated that the prawns were loaded into the container with temperature of minus 14 degrees Fahrenheit. The container set point of prawns was set at plus 45 degrees Fahrenheit for bananas. The prawns were connected at that temperature for three days before being put aboard. The Chief noted that just these two lost prawn loads should have caused some changes on the ground but it had not. The Chief said he was glad to see that they had got me re-involved. I then told both he and the Captain that I had come to General Santos on the request of Mrs. Santos and not the shipping line nor the fruit company.

Nilo and I didn't visit the Tuna plant as it was now called. Nilo said they too were having people problems that the owners fixed by replacing many Philippine workers with Japanese workers. This and I didn't want to see that wall where I had hand wash Joe-Anne's blood off. This made me think of her sacrifice and now the Japanese were replacing her people with theirs. Nilo said this also made him sad. I told Nilo that I wasn't sad, I was mad!

After Nilo drove me by the old bridge he then took me back to the port. Mr. Partridge wasn't there but I asked to use the computer. I wrote Lourdes a message, and got it sent out. I asked Nilo to somehow get three of us on the today's 4:00 p.m. flight out of General Santos. Nilo said he would take care of it. I had waited for the fruit company's Mr. Partridge but he was a no show. Nilo then took me to a small shop in the center to meet Jose. There Jose explained that he had opened a small business that was supplying what material he could to the fruit company's mechanic and container shop. Jose was looking for an investor. Jose didn't talk about the problems of the people as I thought he would. I told him that I would send him a shipment of parts on consignment and would expected a 10% return on my investment. Jose agreed.

There was no mention of the masked man. I then made one last stop, the clinic. The Doctor was happy to see I stopped by, he said he had seen me but couldn't reach me at the funeral.

The good Doctor said that since I had last left, the clinic in the rural zone had closed down. The Doctor said that he and his staff were two months behind with their pay and medical supplies were not being resupplied as they were used. I was quite upset with myself. In my selling off of the shipping company and part of the land, especially the land, I hadn't thought enough about the people. The part about the selling of the Tuna plant, this was not the case. The Tuna agreement both with the Japanese and fruit company had in writing that 90% of all jobs associated with the business would be performed by the local Philippine people. The good Doctor and staff were at once paid from my pocket. Nilo was to place them on the farms payroll. The rural clinic was to be reopened at once, this too having these employees put on the farms payroll. The good Doctor was given how to contact Lourdes and was told that he was to contact her with a list of all needed medications and supplies.

When we left the clinic, I wasn't so happy with Nilo either. I asked him why he hadn't sent me word of the problems of the clinic. Nilo said he didn't believe it to be my problem. That I had done so much for the people and it was they that should respond for the clinics. In a way Nilo was correct, but it was me whom I felt owed the Philippine people for all I had gained from my time and experiences from here. Lori was the best example that I could think of.

When we got back to the house, Lori wasn't ready as she didn't even know we were leaving. We were rushed to make it to the airport on time.

It was the day after Christmas, we were in Manila by 10:00 p.m. and stayed in the same hotel and room as when Lori and I had first spent the night together. This time it really was the honey moon suite. That night I got word that yes, Mr. Crowlbe would see us on December 28th in San Francisco. After that meeting we would leave the next morning heading back to the US. Once landing in San Francisco my Security would head back home. Lori and I would spend the night and see Mr. Crowlbe the next morning.

At the Crowlbe visit we were well received. This time Lori came into the large office with me and we told Mr. Crowlbe that we had just gotten Married on Christmas eve. Mr. Crowlbe had seen but not met Lori in Miami at one of her swim practices. He noted that young Brian would be disappointed to hear the news. We then switch right to business. The line, even with only going out of General Santos at 85% full was still profitable. They now were running the third ship and Mr. Crowlbe offered that as to why they weren't going out full. I asked about a price of me renting space, maybe 15% of the ship. He asked where I would get the cargo? I mentioned moving beef, fish and maybe even my own brand of bananas. Mr. Crowlbe said if I was looking for something to do he could keep me more than busy. I know you don't need the money he said. I said I didn't like the way things were going in General Santos and that I didn't as yet have an appointment with the fruit company, but my visit could see some friction with their management. I mentioned about the Japanese being brought in to work at the tuna factory taking Philippine jobs and about the clinics not being funded. I said that going forward, it was now certain that Lori and I would be adding family that could one day be a part of the General Santos heritage. Crowlbe was shrewd and made me an offer on the spot. 30 slots a week he said, you pay $500.00 for every empty one, $1,000.00 for a full one, if one of your slots is available and we use it, I pay you $500.00, what do you say. I quickly did the math, the offer could cost me almost $800,000.00 a year, but it also was a challenge to force my hand into returning our efforts back to General Santos. It didn't take me long to hold out my hand and say we had an agreement. Mr. Crowlbe seemed pleased with the agreement and himself, he just earned at least another $800,000.00 year. Mr. Crowlbe said that most likely young Brain was in the building and they like to take us out and cerebrate the three Kings. Three gifts he said, Christ, your marriage and this new partnership. I thanked him for the kind offer but said that we had already miss Christmas with the children and we needed to get to Nassau before we completely miss the holidays with them. Only I knew why, but I then invited Brain over to Nassau to meet the entire family. I then opened my briefcase and pulled out the photo of Christina in her black one-piece. She's part of the family and has just resently become available. Mr. Crowlbe took and looked at the photo and then looked at Lori. They could be sisters he said. Can I keep the photo and pass it to Brain he asked? Yes sir I said, by all means. We stood, and again he wished us good luck and a great new year.

Lori and I headed from there to the airport, Lourdes had done a good job of getting us in and now out of San Francisco. Today we would be flying on to Miami and then Nassau. My new marriage would be hardest on Salinas. Christina knew the day would come, just not this quick.

Lori and I arrived in Nassau well after dark. Our taxi dropped Lori off at the beach house, then I would be heading to see Salinas. Salinas now well into her 7th month and the children were asleep when I arrived. I apologized about missing Christmas with her and the children and explained to her about Mrs. Santos's last request of my marriage to Lori. Salinas said that she and Christina had talked about Lori and hoped that Lori would find some nice boy out there before I was ready for her. Salinas said that she knew that she would always have competition with other women but had hoped that I wouldn't take on another wife. Salinas said she would always be here for me and wanted to talk with Lori tomorrow. Please she said bring her to me. Salinas said that Wendy, Johnny and Michelle were asking about me, and Kelly and Jimmy were now enjoying the beach. All had a good Christmas morning opening all the gifts that I had sent. My new Appalachia horse is the most beautiful horse I've ever seen she said. Salinas said she would love me no matter what I did and again asked that I bring Lori to her. I was still holding her when she closed her eyes falling back to sleep.

The next morning I had three children climbing into our bed. Wendy, Johnny and Michelle all saying papa, papa! All wanted to show what Santa had brought them. The first thing I realized was that I needed a bigger bed. We were all up and the eight of us were seated in the kitchen for breakfast. Betty now up there in age was also seated at the table. I didn't realize how many folks it took to run this house. With 5 kids and another on the way, this was going to be quite a house. After Breakfast, I was dragged down to the beach. We were down there until Salinas called us from the baloney to all come on back up and rinse off in the pool. Salinas and even Betty had both of the little ones in the pool with Betty noting that both Kelly and Jimmy had learned to swim before they had walked.

From there it was lunch at pool side and from there a nap for all except me. I had received my marching orders to fetch Lori. Salinas said to bring the whole family if I wanted. But that she would be meeting Lori in privet.

The house chauffeur drove me, we stopped by the apartment first, but Christina and Maria had gone. We then went to the beach house, where we found that Christina and Maria had jogged up the beach to the house. By the time I arrived Christina had received the news. Christina and Lori came to me for their kiss at the same time. From those kisses were the children then Chubby and Lilly. I had forgotten how excited everyone was going to be. Lori had already given them all the news. I then noticed Fernando! What a great surprise. Seeing Fernando and Maria next to each other made something click. Fernando and Maria were a couple. Fernando congratulated me and I him and Maria. Even Christina looked happy. Lori took my hand and pulled me into our room and asked how it went with Salinas? I then gave Lori the news that she and I were invited to return with Salinas's house chauffeur and that Salinas wanted to meet with her. Lori said that Salinas most likely wanted her to bite into the apple. I looked at Lori strangely and Lori said you know, Snow White and the Seven Dwarfs. Lori had only seen that movie a few months ago while it had been more than 30 years ago for me.

Lori changed clothes and we were off. I reminded Lori that Salinas was just last month 18 years old, seven months pregnant and was taking care of 5 children. She's only a little more than a year older than you I reminded her. Lori said they would be fine. Salinas was ready when we arrived. Salinas hugged Lori and congratulated her then took her by the hand and they walked down the back steps off the porch toward the beach. The children were still asleep so I went and sat at the pool. Betty came out and brought me a whiskey. Betty said I might need it. Betty also said that Salinas didn't deserve this. Betty then reminded me that I wasn't that fickle young boy any more, I was almost 40. Betty now in her 70's, had seen and known almost every girl in my life. Seemed that she liked Salinas the best. One by one the children got up from their naps and Betty moved them out to me. Betty asked if I even knew how many children I had, she said ifin I knew how many, she didn't believe that I knew all their names. Usually Betty was hard on me and then Laughed, this time she was serious.

It was almost 2 hours when Salinas and Lori came back up from the beach. Neither girl looked upset. Salinas spoke first, we are now sisters with the same husband she said. Salinas said she wanted all the children including Lori's brother and sister to all grow up knowing each other. One big family Salinas said. Lori then said that Salinas had invited them all over for new year's eve and new year's day dinner. All of this was fine, as long as they were happy.

Lori and I would be leaving within the hour as the Leer should be ready and waiting to take us to Eleuthera. My plan was to get Lori to the Harbor Island house by herself for at least two days.

Lori and I did get off to Harbor Island. It was a short couple of days with us spending most of the time alone, except for visiting the Pink Sands for dinners. Mrs. and Mr. King were formally introduced to Lori as my new bride. We didn't special dress for any of the meals, heck Lori only brought what she was wearing, a bathing suit, a short sleeve shirt, shorts, and tennis shoes. The entire two days we never stopped talking and making plans. After dark, we sat at the table and worked numbers under the lights. We decided that we would go forward with making General Santos one of our strong holds. Partly because Lori was Filipino, and partly because I felt that I owed something to the people, especially Joe-Anne. Joe-Anne's blood on the wall where she stood her ground, was still fresh in my mind.

Instead of spending the summer in the Bahamas we would all go to General Santos. I drew up the General Santos two-story farm house, from there we both started making changes on paper. The front of the house wouldn't change much but the rest of the house would all be remodeled.

We also designed a banana box replicating Lori and Christina carrying bananas. The brand would be named, "Maganda", with the slogan "a touch of the Philippines". Yes, we would stop selling Standard our fruit and market our own brand. By the time we left on the morning of the 31st, we had plans to ship Bananas, pineapples, beef, shrimp and fish. Our farm that stretched out over both sides of the Silway river was 1,300 acres. The Santos farm had been one of the largest working farms in and near the city. Mrs. Santos's cattle business was the largest in the General Santos area. The Tuna factory which we rented to the fruit company and their Japanese partner was boxed in, with us owning all the property North to the river. If they needed to expand they'd have to leave the city. We were thinking of building a larger, better designed, packing facility that would include space for all kinds of cargo. We could also consolidate fruit from several small producers into shipping containers and ship under our brand name. We could have large areas for cold and frozen cargo.

Getting off the leer in Nassau we must have looked like a honeymoon couple. Three days of sun had us both golden brown. Our time at the Harbor Island house went without anyone sending any urgent messages.

CHAPTER XVIII

THE DRUG TRAIL

The Andros project was closed for two weeks, with everyone except the small guard crew going home for the Holidays.

Lori and I arrived at the beach house to find everyone enjoying themselves. Chubby and family had visited Angee's restaurant several times. Christina had taken them all out boat riding too. Tonight, we would all be going to the big new year's party at which Salinas would no doubt mention was Salinas's and my anniversary. Lori was prepared for whatever would be said or take place. Everyone had been invited.

We arrived at the party at 11:00 p.m., we all had taken long afternoon naps. As we entered the house young Brain caught my eye. He too saw us and came directly to us. May I kiss the bride he asked? I said yes, of course, and Brain respectfully kissed Lori on the cheek, noting that her fairy tale wish had come true. Brain then straightened up and said he appreciated the invitation saying he had met the host, plus Christina, Evette and Carol. Brain looked at me and asked? She is available is she not? Of course, Brain was asking about Christina. I looked at Lori and then back to Brain saying, yes, yes she is. Lori already had my hand but then she pulled me in for the kiss. The kiss was no doubt a thank you kiss. Next coming at us was Angee leading Willy by the arm. Willy had suffered a mild stroke and had lost some of his sight and as of yet, only recovered partial movement of his left arm. I didn't know until Angee told me while Willy was standing there with us. Willy asked Lori her age? Lori said she was 16 and Willy laughed so hard that I thought he was going to have a second stroke. Willy then asked my age and when I said 37, Willy still laughing said that he wished he could stick around to see me at 50. You know young lady, the Captain wasn't always attracted to younger women Willy said. I remember when the Captain, at just 16 had the most beautiful woman on the Island, aint that right Ms. Angee Willy asked? That's the Gods truth Angee said and if you don't believe it, yous can ask just about anyone that was here in those days. He had two or three girls then and pardon if I say Angee said, but it looks like things haven't changed all that much. What was she like Lori asked? Who Angee asked? Lori said, Michelle wasn't it. You had better answer that one Willy, Angee said. Willy said she was about 15 when I first noticed Michelle. She started to fill out at about that time. Every man, looked at her walking down the street, if she saw you looking she look right back. They say she had a heart made of ice. Michelle moved right up the social ladder so to speak. The women folk despised her. Any man except for Mr. Bob that wanted her ended up broke and sometimes dead. Michelle was a professional home breaker. Michelle ended up being the wealthiest woman in the town. I's remember the first-time Michelle came a looking for the Captain in my bar Willy said. Michelle and the Captain walked down to the end of the dock and they talked. Michelle left the Captain standing there and she stuck her head in the bar's door when walking back by. "Willy, if you know what's good for you you'll take good care of that boy"she said. Willy said looking at me, that I had first called him Mr. Brown. One day the Captain was upset with one of the other clients and started calling me Willy. Between that client and myself, I was the lucky of the two of us Willy said. I stopped Willy there and said that was enough of the story. Willy said that just about all he could do any more for fun was to tell some of the old King Fish stories. Willy said he loved telling the old stories, some were sad but so far all have had a good ending.

Lots of our people didn't make it to Nassau this time. Jerry and Lourdes were working, seemed that we now were on our third delivery trip to Tehran. Jack and Cindy were there as were Fernando and Maria. Lee and Janie, Peter and Ida, Mark and his wife and of course Odis and Maggie. Tim and Joan weren't there as Tim had been spending a lot of time at the G.D. lab in Fairbanks. Joan was left with the kids and running Omni's businesses. Jack from New Orleans was on stand-by as they were expecting another child. Jody was there with computer Tim's brother, Scott. Looked like this happened when Jody visited Miami's

Omni Terminals while learning some new software that Tim had installed. Bob didn't get permission but had sent Carol. Montibelli was there with his Lebanese girlfriend. The Johnson brothers and their wives also made it. There were several new men and even women that worked with our fishing and tourist boats that I didn't know. We were introduced to everyone. Lori's brother and sister soon found several friends to play with, before we knew it a glass of champagne was passed around. Salinas made it to us and asked me if I had forgotten that it had been our night just two years ago? I said I had not, I reached into my coat pocket and pulled out a small box that held that 10 caret diamond ring that Michelle had once owned. As I put it on Salinas's finger I told her that at least three Queens had once wore this very ring. Salinas turn to show the crowd then turned and kissed me. As the years before with that kiss came the fireworks. Salinas then told Lori that she would be retiring for the evening and that the floor was now hers. Salinas then whispered in my ear that she would be needing me to be around for the middle of February to meet Jacques. She then changed ears and whispered that she was looking forward to her two weeks at the end of March. Salinas kissed me again and then walked into the house. As she walked in Lori took my arm and said she like'd that woman but didn't trust that she'd didn't have some kind of plan. When the fireworks stopped the band started up and Lori dragged me to the dance floor. We entered from the west and Brain and Christina came in from the east. It wasn't two minutes before Evette and Carol joined us on the floor and all of us were dancing together. Soon everyone was on the dance floor.

I don't know how long the party lasted. But we stayed until almost 4:00 a.m. I had a good time but was glad to get home. Again that word home sounded good. Although I hadn't planned marrying Lori anytime soon, I was happy that we would be spending a lot more time together.

We would be traveling back to Miami today in the afternoon. The kids, including Lori were to start back to school on Tuesday morning. Lori had miss a few extra days of class and swim practice. I would make a few calls to insure Lori, as a married teenager could continue with the same school schedule and participate in the athletic programs. Hell I was married and hadn't even told Roy as yet. Roy would have had made up a pre-marital agreement which since Lori was only 16 most likely wouldn't have been legal anyway. The trip back to Miami was good and Lori was adamant that she wouldn't be returning to Chubby's and Lilly's home. Once in Miami she and the children had a surprise. All of them, with the exception of Lori would be staying at the third apartment on our floor. Chubby's home was being completely remodeled and wouldn't be finished for another month. At the same time the house across the street was also adding a second story, it too being remodeled. Lori said she had known for some time that the people living across the street were her security people.

It was Monday morning when I called Roy, I wished him a happy new year then gave him the news. Then asked him about Lori attending the same school. Roy's first question was if Lori was pregnant? I said no. Roy said that there was no law saying that a married girl of 18 or under, that wasn't pregnant couldn't attend public school. Roy said if the school raised any questions, he remembered where the office was. Roy was referencing a school visit he had made with me some 20 years ago. I apologized about not giving him a heads up about the pending marriage. Roy said that I shouldn't worry about any agreement because I didn't own anything. He said that Lori and her family already had a good size trust fund with me being the executor with Chubby next in line. Roy said we should review that trust in a few months to see if things changed. Roy then said the kindest words to me that he ever had. Roy asked when I was going back to work? Find a project he said. If you need and investor I have recently come into some extra money that I'd like to put to work. I told him I'd let him know. Roy wished me and the family a happy new year and I was sure he got back to his golf.

With this cleared up, the very next day Lori and the children returned to school. I wasn't so sure about Lori continuing to drive the jeep to school but that's what she wanted.

Lori didn't get a wedding band as yet and I would hold off on one until she asked, if she would.

My day would be catching up with the Tehran flights, waiting to hear from Fernando's return to Nicaragua and ordering equipment for General Santos. I had decided not to speak to Standard Fruit until we were ready with everything we needed to start shipping. The more I thought about it the more equipment I ordered. I called Mr. Mckee only to find that he was retiring, him now only working part time. Mr. McKee's company was doing the work on our two Miami houses and said they were quite busy. I talked him into sending the same engineer that he had sent to Paix when he had rebuilt the Château. Mr. Mckee reminded me that the Philippines were quite a bit further than Haiti. I thought to myself if he only knew. Although I knew he wouldn't need one, it was agreed that we would send along a translator for Mr. Mckee's man. The trip was set up for the coming week. I just knew that Christina was going to complain, but she didn't. Christina said she would be glad to go.

This meant that I had less than a week to get things ready. My Brother Bob had a customer that made cardboard boxes, I contacted my little brother Dan to do the art work. I met Dan at a downtown bar and gave him several photos of both girls and laid out what I wanted the banana box to look like. Dan had paper an pencil and on the spot drew what I thought a masterpiece. This was exactly what I wanted. Dan was to do some background drawings and have a touched-up drawing by tomorrow.

From there it was time to meet Lori at swim practice. The coach wasn't too happy about Lori's missed day's of practice and warned that this would be the first and last time she would allow Lori to continue with the team if she missed any additional time. Not that it would have made a difference but the coach hadn't heard that Lori and I had gotten married. Lori worked hard and when practice was over asked if she could stay and do laps. Lori had the jeep but I would sit and watch her work.

I had been gone most of the afternoon and when I returned Lilly said that Lourdes and Bob had called. I first called Lourdes. Lourdes said that there had been a fire at our Panama plant where we were turning old tires into asphalt. At the plant we would shred up the old tires, melt them, remove the steel wire, and add the melted rubber into an asphalt mix Lourdes said that the first notice she received was that the fire had started during the night and was still burning. I asked if anyone was hurt and Lourdes said there had been an explosion during the morning that killed several of the men that were fighting the fire. I then called Bob and he gave me the same bad news. He warned that I was not to go there as he felt that anyone connected with the plant could be held. Bob said that the week before Christmas and again last week that Noriega had sent a man that was looking for a sizable contribution for the cause, Bob said that Noriega already received 25% of all sales, not profits Bob said, sales. Bob said he believed the fire was set on orders from Noriega. Bob said to stay clear of Noriega because he was protected by our Vice President.

Bob congratulated me on my new bride and the two year anniversary with Salinas. Bob didn't laugh but I knew he wanted too. Bob mention that Carol said the young Mr. Crowlbe had taken a likening to Christina. Well I said I'm sending Christina off to General Santos to work there for a while, this did get a laugh out of Bob.

When I got off the phone with Bob, I thought about leaving for Panama. Instead I would go another route. I did call Evette and said to make the calls and see what help we could offer to the injured and the families of the dead. I told her she was in no way was to go there.

My next call was to Montibelli, he was now in Miami getting ready to return to Limon. I was adamant that my planes would not touch ground again in Panama. Montibelli said we had two trips of cargo on the ground in Panama. I said to find another carrier.

It was now the second week of the new year, Christina called and asked about us taking an additional passenger. She was asking about young Brain. Seemed that Mr. Crowlbe was sending Brain to get a business education in General Santos. Christina said she learned about his move while Brain was at the new year's party. That's why Christina didn't bulk at my request for her to go. Well they say a photo is worth a 1,000 words. Anyway Christina, Maria, Brian and Mr. Mckee's Matt would be leaving from Mandeville tomorrow morning. One of our C-130s was loaded to capacity. Aboard were 20,000 new design banana boxes with the corresponding cardboard, plastic bag and stickers. Our banana boxes had their new Brand name and the emblem of the two girls carrying bananas. Mr. Mckee's man would be there for about a week. The C-130 was also carrying a new 350 KW cat diesel generator with a separate 3,000-gallon fuel tank. The rest of aircrafts space was used for construction materials that Matt said would be required for the future construction project. Lori and I also flew to Mandeville with the group of four. Tommy was back from his vacation, I was glad to see him once again behind the controls of the Leer. I was going to meet with Jerry, Lori was there because it was a weekend and she could for the first time see the Mandeville house and the airport facility. New Orleans also had a large Filipino population and several good Filipino restaurants. The C-130 took off within hours of our arrival in Mandeville. I wished them luck and told Christina to take it easy on Brain and ensure Matt didn't get bored. I told her that we would need Matt to want to return with a construction crew. Christina's parting words were that Brain was a fast learner and she knew just how to keep Matt happy.

I had my hour or so with Jerry then spent the remainder of the day showing Lori the house and then visiting New Orleans.

We returned to Miami on Sunday and Lori was back at school the next morning. My old friend Robin who was now President of the giant British container business assisted me with the purchase of 30 new refrigerated containers. 20 of those to be 40 foot long, to be used for fruit and 10, 20 foot long to be set up and used for hanging beef or for fish. I also purchased 30 brand new underslung generators that would fit under the rails of 30 new chassis. All of the new equipment would have our new name and logos displayed on the equipment. The equipment should start arriving via Crowlbe's ships within the next few months. I figured that I'd wait until we were ready before we talked to the Fruit Company about our plans.

I talked with Tim and asked if he still had any of our refer technicians that had worked with us in General Santos? If so I needed two men to go to General Santos and stay until they could train someone. I noted that the rebels had been inactive for almost a year and things there were calm. I offered that for the time being these men would stay at the farmhouse.

Evette had got back to me with the information that the the fire in our Panama asphalt plant had been purposely set in 4 different parts of the plant. There had been three men that lost their lives in the next morning's explosion and six men were injured, two from the explosion and four while fighting the fire before the explosion. The plant was a total lost, even the inventory of asphalt was lost. Evette said she had paid out death benefits to the families and set up school trust for their children. The injured were being treated for their burns and or injuries and also compensated. Evette said that she was told that the plant was still smoldering.

I wasn't going to visit Panama but somehow General Noriega needed to feel my displeasure on what had happened.

Lori had now told several of her friends that she was married and was called down to the girl's Dean. The Dean asked Lori several questions that included the whereabouts of her parents, how she arrived here in the US, my age, and what I did for a living. The girl's Dean warned Lori that it was not recommended that she speak to the other girls about married life. I was down there the next day having my own little meeting with the girl's Dean. The Dean when she heard I was there invited the boy's Dean to listen in. At first the girl's Dean questioned the validity of the marriage being it was outside of the US. The Dean even questioned if Lori was legally here. I had brought along Lori's passport which included the correct student visa. The boy's Dean broke in and said that for him that eliminated any suspicions on their part. Lori was an all "A" student with no problems in any of her classes. I could tell that the Girl's Dean wasn't happy but she said that Lori could stay in school just as long as she didn't become pregnant. The boy's Dean asked if I was good with this? I said I was fine with that but noted, that I reserved our rights to take Lori's treatment and questioning to a higher level.

Being in Miami High's office brought back many memories. The agreed end to my high school football days and making a great friend out of the past boy's dean, Mr. Spreen. I felt bad that somehow I had lost track of Mr. Spreen. If still alive he'd be about 80 right about now. Coach Shae whom was still there could be about 47 or so, still a young man.

It was now mid January and no one would be on the football field. Coach Shae taught 11 grade history. Wouldn't it be something if Lori had him for a teacher for one of her classes. I thought about it and laughed.

Back at the apartment Bob had called. It would be one of those sailing club meetings after Lori's swim practice.

Lori left the Jeep and we drove to the club together. Bob was there, I left Lori with Paul while Bob and I walked to the end of the dock. Bob said that President had fired the Director and that the number two was now the official CIA Director. Bob said that New Director wanted an up-date on the Andros project and the Contras. Bob said that the new Director also wanted to see my books on the Contra monies that I had received. I told Bob to tell the Director to bring his check book.

Since congress had sent me my first ever Contra funds, I hadn't touched a penny of the money. Up until we had received the Contra money from Congress we'd been sending our transport and warehouse bills as we always had. The last payment that we had received was the check that the

Colonel had given me. I wanted the new Director to personally approve our invoices before I transferred any of the Congress Contra money to my own group. I didn't want anyone accusing me of mismanaging the Contra money, there was already enough eyes on. The money that it cost me to upkeep my men was my expenditure. I didn't want anyone giving my people orders. It was my small army and I paid their way.

Bob laughed and said that he'd love to be there when I meet with the Director but he was headed to meet Carol for the weekend. I told Bob that Lourdes would call the Directors secretary to set up a meeting on Andros so the Director could see the Vehicle first hand. Bob noted that even he hadn't seen it as yet.

Bob walked me to the bar and personally congratulated Lori on our being married. Keep him closed by Bob said, keep him close by. Lori hadn't told Paul the news, Lori said she was listening to the story of when I was just 17 and crewing for the summer on a 54-foot Yacht named the "Mach-Turtle". Paul had said that his wife was then 16 years old and according to Paul's wife Penny, she was a lost soul until she met Jim on that trip. Paul said that Penny claimed that Jim taught her to laugh, smile and enjoy life. Married to the Captain Paul said, you, young lady are in for the adventure of a life time. Paul said the beer was on him, Lori said she wasn't allowed to drink beer as yet. Bob had a mouth full of beer and almost spit it out with laughter.

Lori and I passed by for the jeep and then passed by Chubby's house. The construction was coming right along. We then went to the apartment where dinner was ready and I checked my messages. Lourdes had called and said that Lee and Jack from Andros had urgently called for me to call them back and that Jerry also had called for me urgently. Lourdes also noted that Christina had made it to General Santos.

I first called Lee, he said there had been a shooting at the Andros airport that had left one of our co-pilots dead and a guard seriously wounded. It looked like the co-pilot was moving drugs and the guard had stopped him. Lee said the local authorities were notified and that they agreed to suppress the incident for 24 hours. Lee said that Jerry was aware of the situation. I then called Jerry and he said that Tommy was on the way for him and that he should be in Miami no later than 2:00 a.m. and at the apartment by 3:00 a.m. I told him I'd be waiting in the lobby. As I turned and put the phone down I saw Lori sitting on the couch in a night gown that was almost X-rated. I asked what that was for and she reminded me that we were married, she was absolutely right. Dinner would be put on hold.

The next morning, I met Jerry in the lobby, I accompanied him up and Lilly had started an early breakfast for us. Coffee was ready and Jerry and I took a cup to the balcony. Jerry first said that all air inbound cargo for Tehran had now been diverted to Haiti.

Then Jerry opened his brief case and pulled out photos of several small aircraft. Jerry had started an investigation and it looked like my buddy Noriega was moving drugs. Jerry was sure that our C-130s were most likely involved without our knowledge. Noriega most likely was camouflaging the drugs into our cargo. Our last return trip from Tehran was diverted to Andros. It was scheduled to return to Mandeville for maintenance but since this same C-130 was going to Haiti, Jerry sent it to Andros for its maintenance. With not much to do on Andros, as the C-130 arrived the maintenance crew was at the airport and ready to work on the arriving aircraft. One of the maintenance crew spotted the co-pilot acting suspicious and watched him. The copilot took a large Navy clothing bag from the cargo hold and walked down the ramp with it. The maintenance crew member alerted the security guard and the guard ordered the co-pilot to stop. The co-pilot then pulled a hand gun and fired on the guard. The wounded guard was able to return fire killing the co-pilot. The wounded guard was transferred to the Navy Hospital and flown via helicopter to Mercy Hospital in Miami. The guard whom was wearing a built proof vest had taken on two shots, one hitting the vest the other his right thy.

We had three C-130 crews, our original that Bob had sent us, one that the Colonel sent us and one that Jerry had hand-picked. This co-pilot was one from the group that had come from the Colonel. At this point we didn't know if the co-pilot was acting on his own or with his other crew members or with the Noriega people. Jerry and I would suspend the entire crew until we investigated them all. Jerry seemed to think that the money trail would tell on anyone that was receiving that kind of money. As for the Bahamas Government, they agreed to only report that they had stopped a drug shipment and killed one and were investigating 3 others. The drugs were taken by escort to the local police station where gasoline was poured on the drugs and burned.

As for Jerry's on going investigation, he and I knew that us not flying into Panama wasn't going to stop Noriega from moving drugs. We figured that Noriega was somehow moving his drugs to the US by either a corrupt group of military personnel or via the commercial flights and cargo ships that left from Panama each day. We decided that we would concentrate on the small aircrafts that were bringing the drugs in from Columbia. Jerry had a plan and I agreed.

Lori and the entire family were now up and sitting at the table. Jerry and I had eaten but joined them at the table with another cup of coffee. I noticed that Lori was having steak and eggs. Lori said that today she would swim as a part of the 200 meter relay team. Lori said that her hard work had gained this spot. You will be at the meet today Lori asked? Wouldn't miss it I said. Chubby said we all would be there supporting her efforts.

From breakfast, Jerry and I went to Mercy to visit the wounded guard. Mikel as they called him was beaming with pride. Mikel knew we had made arrangement to have his mother and a sister here today for a visit. Mikel told the story saying that Fernando had prepared him well. I told him we all were proud of his fast actions. Mikel said that he didn't understand the man he had shot. Where did he think he was going? Mikel asked? Mikel said he was sorry he had killed the man but that the man had already shot at him twice and kept walking in his direction. I had to stop him Mikel said.

Jerry would fly on to Andros to get statements from the crew. We would also get started on our plan for Noriega.

I had a few stops to make that included Miami Diamond, Lori hadn't mentioned a wedding ring so I figured I buy her one. Lori and Christina had once said that jade was worn for good fortune. I ordered up a wedding band that was made with every forth Diamond, there was a jade stone. Of course, the jeweler talked me into having a matching bracelet and neckless. The order would take several weeks to be ready. From the jewelry store I passed by to pick-up the duplicate neckless that I had ordered. The neckless had been ready for weeks. It was quite beautiful. Without the original beside it to come-pare, it looked quite real.

From there I made my way to the swim meet. I was early and got to see the girls warm up.

At the house, I had noticed a big improvement in Lori's left leg. Here at the pool was a chalk board where each event was listed with the names of those girls that would participate in each event. Lori would be the last leg of the 200 meter free style relay. I was told the fastest swimmer was saved for the last. In Lori's case, she wasn't the fastest but that their number one swimmer would have swam in several events prior to the relay and with this being Lori's only event the coach felt she would best be utilized as the whip. The family sat and watch as the other girls competed. Miami's star senior had competed in four events winning three of the four. It was Lori's turn. By the time Lori was tagged we were two full body lengths behind the leader. All 5 of us were cheering her on as loud as we could. Lori knew how far back she was starting. At the first turn, Lori had gained a half body up on the leader, she quickly swam into the second spot and was catching up with the leader. Lori moved through the water with what looked like a propeller pushing her. Lori touched the wall, winning by two seconds. The entire team ran to congratulate her at the finish.

Lori would carry home her first-place ribbon. Later when I asked her if it was worth it she said she now knew why the girl's Dean didn't want her to talk about marriage with the other girls. Why is that I asked? Lori said winning gave her almost the same feeling as being with me.

The next day at school was normal for Lori, there wasn't too much said about their winning swimming team. Lori did get a big surprise at swimming practice. Lori's coach said that Lori's official time in her 50-meter swim, if correct would be a school record. The coach said that come Monday the coach would time her in the 50 meter, if she matched her yesterday's time. Then Lori would be their new 50-meter free style starter.

Lori asked to spend the weekend on the Morgan. We left from the sailing club at about 8:00 p.m. sailing all the way down to Elliot's key. Lori and I had a nice quite weekend. We returned Sunday afternoon and Lori was ready for Monday morning school.

I kept busy Monday morning with calls from Lourdes about the material orders for General Santos. Our second flight had arrived, unloaded in General Santos and was on the way back with Matt. This second trip was loaded with stock for Jose's new parts store. Lourdes sent word that I was to ask Matt about his Philippine girlfriend.

Our Mandeville and Lake Charles flights to Tehran were going as planned. Jerry had hired another Co-pilot and cleared the remaining flight crew of the C-130 that had carried the drugs. That C-130 would depart from Andros later tonight for Haiti.

I arrived on time to see the 50-meter line up on the blocks. Lori looked a little nervous but seemed to be shaking it off. The starter gun went off and Lori got a good start but was in third place at the turn. It was after the turn that Lori poured it on. Lori beat the others by at least 2 feet. Lori's time didn't match her Thursday meet but it was close enough, Lorri, just a sophomore was the new 50-meter starter.

The next morning Lori's name was announced over the school's loud speaker. Lori was accredited with a new school record in the 50-meter free style.

That same day as she exited class to drive to swim practice she found her jeep had been wrapped with toilet paper. At first she thought it was someone that didn't like her, but then she remembered my stories of my days of wrapping my friend's houses. I assured Lori this wasn't the last time it would happen.

Matt had returned from General Santos and we invited him and Mr. Mckee over after work one night. Matt had drawn up the plans for the remodeling of the Santos farm house and improvements at the small fruit packing facility. Matt had visited the local meat slaughterhouse and had taken it on his own to design such a facility of our own. Of course this would include a walk-in freezer. Lori liked all the proposed changes to the house and we would approve all Matt's new designs and drawings. Now I asked, how and when can we go forward. It was now the beginning of February, Matt said with Mr. Mckee's and our approval he would initially take with him 6 men for one month hiring another 20 workers, some from other cities such as Manila. After the first month he'd see how the Filipinos could step up. Matt said he had visited several construction sites in Manila. Matt was confident that the job could be completed using local workers. Mr. Mckee approved Matt's plan and I added that the fruit packing facility needed to be first and the house needed to be livable starting in June. Matt said that by June he could have hot water and maybe some temporary air-conditioning but construction would be on going throughout the summer. Matt was to finish up the material list, having all that material delivered to Mandeville's airport. I noted that the first flight of material could leave within the week. Matt said he and his team would be ready. I didn't mention anything to Matt about what Christina said about a girlfriend. Mr. Mckee apologized to Lori about the inconvenience of us all living in the apartments and noted that she'd be back in her house within the next month. Lori said that only her family would be returning as we had gotten married. Mr. Mckee and Matt both congratulated her wishing us a happy life together.

Evette had sent news from Fernando; His group had attacked and overrun the only Sandinista garrison in the southeast. Fernando had reported that they had lost ten of his local fighters and that he had permitted the Sandinista to truck out there dead and several wounded, the rest of the Sandinistas were marching to the north west, again without shirts. The report said Fernando needed supply's. Evette had sent the supply list to Lourdes and our C-130 that had returned from General Santos would leave for our Nicaragua air strip within 24 hours.

The third and newest C-130 that had the TESS lasers installed was now again at the G.D. Fairbanks location having some kind of special radar installed. Each time we added something new we lost payload. This time we were losing just over 1,000 pounds. G.D. said that this new radar that incorporated a touch of TESS could track even a small aircraft up to 50 to 75 miles away, depending on the weather. Yes, we were going to track the small planes that were delivering the drugs to Noriega. We hadn't decided just what we were going to do about it, but for now the plan was limited to tracking.

As Lori and I got out of our nightly shower we got in bed and talked about General Santos. Summer was only three months away. By then Nilo should be shipping 8 to 12 containers of fruit per week. Hopefully by then he would be also shipping 2 containers of frozen hanging beef sides. I still hadn't met or spoken with The Fruit Company to inform them of my plans and time was running out to do so. The container equipment that I had ordered for General Santos would start to show up the following ship. Tomorrow I would have Lourdes call to see if she could get me into see Shoemaker of Standard Fruit. Shoemaker wouldn't be worried about my shipping my own bananas, he'd most likely feel it was a drop in the bucket and more of a Wim. He'd think that once I didn't get the returns

I wanted, my brand would just disappear. I was sure when he hears, if he hadn't already that I had purchased 30 slots on the Crowlbe ship he'd think I was throwing away money. The problem would come when I complained about the Japanese labor at the Tuna Factory. I wasn't going to threaten him but offer him my assistance in motivating the Filipinos to be better employees. In fact, I'd offer to bring his operational cost down while moving more cargo.

This would be my first trip without Lori since our wedding. I hoped not to miss her next swim meet, but if it was to be Lori said she would be fine.

The next afternoon Lourdes confirmed my meeting with Shoemaker, I had thought the meeting would be in San Jose but it was to be in San Francisco. I was also surprised that Shoemaker had sent an agenda that included their offer of a management contract, plus talks of the purchase of the Tuna Factory building and the land north to the river. Not exactly what I had in mind but it would get me in the door. The meeting was confirmed for this coming Friday at 10:00 a.m. their time, with a Dinner at 8:00 p.m. Looked like I might be spending the night.

The week went by fast and I was now sitting in the pool bleachers waiting for Lori's start on the block. The starting gun sounded and once again Lori was not out front. Again she was a close third at the flip. At the flip, one could see those powerful legs produce that propeller-like splash behind her. Lori's team earned a first and second in the race. Lori took first by an arm's length and our senior took second. Lori also swam in the 200 meter with her pulling up the rear, Lori's team again taking the win. Lori now looked more comfortable with the other girls with all of them jumping and screaming with their second team win. Lori asked if she could go with the team to celebrate at McDonalds? I told her to go and have fun with her friends.

The next morning, I left the apartment at 5:30 a.m. I was on my way to the meeting with Shoemaker. The meeting started on time to include three surprise guest. Mr. Misusocki's son, Mr. Partridge and back from a short retirement Mr. Bozzni. First they all congratulated me on my marriage. Then it was right down to business. They wanted me to take back the management of the maintenance of General Santos. Not the operation, only the maintenance. Then without getting my answer or thoughts, they offered to buy the Tuna factory building and the land. Mr. Partridge noting that Mrs. Santos had passed away opening the way for me to sell the property. Surly Nilo had told Standard that I had promised Mrs. Santos not to sell or change the name on the building. They then waited my response. I then brought up their promise to employ only Filipino workers at the plant. Mr. Partridge then said that the Filipinos had gotten lazy and were talking about forming a union. I noted that we had signed an agreement that included the workers, but more important than the signed agreement, was our hand shake. I asked to see a month by month production showing a decline due to personal and then the increase after the personnel change. Mr. Misusocki said he would get those numbers. Mr. Partridge then asked again about the Factory and the land. I asked if they had prepared an offer. Mr. Shoemaker then handed me an envelope that had in it just such an offer. I looked at the numbers and said that I would consider their offer. I then said that I had met with Mr. Crowlbe and had made an agreement for space on their weekly ships. Mr. Partridge noted that should I accept the management of the maintenance, he was sure that Standard would use more slots on the ship reducing my unnecessary extra cost. I told my friends that I understood that my new brand of fruit wouldn't affect their bottom line but if they didn't fill the slots then I would do my best to do so. The meeting was short and the young Mr. Misusocki said he would have the numbers that I requested sent to my hotel before Dinner. I didn't want to stay over for Dinner but it would have been rude to now decline their dinner offer. Mr. Shoemaker said that I must be tired from my trip and that there was a limo waiting to deliver me to my hotel. Once at the hotel I did numbers for about two hours when there was a knock on the door. I opened the door and there stood a young Japanese girl dressed in a short black evening dress. I thought if she wasn't a ten, she was a 9.9. As I opened the door she walked in and presented me a large vanilla envelope. She said the son had sent the reports and the father had sent her to be my escort for the night. She looked at me and said, you know a wedding gift. I looked at her and thought about it for about 5 seconds and then walked toward the door and opened it. The girl said that Mr. Misasocki would consider the rejection of his gift a personal insult. She said would be shamed by her employer and her family. Please she said close the door. What's your name I asked, Suzy she answered. I told her to make herself comfortable. I then turned and walked to a table. When I turned Suzy had dropped her dress. You did say comfortable did you not she said. I then sat at the table and looked over the numbers. I then called Lourdes and said that I needed to know how many tuna loads were boarded during each ship leaving General Santos for the last six months. I pointed to the couch and told Suzy to have a seat, she did. I told Lourdes I needed the information within two hours. I then continued to check Mr. Misosocki's report and did more numbers. Lourdes called back in about an hour and a half and asked where to send the numbers. I looked at Suzy and told Lourdes to fax them to the hotel. I asked Suzy to put on her dress and go down stairs and pick up my fax. Without question Suzy, did as I asked? With the number of containers shipped, I calculated the production. The report that Suzy had brought me had been manipulated. There had been no such down turn in the tuna production. I then thought about it, I checked my room and found two hidden cameras. This was an old trick that I should have remembered from Michelle's death. It was called blackmail. Not that it would have worked in my case, but I was mad that they stooped to this low. I called the hotel management and the police. Suzy after telling her story was taken away in handcuffs. The police said that what had been done by putting the cameras there was only a misdemeanor crime. I figured just getting caught was worse than the punishment would be. I put in a call to Lourdes and said to have the leer standing by at the airport for a late night departure. I'd be returning home after the dinner.

I showed up to dinner but for some reason Mr. Misosocki didn't show. I wouldn't mention anything about the girl nor cameras but did make my case about the deceptive report. I wasn't a part of the company's ownership nor management but did say that I expected all involved to live up to our agreement. During the dinner, I made it clear that I would not take over the maintenance but would be glad to assist with any refresher courses that their personnel may require. I stated that as Mr. Partridge had mentioned earlier in the day, it was in my best interest for the empty slots on the ship to be filled. I also announced that, at this time, the factory nor the property was for sale.

It hadn't been a very pleasant trip but I did accomplish what I started out to do. I hadn't made any new friends.

I slept most of the way home, we arrived at Opa-Locka the next morning at about 7:30 a.m., this because of the time difference. I had a good rest and Lilly had a good breakfast ready. Lori had already been up and had taken a run, down Brickell avenue to the Miami Marina and back. Before breakfast I joined Lori in the shower. Man, did I enjoy that shower.

After breakfast Lori and I would take out the Morgan for the rest of the weekend. Lori had mastered the Morgan but I still considered her a fair-weather sailor. Lori hadn't ever been in rough seas. Our weekend went just fine. When I was with Lori I didn't miss anyone.

Monday morning I got the news that our C-130 that had the new radar installed was on a practice run off the coast of Columbia and had run into trouble. Our C-130 was tracking a small aircraft that had taken off from a small Columbian runway and was heading to Panama. We were intercepted by two F-15s from the US base in Panama. Our radar had picked up the fighters long before they saw us and our pilots had engaged the TESS laser defense system. What we hadn't figured on was that the fighters were somehow alerted that they were being tracked by a weapon system. We were contacted via radio to identify ourselves which we did, although we were in international air space we were warned to leave the area. One of the jets fired a few rounds of it's machine gun as a warning. TESS automatically activated using it's electric and magnetic jamming system. Both F-15 pilots first talking between themselves stated that their electronics were going haywire and that were having trouble controlling their aircraft. One pilot started calling in a mayday saying they were returning to base but had no navigation and although they were still flying it appeared that the fuel indicators and maybe even the fuel pumps weren't functioning. Our pilots attempted to shut down the TESS system, but the system, still sensing a threat, would not respond. Our pilots decided to register a change of heading, then heading due east at full throttle. Once the F-15s disappeared from our radar TESS automatically went back to stand by. Our C-130 was now on the ground on Andros.

I figured that it wouldn't be long before I'd be getting that call from Washington. It didn't come. It was me that would do the calling. For me it seemed that our F-15s may have been running protection for that small aircraft. If so, this drug smuggling effort was much larger than I had thought. The contras were being funded by congress and we still had a good amount of funds in the bank, so who needed money so badly that they'd be moving drugs?

I decided to meet with Jerry and our old friend Tim from the Miami Herald. I met with Jerry first, laid out a plan and then met with Tim the reporter. Tim had actually spent some time in Panama when he was trying to catch us moving arms during the Iran-Contra affair, he caught us moving farm equipment. Tim also broke the award-winning story of the Cuban's defeat in Nicaragua by Fernando's group. When Tim came to the meeting he was thinking it was going to get him the latest story of Fernando's whipping of the Sandinista's last South Eastern Garrison. Instead I said we thought we had a much bigger story. US fighter jets riding shot gun for aircraft coming from Columbia, loaded with drugs. The story I warned was a dangerous one. Tim said he was told working with me was like playing with fire, only it wasn't just his finger tips that could get burned. Tim was on board.

After the CIA Director thing, I didn't or wouldn't trust anyone with a CIA involvement. Sooner or later I was going to meet up with the CIAs new man and clearly my mistrust was extended to him.

Montibelli on the other hand, while he was the Shaw's enforcer, had chopped many of hands and heads off for drug involvement. Montibelli would do almost anything, but not get involved with selling drugs. Montibelli had heard about the arson of my asphalt plant and said that Noriega was the Colonels friend, not his. Montibelli said that the zone from where the small aircrafts were taking off from in Columbia was controlled by the FARK. Montibelli said, it was a man named Pablo Escobar that was in business with Noriega. Panama was fast becoming the drug capital of the world. Montibelli said it took a lot of power to move F-15s to protect those drug movements. The harbor at the base of the canal could easily have 20 to 30 Cargo ships anchored waiting their turn to pass through the canal. It was settled, we'd use the Miami Herald to slow the drug flow.

This week again Lori shined in their swim meet. That night after the meet Lori said she had informed the coach that we would be traveling for the summer. Lori said she wasn't bored with swimming but that her coach and some of the other girls said that swimming was a year-round sport and that at least during the school year she would be going to swimming practice every day. Lori said that when she was playing tennis she also enjoyed that and asked about modeling? I told Lori that she could do all three. If what she wanted was to be a champion swimmer, she could even reach the Olympics but in doing so it would be almost like a full-time job. Lori then said she already had a full-time job, the one she wanted most of all, she said she was my wife and soon a mother. I came to her and kissed her and said that when I had it in my mind to wait to get married, it was so that she could get an education and have the chance to experience all these things such as the swim team and whatever else she wanted to do.

Before we fell asleep I told Lori that before the season was over I wanted her to not wait until the flip turn to put her legs in gear. Give it your all from the start, don't look back, don't worry about running out of steam. Let's see what you've got. I said, I thought it would help her and the coach define what she would need to do for the next year. I reminder her that she was only a sophomore and had two more years of high school.

Again, the days few by, I had been speaking with Salinas and Betty daily. Betty suggested that if I wanted to be there for the birth of my son I should come today. Today was Thursday, swim meet day. I had Tommy standing by, I would go to the match and then leave from there.

Lori's 50 meter free style went as it had been going, with her winning by an arm's length. The 200 hundred meter was under way and Lori was on the box. As her teammate touched the wall Lori made her dive. I noticed wright away something was different, Lori had stayed under longer, I saw the coach stand. Lori's team was only behind about a half a body length when Lori hit the water. When she surfaced she had already cut the lead. Then I could see what was going on. The propellers were engaged, by the turn Lori was in the lead by a body length. The Propellers didn't stop until she reached the finish line. By then her entire team were on their feet. Lori was up and out of the pool before the number two girl touched the wall. Lori looked at me with the biggest smile and gave me the thumbs up. Her team mates were all over her, all knew that she must have broken her own record. Lori came to me and latched on. Lori being out of breath, she said she didn't want me to go but knew I must. She kissed me saying that she'd be right here waiting. I then informed her that Mrs. Shinner would be at the studio Saturday morning waiting for her. Lilly would be accompanying her and that she should get lots of sleep Friday night. I didn't wish her luck, she didn't need it. I patted her on the butt and was on my way.

By 7:30 p.m. I was at the Hill Top Beach House. Salinas was still there saying, nothing yet. Betty had a good dinner waiting, I took the children in the pool, even Salinas joined in. Wendy, Johnny and Michelle were good swimmers. Kelly and Jimmy were also doing good in the water. Salinas had to hold Kelly while I worked with Jimmy. Salinas had hired a Nanny whom we made darn sure could swim. The Nanny was also in the pool. All had a good time, us being in there until the no seems started in on us. Salinas reminded me that the house at Mandeville had the entire pool area screened in. I reminded her that Mandeville didn't have the winds that we did.

Every one out of the pool and off to bed. That night at about 2:00 a.m. Salinas's water broke. We were only at the hospital an hour when Jacque was born. Salinas and Jacque were doing just fine. Jacque a whopping 9.2 pounds. Salinas said that she finally had giving us a son. Salinas's mom Sharron would arrive the next day. No I hadn't sent a ride for her. Sharron and I didn't see eye to eye on things, even less now that she heard that I had taken on another wife. Salinas and Jacque would stay an extra couple days in the hospital as Salinas said she needed the rest. At the house, there would now be six children for her to care for.

Of course, I kept contact with Lori, Lori said that the modeling went well with Mrs. Shinner asking her to sign a contract, Lori said that she told Mrs. Shinner that I would need to approve any such contract first. Lori said that she had changed clothes at least 20 times and that Mrs. Shinner said she wanted some of these shots to make the mid-March adds for Burdines's Spring look. Lori said that Lilly hadn't let her out of her sight, with Lilly traveling in and out of the dressing room each time. Those were exactly the instructions I had given Lilly.

I brought Salinas and Jacque home on Monday morning. One of the first things that Salinas did was to mark the calendar that was in the kitchen. Thirty days she told me, she also marked the calendar in mid-May saying she was claiming a two-week vacation just the two of us, Salinas had me sign on the calendar. I knew that somewhere during the first week in June Lori, her family and myself would be leaving for General Santos.

I had stayed in Nassau until Thursday morning. Tuesday night I had gone out fishing with a husband and wife on one of the tourist boats. I listened to one of the newer Captains tell a few of the old stories of the white boy who had sailed a small boat from Miami and fell madly in love with the then Queen of Nassau. The story was told that the white boy and the Nassau Queen had found the great treasure of Sir Walter Drake. The white boy was called off to war and while gone the Queen had become sick and died. The story went on to say that the boy went on to become Bahamas most famous fisherman. The story that this particular Captain told, was that the King Fish, as the Bahamians called him had been cursed by Drake's treasure and also lost his next two loves. One of the tourist asked what had become of the King Fish? The Captain sadly said that no one really knew, when the King Fish's second wife had died, the King Fish got in his small boat and sailed off, no one had seen him since.

It had been some time since I had spoken the Bahamian language but I could still talk like a Bahamian. With my heavy Bahamian accent, I asked the Captain if he would know the King Fish if he would see him? The husband of the woman that had asked what had happened to the King Fish broke in and said that this King Fish was only a made up story to tell Tourist. With the boat now anchored and the first fishing line thrown out, I started talking again. It was here I said, in this very spot where one of the King Fish's story had started, here the King Fish made friends with a 14-foot hammerhead shark. I then told the story as the husband and wife listened. The Captain also listened, when I finished the wife noted that I had told the story as if I was on board that night. Yes mam, I replied in my heavy accent. I was here and knew the King Fish. Would you like to hear the entire story as we fish I asked? Even the Captain said yes. I started the story when the King Fish was a young boy dreaming of adventure and continued telling the story as we fished. The couple had caught more big fish than they had ever imagined. At about 2:00 a.m., when they could barely keep their eyes open. I took two of the big fish and cut them up. With the tower's lights pointed down into the water, I threw over the cut-up fish. Within seconds the sharks were there, there I shouted there he is. Yes, as the tourist looked over in the light, he swam by within 6 feet of the boat. It's him I said, he still out here. It was the largest hammerhead shark that I had ever seen. The couple, seeing the shark stepped back. Don't worry mam I said he's and old friend.

As we reached the city dock I informed the couple that the night was on me. People haven't called me the King Fish in quite some time I said, most of my friends now just call me Captain. Oh yes, I said I've now had six wives, all six have boats in the Harbor with their names on the stern. This boat's name is wife number five. The boats name was "Salinas". As I walked away from them I said to come back soon and maybe I would tell the rest of the story.

I had enjoyed my night out, telling that fish story and catching a few big fish. My biggest joy was seeing that Hammerhead once again. Yes, we were both still quite alive.

I was once again headed back to Miami, Lori had been told on Monday that un-officially she had broken the state record for the 50-meter free style. Today it could be made official.

The C-130 with the most up to date TESS was now again back at Fairbanks, they were installing high tech cameras and doing something where the crew could tone down TESS's self-protection devices. The laser system locking on to all aircraft that passed within the 50-mile radius was just a tad too much. Besides what if we got caught up in the middle of the good guys and the bad guys trading shots, TESS would be firing at them both. Ah, life's little problems.

On the ground in Miami, I wouldn't see Lori until the swim meet, Chubby and the rest of the family had just finished moving back into their house in the roads. I stopped by to see the house, it was beautifully done. The children were still at school and Chubby and Lilly showed me what they said was the new house. What I did notice was that the back yard had become much smaller. Chubby then said that he had heard that someone had brought the houses on both sides of them. Chubby said he hadn't even known they were for sale.

It was now time for me to get myself to the swim meet. I got there just as the girls were warming up. Lori just looked to darn good. That one-piece bathing suit was fit onto one hell of a body. Lori was looking more like a woman every day.

Lori wasn't on the roster for the 200-meter relay. I imagined the coach had done this so that Lori wouldn't be concerned that she had to save enough energy for that race which was at the end of the meet.

It was time, Lori was on the block, the starting gun went off and Lori was second getting off the block and into the water but, when she came up she was in the lead. No one even came close, she finished almost three body lengths ahead of the closest swimmer. After a few minutes, the announcement was made that Lori had just set a new state record. The coach then asked Lori how she felt? The coach was asking whether Lori could swim in the 200-meter relay. Lori answered she was ready to continue in the 200-meter freestyle. The coach made the change on the board. Lori and her team mates again won the relay. After the meet when the girls were in changing, I asked the coach, you knew didn't you? The coach said that many times when it comes so easily the swimmer stops working every day. Lori, the coach said could go all the way if she sticks with it. In Lori's case, the coach said she wished that Lori didn't have so much. Swimming could have brought her so many opportunities. The coach with tears in her eyes finished by saying that she could coach all the rest of her life and not see such natural talent. I told the coach that we were building a pool so that Lori could keep up with her swimming over the summer.

Lori and the girls then came out from the lockers, I asked if she would go with the girls to celebrate? Lori said that she was going to celebrate with me at home.

It was great to have Lori all to myself at the apartment. Me I could hang out in my underwear and Lori well you know.

Lori had done as I asked and sent her modeling contract to Roy for review and any changes he wanted to make. I was sure it would ready by tomorrow. I would pass by and check. Lori had several photos to show me, these I wouldn't pay for. I was not surprised in what I saw, the photos were incredible. Lori was beautiful.

Although Lourdes had kept me abreast of what was going on, I got on the computer and doubled checked that I wasn't missing anything.

Fernando was on two weeks of his vacation, he hitched a ride on the C-130 that had taken Matt and his men plus another load of construction supplies to General Santos. I was sure he had gone to visit Maria.

Bob had called saying that new Director was losing his patience with me. I waited until Lori left the next day for class and called Lourdes to see by chance if the Director could meet me on Saturday or Sunday, I told Lourdes I could meet him almost anywhere.

Seemed that the Director had something going on in Las Vegas and would be staying there until Sunday afternoon. I was to meet him the next day for a lunch at one the of the hotels.

Jerry was working on the Columbian project, as we called it, and said he had some film footage that he wanted me to see. The film wasn't aerial it was ground footage. I told Lourdes to get Jerry to Las Vegas for a Saturday breakfast in our room. I had Lourdes call Jack inviting him and Cindy along. I wanted Jack's help with security and I wanted him to know what was going on with our Columbian Project. Cindy and Lori could keep themselves occupied tomorrow morning either at the pool or site seeing. Lourdes said she would have to get to work as there were lots of moving parts.

Today I would be having lunch with Montibelli as he too had some news. We would meet at the usual place. I left the apartment early to stop by Roy's to pick up Lori's Modeling contract then I would pass by Miami Diamond and pick up Lori's jewelry set.

Roy wasn't in but the contract was ready. The large vanilla envelope that was waiting for me had the original plus the newly modified contract. Roy's note said to "have Mrs. Shinner sign the new contract without showing her the old one. Have her sign all three originals then giving her one, delivering one back to me".

My next stop would be Miami Diamond where Lori's Jewelry was there and waiting, it was exactly what I wanted. Of all the jewelry that I had seen, and I had seen a lot, never had I seen anything like this. Jade and diamonds, it all was quite beautiful.

From the jeweler's I was on my way to meet Montibelli. Montibelli showed up with his regular girl and another woman. Montibelli talked to the girl in what I thought was Hebrew, her then going to the bar sitting with Montibelli's security man. Montibelli introduced the next women as an old friend that was in the business. Ingrid, Montibelli said was not her real name. Montibelli said that Ingrid had the coordinates of Sadat Hussein's chemical plant where he was producing his Mustard & Nerve gas. I asked what they wanted me to do with the information? Montibelli looked at me turning his head while raising both hands to his shoulders.

Oh no I said, why me? Montibelli said because you can. Ingrid then pulled out a map, she hadn't said a word until this point. I will clear this route she said. The map showed a flight plan that included Saudi Arabia, Kuwait, Iran, Iraq and back. Ingrid said the same Israeli aircraft that was now refueling our Tehran trips would refuel for this trip. Why me I asked? Ingrid said it was a simple answer, everyone knows your C-130 is coming and going to Iran, no one will suspect until you cross into Iraq. The mustard gas she said is killing thousands of our civilians, women, and children. Please I beg of you she said. Montibelli then said he would go along but that if Khomeini knew he was aboard the Iranians would also try to shoot us down. Ingrid then showed me several photos, they were horribly disgusting. As I looked at the photos, the waiter brought the phone to Montibelli. Talking in Arabic he then hung up and said that Ingrid must go. He then said something to Ingrid in their language and nodded to his man. Ingrid then stood as did I with her saying, "May your God be with you" kissed me on both cheeks and walked away with Montibelli's man. Montibelli then nodded to his Lebanese girl and she joined us at the table. We now ordered our food. Montibelli's girl then asked about my wife. I told her that Lori was at school. The girl asked why? To get an education I said. She again asked why? I then asked who would take care of Montibelli's things when he leaves this world? The girl, now with a big smile said that Mr. Montibelli says he's taking it all with him. Montibelli without smiling said, it's true. I ended giving them both a ride home. As Montibelli exited my car he said to have a good trip to Las Vegas and to give his regards to the new Director. As the car door closed I mumbled,"that old SOB".

I hoped that Lori would come straight home from school but just in case I drove by and left a note on the jeep's windshield. The note said, "we're leaving on a trip, must be ready by 8:00 p.m." This would give her time to do something like visit McDonalds with her team after practice. Me I had a few inquiries to make before leaving for Las Vegas.

Lori got home early, she wanted to know where we were headed. She was thrilled to hear where we were headed. Lori knew that I didn't gamble and that I had only been to Las Vegas once before. The plan was to only spend one night, coming home the next afternoon. Once we showered and were dressed, I showed her the jewelry. Still wearing her engagement ring, I slipped on her wedding ring, we wouldn't be leaving early.

Jack and Cindy were waiting aboard the Leer; Tommy had just arrived from picking up Cindy from Nassau and Jack from Andros.

Of course, Lori showed Cindy her new wedding ring, Cindy looked at Jack, asking if she would ever get one of those. Jack made the comment that it wouldn't be this trip as whatever happens in Vegas stays in Vegas. Lori had never heard that before but Cindy had.

The trip was long with, Lori sleeping most of the way. Once there we got to our hotel to find that Jerry had already checked in. Jerry had brought along his wife with her adding that she trusted Jerry but not Las Vegas. We checked in, with the girls all agreeing that they would dress up. Lori looked so good I thought we never get out of that room.

The six of us saw two good shows, I wondered what it would have been like seeing Frank Sinatra or even Elvis out here. Those must have been the days.

The next morning Jerry, Jack and I got an early start. The three of us had left our rooms and would have coffee out by one of the pools. Jerry had the photos he wanted me to see with him saying that Noriega was receiving at least one air load every other day coming from Columbia. The ground photos were taken from both Columbia and Panama. Jerry was sure we wouldn't see such photos in the near future, as Tim would publish a few of these in tomorrow's Miami Herald. In one of the photos, using a magnifying glass I was shown that Noriega was actually captured in the photo. Jack looking at the same photo picked out an old buddy of mine. Jack handed me back the magnifying glass and the photo and asked if I saw anyone else I recognized? Damn, I said, it was the man that I had shot in the Fairbanks airport. Jack said, the man was fired from the CIA right after the then Director got sick. Jerry said he'd make the call to Tim as this was an important discovery. Jack said that the C-130 should be back on Andros by this morning. He mentioned that the aircraft including the tail section had undergone a new paint job. Sorry boss Jack said, I know how you enjoyed that Traveling Cat emblem up there.

I waited until Jerry came back from his call, then mentioned my visit with Montibelli and Ingrid. Both men immediately said that moving cargo in that zone was one thing but entering the war was another. I said it would be a good test to see how TESS really worked under fire. Jerry said, he rather not find out that it didn't work as good as we hoped. Jack asked how we would find the location without navigation? Then he asked what would we drop to take out the sight? Jack smiled and said that gasoline as we had dropped on a Sandinista base was out of the question. I said it would have to be something that used GPS. Jerry then said, here we go again with the Star Wars dream. I then said it was not a dream. There is such a missile that we could use, the problem was that we'd still be up there and the missile would need GPS navigation to hit its target. Jack asked if this particular missile had been tested? Nop I said, but G.D. has a prototype ready. Before now they just needed a target. Jack asked how much time would it need? I said its range was about 5 miles, so maybe two minutes. Jack said if we were still in the air, we could see the blast. What's it's weight Jack asked? Just over 20,000 pounds I said. Sure would be a rude awaking Jack said. I mentioned that if we did this I would want to be aboard. Jack said he would also go. I told Jerry to speak with the Crews and see if we had the volunteers we would need. Then Jerry asked if it wouldn't be better to try this thing on a cocaine runway? I mentioned that dropping a bomb on Columbia or Panama was out of the question. Both Jack and Jerry then agreed.

It was almost time for my meeting with the new CIA boss, I would not mention the Iraq thing but was going to speak about the drugs.

The CIA Director meeting was a one on one. The new man was much different than his predecessor. He of course wanted to know all about TESS and the Vehicle. I had brought with me the bank statements of the Contra funds and copies of all our invoices that we needed to be reimbursed for. He was surprised that we hadn't spent more money and hadn't touched the government funds. He said that most of what he had seen in the past with Government funds, was that money funded was money spent. He said his secretary would send an approval for the transfer of the money reimbursement. He asked if I'd send the remainder of the funds back and I said, not at this time.

I then asked if the CIA was involved in the movement or sale of drugs? He said he was insulted by the question. I told him that Noriega was moving a large amount of drugs through Panama and that I was sure a big percentage was ending up in the US. The new Director claimed he was aware of the rumors but had no direct proof. I asked him what he would do if he had the proof? The Director said he'd turn it over to the DEA. I asked what if the DEA was involved? He said that was highly unlikely. Would you like me to investigate I asked? He didn't give me a straight answer. I then let him know that I didn't trust the CIA or DEA to do the right thing. The right thing here is to stop the drugs I said. The new Director then said that he agreed with my thinking on this item but couldn't help. I asked if his hands were tied? His reply was an honest one, he answered yes. He warned not to use the Contra money anywhere except for the Contras. I assured him I wouldn't think of it. The way that he said it seemed as he didn't mean it. I came away from the meeting feeling better about him, not the CIA, but about the new man.

I went by our room, Lori's wet bathing suit was there in the bathroom but no Lori. A note written in soap on the bathroom mirror said they had gone site seeing and would be back before 3:00 p.m. With my clothes and shoes on, I went and laid down on the bed with two pillows under my head thinking about it all. Up until now all my, most of my ill thoughts had been focused at Castro. The truth was there were lots of Castro's out there. I thought about Rusty and his drug problem and the millions of kids like him that most likely started by smoking Marijuana then went on to the hard stuff. Then I kept seeing those photos of the dead women and children on the streets of Iran. These people in the photos, all of them suffered a terrifying death. I must of fell asleep as the next thing that I remembered was the door lock switching over to open. I sat up and it was Lori. With me still sitting, Lori came and jumped on me asking how my meeting went? I told her that it went much better than I thought it would have. Lori then asked if we could stay the night leaving tomorrow sometime. I asked about the others? Lori said they'd stay if we did. It was settled, we were staying.

Lori and I got a shower and a well, kind of a nap. Lori had called Cindy and we were all to meet in the lobby at 9:30 p.m. It would be dinner and at least one show.

The six of us had a good time Saturday night and early Sunday morning. We all left in the Leer, as Jerry and his wife had missed their yesterday's evening flight. The Leer would drop them off in Mandeville on our way home.

Lori and I arrived at home at 8:30 p.m. Cindy and Jack in another hour or so. The trip had been a good one. I had picked up the Sunday's news paper from the lobby. Tim had only made a small section on the front page but when I turned the page there it was, the photo that showed Noriega, my friend from the CIA and a forklift pallet full of small packets, all three circled in red. The caption below the photo read "Noriega, the CIA and Drugs". Tim's article said that the drugs were being flown in from the FARC of Columbia under the direction of Pablo Escobar.

Of course, the new Director wasn't going to be too happy with me over this but it might help free up his hands. Knowing that this was coming and the possibility of someone attempting to place the blame on me, Jerry had arranged surveillance of the new CIA chief in Las Vegas meeting with yours truly. Jerry's people made sure they had been noticed by the new man's people.

Lori would get up early for school, I had already been in the lobby to pick up the paper to see the reaction if any. Today, Monday there was no reaction thus far.

As Jack had mentioned our Andros C-130 was back from having the cameras installed. I was anxious to get some of the drug movement from Columbia on film but wanted to pay that well deserved visit to Hussein. I called Montibelli and asked for a meeting. I said it would be nice to have his old friend to join us. Montibelli asked for the meeting to be at the deli on Collins. He'd meet me there in 30 minutes.

Ingrid was a no show but instead I told Montibelli what we would need. A dark night with ground fires getting us in and out. We would also need satellite coverage for the GPS signal not to be lost. I said the coordinates would need to be double checked before our take off. Montibelli said that he'd take care of his end. We spoke briefly about the news article about Noriega and what he thought the DEA would do about it. Montibelli gave me that look taking the salt shaker and putting salt in his hand then throwing it out of his hand onto the floor. In other words, nothing. Montibelli said we'd soon hear about a large drug bust with several arrests with the news claiming that the DEA had stopped the traffickers and the drugs. Before departing from Montibelli, he handed me a check covering all the trips we had made to Tehran up to this point. Montibelli said there was an extra 20% in there so that I wouldn't have to calculate his 50%

of the profits. Montibelli said the difference of the billing and the check besides the additional 20% was the in-flight fuel service. The check was from a swiss bank so I could deposit it in my off-shore companies.

Later that day Lourdes called and said that the CIA office had sent an approval for the monies we had spent on the Contras. I told her to move that exact amount from the Contra account to our Contra expense account. I told her that we had received the Tehran transport money and that I'd have it deposited it our Nassau account. Lourdes reminded me that Lori's birthday was coming up and for me not to forget it. Lourdes said she had seen a photo of that jeep and thought a new car would be nice.

Jack called from Andros and said they would be taking off at about 6:00 p.m. to see how well the infrared worked. I asked that they not get into any trouble. Jack was planning to fly along the Columbia coast, hoping to pick up one of Noriega's small planes leaving from Columbia and landing where ever in Panama.

Me, I got to see Lori's swim practice, Mrs. Shinner was meeting me there so she could get a few photos of Lori at the pool. I had arrived a few minutes early and checked with the coach. Mrs. Shinner did what Roy said she would, she signed all three copies of Lori's contract without even looking at them. Lori was now a model for the Burdines advertisement department. This coming Sunday some of Lori's photos would be placed in the Burdines adds. Mrs' Shinner also asked about Christina saying she also wanted that contract too. Lori and I spent an extra hour at the pool with Mrs. Shinner's photographer taking photos. Lori looked happy but didn't like the attention in front of her friends.

The next couple of days went by fast. Jack had gotten lucky, the filming had caught a small plane coming from Panama and landing at a Panamanian military base. Tim from the News paper would have a field day with this.

Today the C-130 was again at G.D., you guessed it, the plane was being fitted with the new type GPS guided missile. Jerry had ready the all-volunteer crew, and we'd be taking off Friday night.

CHAPTER XIX

STOPPING THE MUSTARD GAS

We took off as planned having an extra refueling over Saudi air space. It was a pitch black night with no moon. We went into Iranian air space then started our run into Irag. It didn't take TESS a minute into Irag air space to start tracking several spots. The TESS Navigation program was started and then it happened. No ground missiles were fired as yet but we were being shot at by anti-aircraft fire. We were sure they couldn't see us on radar and the aircraft was now completely painted in camouflage. They were firing at our sound. At 20 minutes in, we switch the TESS navigation system off to check our coordinates, we marked our watches and turned the TESS navigation system back on. By our watches we'd be over the sight in another 6 minutes. We would then turn the TESS navigation system off and send the missile out the back ramp. Those 6 minutes were pure nerves. Then it happened, TESS navigation system was turned off, the ramp came down and the C-130s nose lifted and out went the missile. Within seconds with the ramp now closed, we were picked up by radar and TESS had fired its lasers twice. Anti-aircraft explosions were rocking the ship. One such explosion was so close it shook us badly. At that same time, I heard an engine alarm, it was our outside starboard. The engine had shut down. We didn't think we had been hit but the percussion was so bad it must have stalled the engine. The captain attempted to restart the engine, but was without success. We had at least two more real bad shakers, one knocking me from my feet hitting the bulkhead before winding up on the deck. I crawled to a seat and buckled back in. Prior to the engine stall out I had been seated and buckled in tight. The copilot now said that he thought the propeller wasn't even moving. At that moment, the pilot said there had been a large blast on the ground behind us. He was sure is was our missile. The pilot then turned the TESS navigation system back on. Then he re-lowered the tail ramp and we dropped what was called an air bomb. As the bomb went out, the ramp was raised and the captain lowered our speed. Just as the ramp closed we were shook once again. This time it was us that had done the shaking. The air bomb had gone off producing a large high altitude explosion, the idea was for the ground to think we had been hit and the aircraft destroyed. This could cause them not to continue looking for us. The Captain slowing the engines was to lower our noise.

Of course, we were now traveling blind. Ingrid had the ground fires going that would help us keep our heading. We would continue heading west until we crossed into Saudi air space. We had until now not used the radio. The pilot said he thought we should land to check the engine that wouldn't start and at the same time make a walk around the aircraft to insure we didn't have any unknown damage. Ingrid was to place a line of 5 fires at the Saudi border. It was as we crossed that the TESS navigation system was turned off. The TESS laser protection would stay on until the Saudi's gave us the all clear. Once the Navigation was again working we attempted to raise the Saudi's on the radio.

We had made the call several times when finally, someone answered in a broken English. We stated that we were in need to land as one of our engines had failed. We were directed to a landing strip that was what the captain thought too close to the Irag boarder. We asked for something further from the boarder but received no reply. The captain said he didn't like it, I didn't either. I asked the pilot about flying on to Israel, he didn't like that either. With-in minutes we had an escort then another. We had past the landing strip that they had given us. The pilots of the fighters then spoke in English telling us to return to the designated landing strip. Our pilot explained that we were a US cargo plane and that because of only flying on three engines we would need a runway with emergency services. Our pilot warned that our auto gun worked in conjunction with our radar and our radar was giving us problems. We asked them to keep their distance. At this point we again turned on the TESS navigation system. Again leaving us and of course the fighters without navigation and in some cases causing their electrical equipment to fail. At present, we were flying in the dark without knowing what we were coming up on. The fighters soon disappeared and we once again turned off the TESS navigation system. We were now well into Saudi air space and again requested to land to check our failed engine. By now the word of an Iraq air attack had reached most of the area. The Saudi's gave the permission and landing directions. As we change our directions we could see landing lights. Within minutes we were on the ground. When reaching the end of the run way we pulled off to a parking area that was well away from the terminal. The inflight mechanic and Jack exited the plane with no more than flash lights. They returned and we helped them with a ladder and tools. By now we had onlookers, they stayed their distance but were there just the same. Jack and I set up a perimeter, we were both wearing armor and heavily armed. Within minutes the mechanic said we may be in luck as he had found an electrical connection that had been disconnected by the strong jolt. The mechanic gave the pilot the signal and the propeller started to turn and then boom she started. The mechanic then checked the rest of the aircraft's outside shell finding 50 Calabria holes in the rear fuselage and tail. The mechanic said that he couldn't find anything leaking so we were good to go. We put the ladder and tools back aboard, climbed on, the other engines were started and we asked the tower for permission to take off. Permission was given and a good luck was added in English. We took off heading back for home with less than 500 miles left of fuel. We hoped our Israeli friends would be close by.

This was our first breathe easy moment. Jack unbuckled himself and came to me saying I was bleeding. I had noticed the blood but until that moment had been just wiping it with a rag. I had a golf size bump and a small cut over my right eye. Jack went and got the first aid kit and cleaned up the cut with some iodine and placed a stickum on it. Jack said that should do for now. The pilot now called me to the cockpit saying that the Israel's wanted us to land and they would refuel us. He was shaken his head no, as did I. The pilot told the Israeli's that his's orders were to ditch the aircraft in the Red Sea, this if we were to run out of fuel. To make our point clear, the pilot then changed heading out to Sea. We had only been over the water 10 minutes when our fuel arrived. While we refueled in the air, the tanker pilot congratulated us on a job well done. The computer started buzzing with calls. Before I answered back, Jack and I checked the on-board camera. What a show it was. I thought about when Liz watched our small show on Andros. At night one could clearly see the lasers at work. We had thought that TESS would only respond to a missile heading our way, but it had fired back at the big guns too. There were several explosions on the ground before our missile hit its target. After reviewing the film two times I sent Lourdes a coded message that I believed we had hit our target.

From reading all the computer's messages, I noted that Christina and Maria had returned from General Santos, and they would wait for us to return to Mandeville. Someone must have let the cat out of the bag because one of my message was from Lori asking if I was ok. Cindy had also sent a message to Jack from Mandeville. The message had come from the Mandeville house. It was Monday morning when we landed in Mandeville. Needless to say, there was a crowd there waiting for us. With us now landed, the tail ramp lowered, Lori was standing there with Cindy waiting to see our faces. Before we landed I had Jack remove the stickum from my head and put on two butterfly band-aids on holding the cut together. During the flight, home my left shoulder stiffened up on me. One of the near-miss explosions had made me lose my balance bumping my head then my shoulder.

As I walked down the ramp, Lori and Cindy were coming up. Lori latched on, then kissing me. We continued walking down then stepping of the ramp. Christina, Marina, Fernando, Lourdes, Jerry and his wife were there two. I hadn't been gone that long, but I hadn't seen Christina in what seemed like months. It was a happy reunion. The entire crew was most certainly happy to be back home. I looked at Lourdes. Lourdes said she didn't tell them where we had gone fishing, just that we had gone. The Captain which hadn't seen the holes in the fuselage until now, said that the C-130 would patch up just fine. He looked at me and asked how many days they could have off. I looked at Jerry and he said that Tim had stirred up a bee's nest, and he'd like to get the bird back to Andros as quickly as possible. I asked Jerry if he had another crew and he said yes of course. I looked at the Captain and said to take a couple weeks. Lori asked me too? I turned and hugged her lifting her up, my shoulder was giving me problems. Lori didn't notice it but the shoulder was not good. I told Lori that she had already missed a day of school. With all the crew standing there, I then thanked and congratulated them on a job well done, we made a difference I said. Lori and I would spend the night and head back in the morning.

Once back at the Mandeville house. Christina said that she hoped that I had put in our divorce papers. I looked and my rings that had been on her left hand were now gone and something new had taken their place. Christina said that Brian had asked her to marry him. I was happy for her but Lori was the happiest. Christina was all smiles. I looked at Maria and asked how that could have happened if she had done what I had said and not let Christins out of her sight. Maria then also held up her left hand. Oh my Lord I said, not you too. Maria said Yes! Fernando had asked Maria to marry him. I looked at Fernando and said he was a sly dog. Fernando then said that I might not get an invitation to the wedding for not taking him along on the fishing trip. Well I said, all is fare in love and war. You were too busy with the love part. Cindy then gave Jack a kick in the butt and told him that he was a horse's ass! Well, Cindy said I don't have a ring but I can show you all something I do have, Cindy pulled up her shirt. She was pregnant, everyone but Jack was congratulating her. Jack was in shock, no he really was, he looked at Cindy and asked, I'm going to be a father? Cindy looked at him and said "such an ass". Cindy then went and hugged him. Although Jack was probably going to get a spanking, it was a happy time for us all.

Lori got me in the shower kind of taking inventory. It was the first time I had seen my shoulder; it was swollen and badly bruised. I promised Lori that I'd get it looked at tomorrow in Miami. I wasn't sleepy so after the shower and some bed time Lori changed into her bathing suit. I had one around somewhere.

At the pool, the gang was already in the water. What stood out right away was that Christina was still wearing our rings around her neck. Lori didn't say a word but I knew she saw them and what was on her mind. I had of course thought about how all of this would work out. If the Brian thing hadn't happened, Christina and I eventually being alone would have been odd. I had never talked about my marriage to Lori with Christina. Still that first reunion was going to be odd, but with Brian in the picture it sure should make a big difference. Lori spoke up and asked Christina about her plans. Christina said if I still wanted her she'd keep right on working with the group. Brian had taken a temporary job with his Grandfather putting him in charge of their Southeast Asia operations. Christina said she hoped to talk me into her staying in General Santos but if not she was prepared to go wherever I needed her. I knew this would bring conversation with Lori and I. Christina said they were planning a December wedding.

I had thought we were spending the night but Lori asked if we could get home earlier. Lourdes still being there made the call to Tommy. We, meaning, Lori, Cindy, Jack and I would leave Mandeville by 7:00 p.m. arriving in Miami just after 11:00 p.m. Cindy asked if they could spend the night. Of course, Lori said they were always welcome.

Once at home, I was tired and was ready for bed, Lori wanted to talk about Christina. Lori had asked Christina about the rings and Christina said she kept the rings close by for any moment that I needed a wife for the business. This was the first time that Lori said she didn't like something. Lori asked me point blank if I would ever sleep with Christina again. This was a hard question, but I didn't fall into the trap of not saying no. Lori said that if I needed a wife for business, she would stop going to school and become that wife. Those words, besides Lori telling me how much she loved me were the last words of the night.

The next morning I went to the lobby and picked up my today's News paper, plus the days that I had missed. In today's international news, The Iranians had claimed to had successfully destroyed Iraq's chemical weapons factory and storage. The Iraqi's were claiming that the US had intervened into the war by not only supplying Iran with weapons but now had bombed Iraq. The US only said at the time of the bombing, all of their bombers were on the ground.

When I opened the Sunday paper, now there, were some photos. This time even the small planes wing numbers were visible. The owner of the plane was named as a well to do Panama banker that had several US properties to include being a neighbor of Jena's on Starr Island. In Monday's News Paper the Banker came up with paperwork that the aircraft had been sold months before. Tim had been doing his home-work as he had gotten several photos showing the banker with several Senators and you guessed it, Noriega himself. All of this was in the same Monday's Paper. In reading on, I found a name I was more familiar with. It was Liz, Liz was among the list of Congressmen and Senators that had received political donations from the Banker. As I read the paper the phone was ringing. Lori was on her way out the door and picked up the phone, it was Lourdes looking for me. I took the phone, Lourdes said to check the computer, the big chief's office is calling plus Bob and Tim. I told Lourdes that I would check the computer and call or write her back. When I turned, Lori was still standing there looking at me. Lori said I'm not going to lose you. She put her books down and refused to budge. I went to her and said that she wasn't going to lose me and that she only had two more swim meets before States. I wanted to see her take first in the 50 meter. I picked up her books and put them in her hands, kissed her, turned her around, opened the door and gave her a pat on the butt. Now out the door she turned for one more kiss and asked, see you at practice? I said yes, she then said to look in the Sunday's advertising section.

With Lori gone and Jack now up, I handed him the news-papers, all except for the Sunday's adds. Damn I said as I spotted Lori's several photos. I asked myself how many of Lori's classmates would see these? After looking several times at the photos, I then called Bob. Bob sounded concerned, he said that Liz wasn't too happy about being in the news. I said that I had only seen the paper a few moments ago. I told him that I had called him first as White House had also called. Bob asked if the articles were coming from me? I said we only assisted with a few photos. Bob then asked if I had seen the news about Don? Don who I asked? Bob then said that Don Aronow had been shot and killed on Saturday afternoon. I said that most likely someone didn't like Don building those faster boats for the DEA. Bob said that Columbians played for keeps. Bob said he'd meet me at the sailing club at 12:30 p.m. I said I'd be there. Jack then asked how many men we would need? I told him two for now. My next call was to find Tim at the Herald. Seems he wasn't taking calls, I left the message to call the traveling cat. I then got on the computer and let Lourdes know that I could see the president any time starting this Friday morning.

Tim called back agreeing to meet at the sailing club at 10:00 a.m. Jack mentioned after reading Tim's articles and now seeing the Don Aronow artical that Tim too should think about some security. Jack said that those kind of people, used brutality to get their message through. I agreed and said that I would talk to Tim about it. Jack said that Cindy would stick around until Christina and Maria arrived. Fernando would be headed back to Limon to give Evette a breather from the Radio. Fernando had said that everything in his southeastern zone of Nicaragua was under control. Jack offered to tag along to the Sailing Club.

At 10:00 a.m. I was waiting on the Sailing club's lawn. Tim arrived and we walked out on the dock. The first thing Tim wanted to say was that the Bankers list of political contacts and donations included our sitting President. The Banker had also contributed to both of the President's election campaigns. Tim said heavy money. Tim said that he hadn't mentioned the connection to the President but that given the attention the story is getting, it wouldn't be long before this too became public. While standing out on the dock, shots rang out to our north east, we then heard the squealing of tires and more shots. I told Tim to follow close behind as I ran toward the shots. It was one of Big Ted's men that Ted had sent in to assist with security. No one was hurt, the plain clothes officer said that two men were taking what he thought was a spot to do some shooting. One man with binoculars, the other with what could have been a rifle. The officer said he drew his gun and was heading their way when the two men spotted him, one drew a gun and started firing at him. The officer said he returned the fire and he could have wounded one or even both as they jumped into a waiting car. The officer said he had called for back-up and that the car was a black late model SUV. The officer said that he had at least shot out the back window and maybe flattened one back tire. Jack had arrived from the park side of the club and we could hear sirens heading our way. Jack said that both of us should walk back to our cars and leave. As I walked Tim to his car I didn't have to tell him of the danger that this story could bring him. He said that the paper had offered someone to look after him. Tim said that he had sent his family to stay with his grandfather that was living in Texas. Tim said that he couldn't hold off on the money trail very much longer. Tim got in his older Buick and left. I knew what he meant when he said he couldn't hold off much longer, he meant the information about the drug money reaching the White House.

Me still not used to carrying that darn cell phone, I walked back to the sailing club to use the pay phone to try and reach Bob. By now Big Ted himself had arrived on the scene. There were cops everywhere. It had been less than 20 minutes since the shooting, the police had located the car, it was abandoned just one block off 27th avenue. The car of course was stolen and had a good amount of blood in the back seat and driver's seat.

This meant that the officer had at least winged two of them. Big Ted said a man hunt was on throughout the City. Bob's office didn't get to him and he showed up at the club. Almost an hour later, the police were still on the scene. Bob said anybody but me, and someone would be dead. Bob had some white crap on his lower lip but again he had that Cuban cigar in his hand. Bob said not to say a F___ing word that it was all my fault. I then told Bob what Tim had said about the President receiving campaign money from the same banker. Bob said when you got that much money you either spend it on making friends or use it to wipe your ass. Bob's thinking was that the shooters were here for Tim not knowing whom he was meeting with. Bob said they most likely would have popped us both thinking Tim was meeting with a source. Bob asked what would be my next step? I told him that I had sent a message that I could meet with the White House anytime after tomorrow but, with this new information I had already called Lourdes. Lourdes said my meeting was set up for Friday morning. I told her to call them back and let them know I was on the way to DC. Bob said that Liz also wanted to meet with me but not in DC. Bob said Liz was thinking Nassau. Bob also wanted me to know that our Panama partner in the asphalt business had been arrested for setting the fires at our plant. Yeah I said, sarcastically, he had a lot to gain. Juan was making good money and there was no insurance for the fire. This was just one step for Noriega showing a bit of his displeasure. Well I said, see if you can buy Juan out of jail and get his family out of there. Bob said he had already moved the family to Costa Rica. Then Bob changed the subject, saying I was foolish to have helped the Iranians but that those who knew it was me, especially Iran and even the Israelis, were grateful. I told Bob that I hadn't picked a side but that civilians were being targeted by that madman. Bob said my show had put Hussain on notice that he too could be reached.

Bob asked how married life was and said he had heard that I was starting my own fruit business. Bob said that Nassau was much closer to home and that with money even the Bahamas could grow fruit. But he said I'd always have somewhere to send the wife. I asked about Carol and he said they were doing just fine. I told Bob that if I got in to see the President before then, that Liz could find me in Nassau on the weekend.

Before Bob left, Big Ted and Jack came to give us the news that the police had located two bodies in a second car at Miami International. They were now looking for one man attempting to get out of the country. One of the dead men had died from the officer's return fire, the other that the officer had wounded had been shot in the head execution style, most likely by the third man knowing that the wounded man couldn't have made it onto the flight out. Big Ted said unless the third man had blood on him or was stopped for looking suspicious he didn't think they had much of a chance of finding him before he boarded a flight out. Big Ted said that most likely his man had saved my life. Bob was fast to say that at least the assassins had either been killed or were on their way out of the country. Big Ted said that with groups that worked like this, there was most likely a back- up group. Bob said that should make us feel better. Big Ted said he put an extra man on Lori.

When Jack and I arrived back at the apartment Christina and Maria were there. I informed them on what had happened and that I'd be leaving for DC just as soon as I could get to the Opa-Locka airport. Christina followed me into my room and shut the door behind us. Christina said that she was still in love me but understood what had happen and knew that we weren't going to be continuing our relationship as it had been. She wasn't sure she would marry Brian but he had asked and yes seemed like the right answer. She was committed to the group and was not going to leave me not even if I sent her away. Christina said not to worry about Lori while I was gone she and Maria would watch out for her. I told Christina I would like for her and Maria to go to Nassau and kept an eye on Salinas and the children until this was over. Christina walked to the door, put her hand on the handle and turned and said that if I ever wanted her she was there for me. I then told her that there was a modeling contract on the dining room table, she could look it over, and then sign it. It's kind of a gateway I said, a gateway to anywhere.

I put on one of my black suits wearing my ultra-light weight armor vest under my dress shirt. I carried and extra change of clothes and my brief case.

It wasn't long before I was on my way aboard with my old friend Tommy. Tommy had purchased a new ride that was about the same size but had a few more gadgets and an extended travel range. The Computer system had also been up dated and the leer was equipped with you guessed it, a modified form of TESS.

We had arrived at the DC airport, Lourdes had contacted the White House and they were expecting me.

I wasn't expecting not to sit in some hotel waiting, but wait I did in the Oval office reception. Security had checked in my two guns and this time checked my brief case better than normal. I was sure than Lori had gotten my message and I had promised to call her by 9:00 p.m. if I wouldn't be returning tonight. I only had an hour left so I asked and called Lori from the waiting room. Lori was happy to hear from me, she mentioned that she now had more than one shadow and asked what was up. I told her that Big Ted was training a few extra men. I told her that it was a possibility that I'd make it back tonight but that in any case I should be there for her tomorrows swim meet. While talking, I was called to enter to the President's office. I told her I loved and missed her.

The CIA Director and Secretary of State were there with a projector all set up for the film I had with me. The Secretary said the President was running a bit behind and asked that we talk a bit until he could make it. The Director had heard the news of the morning at the sailing club, his Miami office had heard from the Miami police. He asked what I thought? I said that they were most certainly after Tim to silence his articles about the Noriega drug trail. The Secretary noted that I was quick to pass judgment. Judgment I asked? I haven't passed anything but a few photos. The News paper I said, was doing a good job of following the money trail. The Secretary asked what I thought should be done about it all. I said to stop the drugs. And just how that should be done he asked? Well I said its obvious that whatever and whoever has been overseeing the drug business down there is sleeping on the switch or something worse. The Secretary started to reply but was interrupted by the President's arrival. We all stood, the President asked to get right to business. Looking at me he said that once again I had taken it upon myself to work as a lone wolf and drop some kind of bomb on Iraq. I want you to know, he said that this will not be tolerated. Now he said that being said, let's see the film.

The lights were dimmed and I started the film. The quality of the film was good, being dark, one could only see a few ground lights.

All of a sudden, without warning there was one then another what looked like a blast from the ground. Simultaneously the C-130 sent two then two more laser shots downward. The laser shots were followed by two blast on the ground and two in the sky. The Camera then caught the missile that we had dropped, the film showed the missile's flame right until the blast. During and right after the missiles take off, the film showed several blasts from the ground that were unanswered by TESS. At about the same time the C-130's camera was catching blasts that were hitting all around the C-130. The camera showed for each blast from the ground, in just seconds, there were explosions all around the aircraft. During all this the camera showed the aircraft shaken by a few near misses. That first shake was the one that had knocked out the starboard engine, the next one was the one that knocked me off my feet. Once we could see the large explosion on the ground from our missile, TESS again started answering back with its lasers at the big guns on the ground. The film only lasted about five minutes. I turned on the light and again asked if there were questions? The President asked why TESS had appeared to stop firing back for a time. I explained that in order for our Missile to be launched, that TESS had to be shut down. This for two reasons, the first our Missile required the GPS from the above satellite to be working and the second that if left on, TESS would have also taken out our missile. The President then asked, If TESS would have been left on, wouldn't it have knocked down the incoming small rounds? I said no, TESS only searches out heated flame and that the antiaircraft rounds didn't have a flame. The President then said you mean if they were better shots you wouldn't be here with us today? I answered, exactly. I then mentioned that when the TESS navigation system was activated that the ground radar shouldn't work. The President then asked if I had risked my life to see how this TESS thing worked or to take out that chemical plant. I said that I disliked Castro and the Soviets but that anyone using chemical weapons on civilians should be dealt with by the entire free world. I added that soon the missile that we had used would have a much greater range and could be sent up by destroyer and or Submarine. I said, we needed someone out here willing to do live test to continue to make progress.

The Secretary then brought up the fact that my aircraft had chased off two F-15s from off Panama. I answered back that what he claimed was a half truth. Looking at the President I said that one of the problems with a young TESS is that it didn't distinguish between whom was on its side. The F-15s were tracked from 50 miles out heading our way, them being locked on by TESS. If the F-15s had fired a missile then TESS would have shot at the missile and as we saw in the film, maybe even fired back at the F-15s. I then said that I had a surprise recording of the entire conversation between the F-15 pilots and our C-130 pilot. I say surprise because that same tape you can hear the small plane call for assistance, shortly thereafter the two F-15s showed up. I believe that the F-15s were being used to watch over the drug traffickers. The Secretary then asked, did you or didn't you supply the information for the News? I then looked at him and said that we had only supplied the air photos. The Miami Paper, I said had not printed the part that the same Banker, Mr. Gonzales had contributed to both of the Presidents election campaigns. I then took out a photo from my brief case and handed it to the CIA Director. Did I take this photo too I asked? He looked at the photo and passed it to Secretary. The Secretary then looked at it and passed the photo to the President. That's Gonzales, the President asked? Yes Sir, I said, I wish we didn't recognize the other man. The President then asked if this was the only photo? I then told the President that the photo was given to me this morning by a reporter. I then added what had happen while the reporter and myself had met this morning at a Miami sailing club. The President then asked the Director if he knew about the morning's situation? Of course, he said yes and mentioned that the Police and FBI were working on the case. The Director said that most likely that the only survivor of the three was back in Columbia by now. Well the President asked what are we going to do about this. I suggested giving Gonzales his money back. The President said, yes of course. The Director then said that this would be a combined effort of the DEA, FBI, the Police and the CIA. The President asked if the reporter would hold the photo? I said the reported said that this was our heads up as if it wasn't him, that soon enough someone would connect the dots. The President said, yes of course. The President then went back to my lone wolf actions saying that the Secretary said that all this was my fault. Yes, the President said you didn't create the problem, but we can't investigate everyone that donates money. I then added that not to worry I hadn't donated any money to his or any other political party.

The Director then asked again about the Contra money, him adding that he had asked me for the amount unspent to be returned. What about it Captain the President asked? I asked if the President wanted me to keep up the pressure on the Sandinistas? The President said hell yes! I figure they won't be able to last another two years. The Secretary then asked, they being whom? I said they being all three parties. The Sandinistas, the Cubans in Nicaragua and the Soviets. Why the Soviets the President asked? The money factor I said. The Soviets are running out of money. I wouldn't be surprised if Noriega was also throwing drug money at the Soviets, the Nicaraguan war helps Noriega stay in power. With the Sandinistas gone, Panama could then become the center of our attention. I said the Soviets were well aware of the existence of the Vehicle and TESS. I was sure that they were aware of the Iraq operation too. They had to know that we just didn't drop a bomb on that factory, that it was some kind of GPS guided missile. They most likely don't know what its range is and they are throwing as much money as they can to keep up. The Soviets also now know that we have lasers that have knocked out a traveling ground to air missile. As we know, they can spend all the money they want, but without stealing the technology they will not have it. The Soviets now know your Star Wars speech wasn't a bluff.

The President then said that his military was concerned that such technology was in the hands of a civilian group. I smiled and said that with his approval I would send G.D. $50,000,000.00 of the Contra money. The military should be working with G.D. TESS I said, is still in the development stage. I asked if our military could have taken out the Iraq chemical plant. The Secretary answered of course we could have. I looked at the President and asked, then why didn't they? I looked at the Director and asked why haven't you stopped the drug movement? I then opened my mouth a bit too much implying that drugs were being moved to the US via our own Military, maybe not knowingly but its happening just the same. The Director didn't respond but the Secretary became furious saying that I must prove what I was saying. Yes Captain, the President said, then he asked if I indeed had the proof? If you want it, I said, I will get it. The President then said it was getting late, the Director and the Secretary excused themselves, all three of us standing up. The President asked me to stay, he then asked why I had to rub his people the wrong way, why he asked can't you work with them. I asked if the new Director had objected to any of my actions? The President said that the Director had asked to be free to work with me but warned that in doing so he himself could be pushed aside by the so called, establishment. The President said that the Director was concerned that unwillingly I could hurt our countries interest. Not everyone has the Presidents ear he said. I promised to use the Director as my contact and said that I would not revisit Iraq unless it was requested or cleared my himself. I noted that I would not back down on the drug war or Noriega. The President ask if TESS could protect his Air-force One? I smiled and said that TESS still had several problems that were being addressed. One such problem was that while the Navigation System was activated that our aircraft was effected in the same manner as everything within a 100-mile radius. The other thing was that as yet, TESS couldn't separate the good guys from the bad guys. If for an example, one of your escorts fired at an intruder, TESS could respond with a laser at the fired missile and or our aircraft. Anything that had a working radar could feel threatened by TESS's lock on. Sounds like you have a great deal to work on the President said. He then asked about how the Vehicle was coming along. I said that for now the Vehicle needed to stay grounded as we wouldn't want to lose it. Remember I said, we moved it by remote control.

The President asked about my children and when the wife and I could come visit them out at the ranch. The President said that he remembered one of my wives was a horse person. Yes I said, that would be Salinas, she just had given us a son that we named Jacques and that I would be seeing them and all the children on Saturday. The President said that the first lady had mention that it was difficult keeping track of all your wives. I smiled and said that I really only had one wife. We both stood and shook hands with him saying to keep in contact with the Director.

Seemed that I had gotten the green light on the fight on drugs, well there wasn't a no or a yes but since I hadn't gotten a no, I took it as a go.

The adventure would continue.